Justin The Just

Robert Butler

Dedication

This is for my granddaughters, Kenslie and Luna, who showed such interest in the book.

Acknowledgment

I want to thank my sister, Lynda Crider, for constantly badgering me to finish this book and not give up. Also, I would like to thank my wife, Cathy, for listening to all my petty grievances.

Contents

Prologue

Looking to the future was all this boy had, for his past hadn't been all that great. But then again, his future didn't look much better either.

As an eternal optimist, Justin always tried to look at the bright side of things. Lately, that had been hard for him to do.

His troubles started about five years ago when his father passed away. His world had been pretty good until that fateful day, but things had worsened.

These past few months were the worst so far, and it appeared that things wouldn't get better anytime soon.

The problem? Well, it was his stepdad, or soon-to-be stepdad named Mark. This guy was a work of art, but not in a good-natured way.

When Mary, Justin's mom, started seeing Mark, he seemed like a good guy. He was always attentive to her needs and did things for her.

I guess most couples are like that when they first start dating, and for the most part, it was good.

But as time passed, Mark's true character came out. Once he moved in with them, he seemed to change somewhat. He became very belligerent and downright cruel to Justin and sometimes to Mary.

There were other times when he was just plain evil and full of hate. Not only was Mark hateful, but he also had alcoholism. With this disease came a lot of destructive behaviors.

Sometimes, Mark was very volatile, and his mood would change without warning. This seemed to happen more when he drank too much.

Another awful behavior was that he always seemed to want to control them. He was almost to the point of being a control freak, wanting to know everything they did every minute of the day.

Mark also had a total lack of empathy toward them. He lacked any compassion for anyone or anything.

With Mark this way, Justin did all he could around the house to help his mother. Not just his chores but other things that he knew needed to be done.

Justin would do dishes, trash, laundry, and anything else that might come up. This way, it took the so-called spotlight off of her and made her life a bit easier.

Don't get this narrator wrong, but children should have chores. This will help them learn to be self-sufficient and give them a sense of belonging to the family.

The real problem was with Mark.

If Justin didn't get his chores done fast enough or exactly

how Mark wanted them done, that brought on a specific punishment. This punishment Justin received wasn't just being grounded like most kids. No, that would be far too easy. Mark would take it to another level altogether.

Sometimes, when he was in a good mood, he would deliver a slap across the face or a kick to the nearest leg.

Now, what would happen if he were in a bad mood? When this happened, the punishments would be delivered by a piece of wood that Justin had nick-named 'the stick.'

Mark would use this stick across Justin's rear or the back of his legs. His favorite spot was the back of his legs because he left so many bruises. He knew that this hurt Justin the most, so he made sure he hit him there the majority of the time.

Mark also knew that if he did this, then there was a good chance he could see the kid cry out in pain. Also, there was less chance of anyone seeing the bruises because his jeans would cover them up.

The funny thing was that it didn't make Justin cringe or hide. If anything, it seemed to make Justin stronger somehow. No matter how much punishment and pain Mark inflicted, it didn't stop Justin. The kid always stood up to him and didn't care what he did to him.

Thankfully, the punishments were rare and few. But if his

mother were home, she would stop them when they did happen. She would tell Mark that she would discipline Justin if needed. But things always turned out bad for the kid if she wasn't around.

During these episodes of 'correction,' Mark always seemed to be in the right. It was never his fault. Justin was to blame every time, no matter what the crime was.

What was clever about Mark was that he made sure Mary was never around when he applied his so-called 'corrective measures.' Of course, if Mary found out, Mark would always come up with some answer for the corporal punishment he had delivered.

He would say that Justin talked back to him or was disobedient. Mark was very good at lying on the spur of the moment. He would come up with an excuse or a lie at the drop of a hat.

It didn't matter to Justin, though, for he was unafraid of his so-called stepdad. No, he couldn't care less what he did to him when he was punished.

The only real fear Justin had was for his mom and her safety.

You see, this Justin kid was a good, brave, and honest lad. All these things were hard for him to live up to, but he did every day.

The only thing he did that might be considered an act of rebellion was that sometimes, when he got out of school, he would take a little longer to get home. The longer he was away, the better he felt. His home environment was not something he enjoyed being a part of most of the time.

So, each day, he would take a few minutes longer than the previous one. Not only did he take longer, but he also took a different route.

What he was doing was something he hadn't even realized until it came to him one day. He was headed over to a large wooded area. This place was like a forest, for it had a lot of trees and bushes in it.

Justin would get closer to this area but pass it by each time.

Justin and Steve, his best friend, had gone over there a few times in the past and played around this area. They never went inside, however. It had always seemed like a place that was better to look at but not touch. Too many fables had been spoken about this forest, which seemed to tell even the most curious to stay away.

People described this forest as ominous, dark, and forbidden. But to Justin, it looked like some kind of retreat. It seemed like an area he could go to and hide or relax. He might even find some adventure inside of this wooded area.

"An adventure behind every tree," he would say to himself. That's what he was looking for, an escape of some kind.

Then, one day, he found it. He ventured farther than he had ever been before and made it to the trees themselves. And then Justin's life changed. It changed so much from going inside this forest known as The Woods.

The Woods

It was a cool and breezy evening in late May. The breeze felt good as it gently pressed against his skin.

Justin didn't give it much thought, though, for there was something else on his mind that was far more important.

He was thinking and worrying about his mother. She was all he had left since his father had passed away.

As he lay on his bed, his mind drifted to his father and the time he had said goodbye.

From what Justin could remember, his dad was very healthy and athletic. He was six feet tall and very agile. The two loved hiking, bike riding, and other outdoor sports.

Still, his dad got sick.

So how could someone be so healthy and in such great shape yet still get sick?

Chris, Justin's dad, came home one day and said he wasn't feeling good. As time passed, he didn't get any better, and doctor after doctor couldn't figure out what was wrong with him.

Then, after a few months, a specialist found the problem. What was discovered was that Chris had an incurable disease. It was one that Justin couldn't even pronounce. No matter whether he could pronounce it or not, it was not good.

A few weeks later, his dad came home and told his family he was going to a clinic for treatment. He had done a lot of research on this clinic and added that he would be gone for a while.

Chris was insistent about leaving, and he also had one stipulation. He did not want anyone to contact or have anything to do with him until he returned home. This was because the clinic he was going to was very private. They did not allow any outside calls or letters to come in. He would have to be the one who called or wrote when he got the chance.

He also told them this place was a secretive institution in another country. With the information that Chris had found out, he felt this was the best way to treat his disease.

Chris then let them know of a couple of other disturbing things. He said these treatments would be very tough on his body, and the medication would be even worse.

He also let his family know that there was no way he could get treatments like these here in the United States. These were experimental treatments and medications; they had not been approved in the States yet. This was the reason he chose to seek a cure so far away; he knew time was running out. The doctors had only given him another two or three months to live, so time was not his friend. He needed to start a treatment program as soon as he could.

Justin and his mother were totally against this but followed his wishes. This way, they would not interfere with his quest to get well.

A short time after his departure, the unthinkable happened. They were notified in a letter that Chris had passed away in this European clinic. It sounded mysterious, but what could they do? This place he had gone to was so far away, and there wasn't much information to go on either. Chris had taken care of all of the arrangements in advance. Mary did her due diligence but still could not find much information about this clinic.

Another thing the letter said was that his body would not be returned. This was because the treatments he had received had been very devastating. The letter said that he had been cremated, and not even the ashes were allowed to be brought back to the States.

When she finally contacted them, they said they could not give out any information about patients at the clinic. They couldn't even confirm whether he had been a patient or what had happened to him while he was there.

So, Justin and his mom still gave Chris a funeral. In a way, at least to Justin, since there was just an empty coffin, there was a chance that his father would return someday. It was a crazy idea, but to a nine-year-old boy, it seemed logical.

When his father passed away, Justin the Just, that's what his dad and best friend Steve used to call him, would keep to himself a lot. He would hide away from the world and never seemed to venture out much. As for friends, he didn't have many of those either.

Now, it had been five years since that awful day, and for the most part, Justin was just getting by. His mom said she thought he needed a hobby or to get back into sports. So, for her, he tried to find one. He even went so far as to try to socialize more with kids his age.

Deep down in his heart, Justin knew his mom was right about trying to find something to do. He knew this would help keep his mind focused and not dwell on the past so much.

What she didn't realize about her son was that he had lost the will to play sports when his father passed away. These things didn't interest him anymore.

But there was something else his mother didn't know about her son. She didn't know that he didn't need any activity to keep him busy, for he was already too busy saving the world daily.

Saving the World?

Yes, saving the world.

Justin didn't have time for anything else because each day, while walking home from school, he would encounter some damsel in distress or evil villain he had to fight.

And so far, each day, he had saved them. Whether it was from the cars in the streets or off the railroad tracks, he saved them.

This was just a fantasy that he had developed over the years. It was just a game he would play as he tried to cope with the emptiness in his heart from losing his father.

As time dragged on, though, Justin noticed something was changing. He couldn't quite grasp it, but something was different.

The more he thought about it, the more he realized that it might have something to do with him saving the world.

"Am I getting tired of doing this?" he asked himself. "I've done such a great job for the past five years, so who would take my place if I quit?"

Would it be his best friend, Steve?

"No. Steve wouldn't know where to begin. He would probably get hurt the first day, and then they would have to call on Justin the Just to make things right. Bring me out of retirement," he said, smiling at this thought.

Or was it something else?

Could it be that Justin was growing up? Maybe that was why things seemed to be changing. After all, he would be heading to the ninth-grade next year, and everyone knows that when you get into high school, you're all grown up and know everything.

Well, whatever it was, he knew that he would have to figure it out soon, for summer was coming, and this year, he might finally get to do something fun and not have to stay home.

One more week left of school, and then summer vacation would be here. He was so looking forward to this one. His mom had promised him that he would get to go to camp this summer.

It was called Willoughby's Boys Camp and was located in the Lone Pine Forest about a hundred miles from his town.

From what Steve had told him, it was a great camp to be a part of. Steve had gone last summer, and Justin was supposed to go too, but something came up to prevent him.

The something that had come up was Mark. Last year, he made sure Justin couldn't go. He told Justin's mother that he had lied to him and convinced her that he shouldn't get to go to camp because of it.

"Why is Mark always against me?" Justin must have asked himself this question a hundred times in the past.

This was one thing that he couldn't figure out. From the first time Mark started dating his mom, Justin could tell he didn't like him very much.

The only thing Justin could come up with was that maybe Mark was jealous of him for some odd reason. It was the only possible answer.

So, Justin ended up staying home last summer. He was a little upset about this, for he knew that Steve and he would have had a lot of fun together at camp.

It was sad to say, but the kid already knew that Mark would come up with another reason for him not to go to camp this year.

Justin hoped he was wrong, but lately, he had become increasingly pessimistic. This was because Mark had recently become a big problem for Justin and his mother. In Justin's eyes, he hadn't been treating his mom very nicely.

Lately, Justin noticed that Mark had been abusive to his mother in the last week or so. Not physical abuse, but more verbal. He seemed to enjoy belittling her, especially in front of Justin, which worsened things.

Plus, Mark would always threaten Justin without his mother knowing. He would tell Justin that if he told anyone how he 'corrected' him, there might be an accident involving his mother. He always said these things with such malice that it did its job. It kept Justin from saying anything to anyone.

When you're young, you tend to believe the so-called authoritarian figures in your life. So, to ensure his mom would be OK, Justin never told a soul.

"Do what you want with me, but leave my mom alone," is the true way Justin believed.

Another thing Justin didn't like about Mark happened last week. When Justin came home from school, Mark said he had something he wanted to ask him. What he wanted was for Justin to call him dad.

As you might expect, this almost made Justin heave a big load.

"Yeah, right. Like that's ever going to happen," Justin said to himself with loath in his voice. "I don't care how bad he beats me; I'll never call him dad!"

But once again, succumbing to the possibility that his mom might get hurt, he gave in to Mark's demand and called him the dad's word.

As he woke up from a restless night of sleep, Justin looked out his bedroom window, and for a few moments, life was good. Then, back to reality, he came. His face went from a smile to a sad frown.

Quickly, he was up, ate breakfast, dressed, and headed to school, all before Mark woke up from his drunken stupor.

While walking to school, Justin was absorbed in his thoughts, for so many things were on his mind.

What did his mom see in this guy? How did she ever get mixed up with him? He was a horrible person, one that no one cared for.

Justin's mom had been with Mark on or off for over a year, but things weren't improving. If anything, they were getting worse. They split up several times, but Mark always weaseled his way back into Mary's good graces.

It seemed from the moment Mark came into their lives that he had a chip on his shoulder for one reason or another. He always blamed others for anything that went wrong or didn't work out for him. But in reality, it was mostly his fault. He was not man enough to admit his failures, so the blame went elsewhere. And most of the time, it went toward Justin.

Mark was short in stature, but so was Justin. The only difference was that Mark outweighed Justin by fifty pounds or so. Being short also gave Mark that so-called 'little man syndrome, ' which, when it appeared, was always filled with anger and hate.

So here Justin and his mother were, trapped, with no hope for any future. He knew that things needed to change, but he had no idea how to do it.

Suddenly, he heard a loud ringing sound. As he looked up to see what it was, he realized it was the school bell. If the bell hadn't rung, Justin could have just walked on by and would have been tardy for his first class. Quickly, he went inside.

When he walked into the school, he discovered it was a short school day. All the kids got out at eleven because of some teacher's conference. Plus, Friday was always the best day of the week because it meant the weekend was here.

Since it was Friday, Mark would be going out of town for work, or at least that was what he always told Justin's mom. He would either go to work, hunt, or fish with his so-called friends.

It was always a good thing when Mark left. Justin and his mom didn't have to worry about upsetting him then. They could be themselves for a while, and that was always fun.

Another good thing was that his mom and Mark didn't know it was a short day at school. This meant that he could take his time getting home.

"I might even get enough courage to go over to where all those trees are," he said with wonder.

The area he was thinking about was like a forest. It was called The Woods. Only a few had dared venture into this place: the few, the brave, and the strong.

The trees in this so-called forest were very thick and old. If truth gave way to legend, then a sort of mystery was associated with this area. Most of it was fabricated, but a little truth did surface.

The real truth was that hardly anyone went into The Woods, but it wasn't because of what you might think. It was mainly because once you did go inside, there wasn't anything to do.

As far as he knew, there wasn't even any game to hunt, at least none to speak of. Also, there were no areas where someone could go and have a picnic or enjoy family fun. All it had in it were thorns, bushes, trees, and sometimes poison ivy. So why go in?

Another reason people wouldn't go in was that there were a few 'No Trespassing' signs in and around The Woods. Now that it had been so many years, though, they were all faded.

But if legend had its way, and it mostly did with young boys, then it was a dark and mysterious place that people should avoid at all costs. So, most of them did, but not Justin. Not this time.

These were some of the things that Justin's young mind was thinking about as he sat and waited for the minutes to tick away.

Shortly, the time did just that: the school bell rang. Justin then headed for home, sort of. Home was on his mind, but The Woods was where he would go first.

First, he took the street to the end of a cul-de-sac, then up and over the railroad tracks. Once he had passed the tracks, he reached the main road, which went past a cornfield.

The cornfield was owned by an old farmer named Tucker.

No one knew where this old man came from, for he kept to himself most of the time. He did seem to be your typical farmer, though, for he had a straw hat, overalls, and a scarf around his neck.

Most of the time, you could walk right through his field if you wanted to or take the dirt road that was adjacent to it. But sometimes Tucker would send Red out to chase you.

Red was Tucker's old basset hound. If his dog ever caught you, he would just waddle up and lick you.

But this time, there was no dog, farmer, or anyone else to stop Justin from walking to The Woods.

Stepping off the main road, Justin walked down an old dirt road. As he continued walking, he approached an area that seemed to have an opening where one could quickly enter, a sort of hollow.

He suddenly stopped just outside and waited. A few moments passed, but he still did not move any closer.

Instead, he just peered inside the thick overgrowth. Justin tried his best to see what he could inside the forest, but it was dark. The more he looked, the darker it seemed to get.

So, once again, he waited. Justin waited so long that one might think he was looking for some signal or a sign. Or, some clue that would tell him to go in.

Looking at his watch, he noticed it was almost eleven thirty, so there was still plenty of time to go inside and explore. After exploring, he would head home to do everything he knew would await him.

Even though Justin knew that Friday was the best day of the week, it was also the worse in some ways. Friday was the day Mark would leave, but he always had more chores for Justin to do.

Justin knew there would be heck to pay if he didn't finish them all by Sunday evening before Mark got home.

Suddenly, a slight wind blew past him. He could feel it oh so soft against his skin. Justin felt like the breeze was pushing him and saying, "Go on in. Life awaits you."

"Well, here goes," he said with some trepidation.

Forward, he went into the darkened trees, leaving the safety of the cornfield and dirt road behind. Not once did he look back.

Justin gallantly moved past the first row of trees, all the while noticing that the light inside this area was growing dim.

He then realized that he had his backpack on. It seemed to be slowing him down, so he took it off and hid it by a tree stump.

"This should be safe here because no one in their right mind would enter these woods. But here I am, so what does that tell you."

He had said this out loud to himself, hoping it would help him muster up some courage as he moved forward into the darkness.

As he continued walking, slowly pushing aside shrubbery, his eyes grew accustomed to the dark. He noticed that the further he went, the more things he could see.

He could mostly see green bushes and trees, but there were also other colors as well. There were lots of plants and shrubs here, some of which were unfamiliar to him.

His eyes had now adjusted to the darkness so much that he could see some kind of path. It wasn't much of one, just one that a person could walk on without fear of stepping into something.

Then, as he trudged further, he thought he saw something ahead. It was a light that seemed to be shining at the top of the tree limbs above. His pace picked up a little, for his curiosity was heightened.

A short time later, Justin found a rather sizeable moss-covered rock. It was big and long, and there didn't seem to be any way around it. Too much foliage and trees on each side of the rock made it almost impossible to go around.

He could still see the light as he looked to the top of the rock. Now, it seemed to be shining dimmer, however. His need for an answer was increasing, and he knew that if he wanted to find out where that light was coming from, he would have to climb. This didn't look easy, but he felt he was up to the challenge.

Quickly, he scaled the rock and then sat at the top to rest for a moment. As he looked in the direction of the light, he saw that it looked as if it were coming from some kind of an opening. If it was, then it was a very small one.

Shortly, Justin realized what he would have to do. He would have to slide down and go to where the light came from.

So slowly, he started his descent, doing his best to keep from falling off the side of the rock.

Reaching the bottom, Justin now headed toward the light. A few short steps later, he stopped in mid-stride.

He heard a sound. The sound was almost like a rushing river, but he knew this couldn't be true, for there were no rivers close to this area, especially near this forest.

Casting this thought aside, he continued walking toward where he saw the light. As he did, he noticed it grew dimmer and faded somewhat. Now, he could see that this was indeed an opening.

Arriving at where the light came from, he slowly peeled back the last brush in his way. When he did, the light grew brighter as the foliage was removed.

Walking out of The Woods, he looked out over a beautiful valley.

Justin was now standing on a flat area covered with grass.

This spot, which was slightly elevated, gave him a great view of the valley below.

What he first noticed was that everything here seemed so fresh and clean. He was awestruck, to say the least.

Justin then noticed something else. The daylight here seemed brighter, and this valley seemed to have no smog. Where he had just come from, there happened to be a lot. Primarily agricultural, but still smog.

Then, he also realized that the air smelled better. He figured this, too, was because of the lack of smog in this area.

As he stood there in disbelief, Justin looked to his right. There was the river he thought he had heard a few moments earlier.

Looking out past the river, he noticed a mountain to the left of it. To the left and right of the mountain were more beautiful trees. It was lush with greenery, almost picturesque.

As he continued looking out over the valley, he saw something else. There was a path that led to the river. It looked as if it had been used many times in the past. He also noticed that it branched off. One way led around the mountain, and the other followed the river.

Standing on top of this grassy plateau, Justin realized that if he wanted to explore this area further, he would have to slide down the hill he was on.

First, he looked for other ways to descend, but none were found. There were also no steps or handholds to wedge his way down.

After debating whether to do this, he moved forward. Without hesitation, he said, "Geronimo," and started to slide.

As he slid, he could feel the wetness coming through his clothes. This was fun, but it was fleeting. It only took a few seconds to get to the bottom.

Once he was at a complete stop, he turned and looked back up to where he had slid down from.

"Wow! That sure looked shorter when I was up there."

He thought it was only about fifty yards, but now it looked as long as a football field.

"Incredible. Now, how the heck am I going to get back up there so I can go home?"

Justin felt slightly worried about this prospect, but somehow, he knew he would find a way to get back up. Shrugging his shoulders, he moved toward the path and the river.

Once he started moving toward the river, he saw a large tree. Justin realized he would have to go around this to get to the river. This tree was almost up against the hill he had just slid down. It was not only tall but very dense.

As he made his way around the tree, he approached the river. When he did, a loud noise pierced the air. This made Justin stop and look all around. Shortly, the noise seemed to fade and then stop. This strange noise seemed to rattle him a bit.

A short time later, Justin continued walking but kept a close watch on his immediate surroundings. He couldn't see anything wrong, so he continued on the path. Still, he was a little unnerved by that sound, what it was, and where it came from.

As he reached the river, he noticed that it seemed to come right out of the side of the mountain. There was a beautiful waterfall with a deep bluish color as it cascaded into the river. Another thing he noticed was the sand by the river. Somehow, it looked different.

He then walked up to the river. Bending down, he grabbed a handful of the sand. Shaking his head, he examined it. This sand felt soft to his touch. Plus, it didn't have that grainy feel when you held it.

Then he noticed something else about the sand. It seemed to melt in his hand, sort of. Also, it had a fluffy texture.

"Now that's different," Justin said, trying to figure out what he saw and felt.

Justin then walked up to the river and examined it some

more. He noticed that there seemed to be a lot of fish swimming close by. Some of them were fish he had never seen, almost odd-looking in their shape.

Also, as he watched them swim, he noticed they had different colors. Some were stripped, and others were solid black, yellow, and red.

Then he noticed the water itself; it looked so clean. It was some of the cleanest he had ever seen. Plus, it was crystal clear, except for a bluish tent.

Justin finally turned away from the river and started walking on a different path around the mountain.

Suddenly, he felt something was wrong. Stopping, he looked at his immediate surroundings once again.

Finally, it came to him. The light was beginning to fade and getting dark here rather quickly.

"OH, NO! The sun is sinking. I have to get back home, and fast!"

He knew the penalty would be harsh if he were late. All he could think about was how bad Mark would treat him if he didn't get home and finish his chores.

"How could this be? I've only been here a little while; at least, it seemed like it."

He was almost shouting this as he ran back to the hill.

Quickly, he looked at his watch. He knew he came into The Woods at about eleven thirty. But if the sun was sinking, then he must have stayed way too long in this valley. He must have lost track of time.

As Justin stared at his watch, he noticed it didn't seem to be working. That might explain why the sun was now going down. He had enjoyed this place so much that time had flown by.

"That has to be it," he said to himself, trying to find an answer to his dilemma.

"Or my watch was broken when I climbed the rock or slid down the hill."

That was another explanation he came up with as he returned to the knoll. Still, these explanations just didn't seem logical.

As he stood there, the small hill looked like a mountain. Justin started looking around the area to find a better way up.

There were rocks on both sides of the area that he had slid down, and they went almost straight up. There was no way he would be able to climb them, for they were slippery. They, too, had some type of moss that covered them. The only way he could have climbed them was if he had some climbing gear.

Now panic began to sit in. What was he going to do? He had

to get home, and the faster, the better.

Stepping back a few yards, he began trying to run up the hill. As he did, Justin noticed he had made a little headway at first. He was delighted at this prospect, for there was hope he might make it after all.

That didn't happen, however. Justin lost his footing and tumbled down to the exact spot he had started from. The hill was just a little too slippery for him to try and run up.

He realized that it must have rained in this area briefly before he came and that the ground was still wet. That would make the grass on the hill slippery and too hard to run or climb.

Now despair started to sink in. He tried several more times but to no avail. Justin stood there all the while looking up and wondering how he could get back to the top.

"I don't think I can do it," he said out loud. "I don't think I can run up that hill."

Suddenly, a slight noise came from that large tree he had to go around to get to the river earlier.

As he turned toward the tree, he heard someone say, "Then don't."

The words seemed to come from behind some long vines that grew from this tree. The tree looked a lot like a weeping willow. If it was, it had to be one of the largest weeping willow trees he had ever seen. It was almost impossible to look through it, for it had so many vines and leaves.

A moment later, after being startled by hearing the voice, Justin regained his courage.

"Hello! Is someone there?" But there was no answer.

"Did I just imagine those words," he said.

He tried to remain calm, but the thought of someone watching him in this strange place seemed to unnerve him somewhat. Plus, he was still a little edgy from hearing that alarm earlier.

Suddenly, the vines moved apart, and as they did, he saw a figure behind them. The figure then walked out towards Justin.

At first, Justin took a few steps backward just in case he needed to run from whoever this was.

When this person walked up to Justin, he could tell it was a man. The man then shook his head and started to speak to Justin.

"Then don't. Don't run up the hill. You know you don't have to, don't you?"

He then looked at Justin to see if he knew the answer.

As Justin stood there in disbelief, he noticed that this little man was just that, little.

Justin was only five foot six, but this guy could only have been five feet at the very most.

He then looked at Justin with an annoyed look on his face. It was a look that seemed to show some irritation and seemed to be directed at Justin for some odd reason.

Motioning to Justin, he said, "Follow me."

Quickly, the two of them headed over to the side of the hill that Justin had slid down.

As they approached the hill, the little man walked over to the rocks. Then, to Justin's amazement, he started to walk up effortlessly.

Justin noticed that the man was not walking up the rocks. He was walking between the rocks and the hill. Apparently, there were some steps here.

Deciding to follow him, Justin tried to step exactly where the man stepped. As he did, he could see the steps now, for they were in plain sight. They were very steep, but he didn't care. All he cared about was getting home, and now it looked like he would be able to.

"Funny, I didn't see these steps before," Justin said but under his breath.

These steps were almost hidden from the naked eye. They

were made just for your feet and fit perfectly with each step he took. He also could see them better as he continued to climb. It was as if the steps cast a small light as he walked up them.

When they were almost to the top, the little man stepped to the side and let Justin go first.

Using these footholds, Justin quickly reached the top. He knew now that he would never have found the steps without this little man showing them to him.

As Justin reached the top, he turned around to thank the man.

"Wow! I would never have been able to climb this without your help, sir. Thanks a lot!"

But there was no answer. The little man had disappeared.

"Where did he go?" Justin said out loud. "I wanted to thank him."

Justin then quickly started to turn in a circle as he searched for the little man. But try as he might, he could not find him. Somehow, he had just up and vanished.

After a few moments, Justin shrugged and took one final look at the beautiful valley. Justin was hoping that someday he would get the chance to come back, but for now, he had to get back home or feel the wrath of his stepdad. This had been too good of a day to end like that.

"Now, which way did I come in?"

As he said this, he started scanning the trees and bushes nearby.

At first, when he looked back to where he thought he had come in, he could not see the opening. It seemed to have disappeared.

As Justin continued searching, he could feel some anxiety building up, increasing as time and the light faded. It almost seemed hopeless now, but still, he searched.

Suddenly, when he had almost given up on finding the way out, it appeared.

There was the path and the hole he had stepped through. He could now see the darkness from which he had emerged.

Somehow, the opening had been camouflaged, making it look smaller and almost completely hidden.

Giving the valley one last look, he glanced over his shoulder. There wasn't much to see, for the light was completely gone.

As Justin ran through The Woods, he knew he had to get through them as fast as he could. There was no time to linger.

Justin reached the vast rock rather quickly. He made it to the top with little effort.

Quickly, he slid down the other side. Once again, he could feel the wet moss seeping through his clothes.

As Justin hurried through the wooded area, only one thing was on his mind.

"Got to get home and wash my clothes before Mark finds out!"

Since it was so late, Justin hoped Mark had already left for his weekend rendezvous with his buddies. If he had, this would solve his dilemma.

Justin was now at a full run. As he ran, a strange feeling came over him. He felt as if someone or something was watching him. All he wanted was to get out of there and get home as fast as he could, so he did not stop to see if someone was in the area.

Up ahead, he saw where he had come into the forest from. He also could see that there was still light at the opening of the hollow.

"How can this be?" he questioned himself out loud. "It should be dark outside now!"

As he looked down at his watch, he saw that it was moving again and that he had only been inside for about half an hour. He could have sworn that his watch had stopped when he was in the valley.

"What is going on here?" he said under his breath in a low disbelieving whisper.

Now, he was perplexed. On the one hand, he was glad time had slowed because he could get home in time to wash his clothes and do his chores. But on the other hand, he didn't want to leave The Woods and the valley. For some reason, he felt safe there. Also, he thought that he had found a home in the valley.

Just before he stepped out of The Woods and onto the dirt road, he remembered his backpack by the stump. If he had forgotten it, he would have gotten another beating. A sigh of relief came from his mouth as he picked up his backpack and threw it over his shoulder.

Once again, as he left The Woods, he had that strange feeling—the same feeling he had when he had run through The Woods earlier—as if someone or something had been watching him.

Justin knew one thing for sure: whoever might have been watching did not want to hurt him or cause any trouble. If they did, they could have gotten him at any time when he was inside.

Now Justin started jogging up the dirt road by farmer Tucker's field. He knew he didn't have to hurry, but the sooner he got home and hid the fact that his clothes were dirty, the better it would be for him. That way, there would be fewer questions asked. Plus, he wanted to ensure the time on his watch was correct.

Leaving The Woods, Justin kept shaking his head back and forth in total bewilderment from what he had seen in the valley.

"Now, that was crazy. Crazy or not, I can't wait till I get a chance to go back inside." A big smile was on the kid's face as he headed home as fast as he could.

As he reached the paved road, he felt he didn't have time to look back at the field or The Woods.

If he had looked back and to his right, he would have seen someone watching him. Farmer Tucker and his old dog Red had been outside when Justin went into the wooded area and when he came out.

The old farmer also smiled as he watched the kid leave his property. Tucker then called to his dog, and the two of them quietly headed into the farmhouse.

Confrontation

Justin hit the front door of his home at full speed. The first thing he did was go into the laundry room. Off came his clothes, and the soap followed. Quickly, he ran upstairs and put on some clean clothes.

Running downstairs, he went to the kitchen to check the clock. He wanted to ensure the time was the same as his watch. When he did, he sighed a sigh of relief because they were the same.

"Thank God," he exclaimed out loud. Now he knew he had some time before Mark got home. Justin felt confident that he could cover this all up.

If his mother got home first, there wouldn't be any problem. She would understand, plus she wouldn't want him to get punished again for being a boy.

Guessing the time frame of the washing and drying cycles, Justin decided to do his homework while he waited. He knew that if he wanted to do something later or even spend the night at Steve's house, he would have to finish his homework and some of his chores.

He wanted to see his friend because he had so much to tell him. He wanted to let him know all about what he had discovered.

A short time later, he ran down the stairs and put the clothes from the washer into the dryer. It would only take a little longer, and he would be done. Things were finally looking up for him.

Suddenly, as he was about to run up the stairs, he heard a door shut behind him.

"What the heck are you doing home so early? Did they kick your worthless little butt out? They should because you're not a very smart kid anyway."

Justin froze, and his heart sank. He looked defeated and knew now that he had run out of luck.

Mark was home, and by the way he sounded, he was already drunk. Nothing new here. It was almost a daily occurrence.

The bad thing about Mark getting drunk was that he would get mad about anything. The slightest thing could set him off. He always took it out on Justin or his mom when this happened. It brought out the worst in him. Also, his punishments seemed more severe when he over-indulged.

Slowly, Justin turned toward the voice and realized that he could see the pure hatred in this man's eyes. He could also sense that he wanted to hurt someone badly.

"No. I didn't get kicked out. It was a short day at school. Some kind of teacher's meeting. I just forgot to tell you and Mom."

Stepping back a few feet, Justin added, "I was about to finish my homework. Plus, I have some clothes in the dryer. I've already done some of my chores."

He was praying that this would stall Mark for a while and that he would let him go and finish the rest of his tasks. But, once again, this was not the case.

Justin quickly turned and moved away from Mark, knowing he wouldn't make it.

"Where do you think you're going, little boy? I'm not through with you yet! I have something very important to tell you."

The only thing Justin wanted to hear Mark say was that he was leaving and would never return. But Justin knew he and his mom could not be that fortunate.

Mark stopped momentarily and stood there, swaying a little from side to side. He waited a few more seconds, and then his wicked smile appeared.

"Your mommy and I have decided to sell her house, and we will all move away. In fact, we are going to be moving out of this state. I just wanted to be the first one to tell you."

Mark was now looking very intently at Justin. He must have been waiting to see how Justin would react to this new revelation.

As he stood there, Mark laughed and even loudly belched from all the beer he had consumed. His laugh seemed to get louder and louder as it cut right through the boy.

Then Justin thought about what he had just told him.

"Moving out of state! I don't want to move out of state, or anywhere else for that matter," Justin said to himself but quietly.

Mark still wanted a reaction from Justin, but none came. Nothing whatsoever came from the boy. Justin's face showed no sign of hurt or sadness. All he had was a blank expression. Justin was not about to let Mark know that what he had just said had hurt him deeply.

If they moved away, what would happen to his best friend Steve? What about all of his other friends at school? And what would happen if his real dad came home? He wouldn't know where they had moved and couldn't find him and his mom!

Justin knew this last thought was nothing more than a fantasy he used when things got tough. It was his defense mechanism for blocking the truth about his dad. Deep inside, he knew that if his dad was still alive, he would have already come home and saved them.

Suddenly, he heard the dryer alarm. Slowly, Justin moved past Mark and into the laundry room.

"Saved by the bell," he said as he gingerly walked by.

It was good that the alarm sounded because Justin could tell Mark was in a bad mood. It looked like he still had punishing someone on his mind.

Justin then moved as fast as he could out of range of his stepfather. He walked swiftly into the laundry room without looking back.

As he took the clothes out of the dryer, he knew Mark had followed him.

Justin took his clothes without hesitation and headed to his room. Once again, he could feel Mark closing in. He wasn't out of trouble just yet.

Then suddenly, Justin could smell his stepdad's breath. He was close, too close.

Justin knew that something terrible was going to happen. He could sense it.

Suddenly, Justin was grabbed from behind. He felt his shirt almost being ripped off of him. He was then spun around to face his attacker.

Quickly, Mark's arms had Justin in a headlock. The pain was tremendous, and Justin tried to fight back, but it was useless.

After a few moments, which seemed like an eternity, someone shouted, "Get your hands off him."

Mark was so startled from hearing the command that it took him a moment or two to realize it was Mary yelling at him.

Quickly, the excuses began.

"It's not what you think. He had it coming to him. He smarted off to me again, so I showed him who was in charge. That's all!"

Once again, he had come up with a lie on the spur of the moment. And it was a good one. All the while he was saying this to Mary, he was making it sound like his feelings were hurt. He was good. You had to give him credit for that.

Then he continued. "Isn't that right, Justine?"

He said this last question in a smart-aleck way and with quite a condescending tone.

Justin didn't say anything. He just nodded. He knew it was better not to let his mother know the truth for her sake. It might put her in harm's way, and he wasn't about to let that happen. Justin was glad she had come home when she did because he could tell that this beating would have been bad if it hadn't been stopped.

Finally, Mark stumbled back and away from Justin. Somehow, he got down the stairs without falling. Justin could hear him getting into the refrigerator and popping open another can.

His mom then moved over to Justin to ensure he was all right. Finding out he was, she kissed him and told him to finish putting away his clothes. She also said that she would talk to him later.

Justin then looked at his mother and said, "Mom, do you

think I can go over to Steve's and spend the night? I'm almost done with my homework and my chores."

He said this in an almost pleading sort of way. There was no way that he wanted to stay home after what he had found in The Woods.

"I'm sure you can, sweetheart. I don't care what he says. Go ahead and go. We can talk later, OK?"

After his mom left his room, Justin called Steve to ask if he could spend the night. Steve then asked his parents and got their permission.

Justin told Steve that he had something important to tell him. It seemed almost magical. Justin knew this would pique his friend's curiosity, so he told him he would be over around six that evening.

A short time later, the tension in the house had eased a little. This was mainly because Mark was leaving to go away for the weekend with his so-called 'friends.' They were supposed to be doing some hunting and fishing. Just as long as he was away from him and his mom, Justin didn't care where Mark was going or doing.

Justin couldn't hardly wait till it was time to go to Steve's. He had so much to tell him. He wanted to tell him about The Woods and his discovery of what he had found inside.

Yes, he had a lot of good things to tell his friend, but he also had something terrible to say to him.

He had to let Steve know about the possibility of moving away. He still didn't know when they planned on moving, so he felt he might still have time to convince them not to.

Justin knew he could not leave this place, especially now that he had discovered what was inside The Woods.

The Plan

The evening, it had finally arrived. It seemed to have taken forever, but Justin knew it was because he was excited about telling Steve what he had discovered that day.

As Justin slowly rode his bike to his friend's house, he was in a good mood. Mostly, it was because he was out of the house and away from Mark. Justin would have been worried about his mom any other time, but Mark had already left for his weekend camping trip with his buddies.

It was sad, but Justin and his mom were only cheerful when Mark was gone. It seemed whenever he left, a huge weight was lifted off their shoulders.

Continuing on his way to Steve's house, the young boy had a chance to think about his situation and home life.

"So what! So, what if he hits me? I can take care of myself. I can handle anything he throws at me. He isn't that tough!"

Justin was still thinking about his earlier encounter with Mark when he had put him in a headlock.

But this time, there was vindication in Justin's voice. He knew he could take anything Mark dished out; at least, he hoped he could.

Knocking on the door, Justin noticed that Steve had

answered it rather quickly. This came as no surprise to Justin. He knew Steve would be anxious to hear his news about what he had found.

Quickly, they put Justin's bike in the garage and headed inside to tell Steve's parents that Justin had arrived.

A few seconds later, both boys had run upstairs to Steve's bedroom. But before Justin said anything, he slowly walked over to the bedroom door and ensured it was locked.

All this so-called secrecy had Steve's interest at a peak.

"OK. What is so important that you won't tell me over the phone and want the door locked? Come on now, out with it!"

Steve was quite anxious at this time. After all, he had waited almost three hours for his friend to come over and tell him what he had discovered.

So, after Justin thought Steve couldn't wait any longer, he began to tell him all that he had found in The Woods.

"You won't believe what happened to me today and what I found! It was simply incredible."

Justin had now moved from the door and sat across Steve's bed.

As Justin was about to tell Steve about his discovery, he stopped abruptly. Steve suddenly put his hand over his mouth and whispered to Justin to be quiet for a second.

"Just a sec," Steve said softly.

Slowly, Steve stood up and quickly ran over to the bedroom door. Without a split second of hesitation, he unlocked it and yanked it open.

Steve's little sister, Rhonda, was on the floor. Her ear had been pressed against the door so hard that she fell into his room when Steve opened it.

"Are you spying on me again, Rhonda? You are becoming a little pest! You are always sticking your nose in somewhere it doesn't belong. Now get out of here before I tell Mom, you little brat. Go on, get!"

Steve had said this with a lot of force behind it. He was hoping that it would make her go away and leave them alone.

Rhonda was only twelve years old, and her brother would turn fifteen this year. He was all grown up in her eyes, and she listened to him, at least sometimes.

Reluctantly, Rhonda got off the floor and left the area with her head down. She obeyed Steve but only to a certain point. As soon as the door shut, she was back trying to listen more.

With the door closed and locked again, Steve returned to the bed.

"OK. What have you found? This better be good because this waiting is killing me!"

Justin then began.

"On my way home from school today, I stumbled onto something. I took the long way home, the one that goes by farmer Tucker's field. As you know, his field is right by The Woods."

He stopped for a second because he could tell that Steve looked a little puzzled and confused.

"Yes. The Woods. You know, the wooded area that no one ever goes into. The one they say is haunted or some crap like that! The one you and I have been to but never went inside."

Justin knew he had his friend's attention now. He could see him sitting on the edge of the bed, listening to every word. He also knew Steve had realized precisely what and where he was talking about, for he nodded in agreement.

In the past, both boys had gone to this place but never really went in, or at least not that area. There were other entry points, but it was always the same thing. The Woods were an area that people stayed out of.

"Anyway, I went there by myself. And listen to what I discovered!"

Justin went on to tell Steve the whole story.

When he finally finished, he saw he had captured Steve's imagination. All Steve did was sit there with his mouth half open. A short time later, a dumbfounded look appeared.

Finally, he spoke.

"Are you kidding me? You had me going at first. I almost believed you. You're telling me you went to The Woods and went inside! Sure, you did!"

Now, Steve's demeanor changed somewhat. There was disbelief written all over his face. Steve was not buying any of what Justin was telling him. He also started to laugh a little at Justin. He felt that his friend was kidding around with him.

"Look, everything I told you is true. It was incredible inside there. I know I will go in again tomorrow if I get the chance. Mark is already gone for the weekend, and my chores are almost done. It would be great if you came with me. You won't believe it until you see it with your own eyes anyway."

Justin sat there in a challenging way. He wanted Steve to come with him the next time he went. It would be more fun if someone else came along.

Steve sat there for a second and thought about what Justin had told him about The Woods.

Then Steve announced, "I have a lot to do tomorrow. I'm

packing for summer camp and must get more supplies for my trip."

Steve looked slightly perplexed at this slight dilemma, but Justin could tell he was still thinking about something.

A few moments passed, and Steve asked Justin, "Did you find out if you could go to camp this year? Maybe your mom and Mark will let you this time!"

Justin snapped back without much thought about what he was going to say.

"He would never let me go. I've just been kidding myself, thinking he would let me this year. But I might as well forget about it. Besides, I would feel better if I stayed home and kept an eye on my mom. Mark might hurt her or do something worse, and I wouldn't be there to help her. This guy is pure trouble. If I disappear someday, you can bet it's because of him. I hate being around him. He's always mean and drunk!"

Justin stopped for a second. He realized he had been carrying on way too long and told Steve some things he had kept bottled up. It was good to get it all out, but he still felt he shouldn't have said some things to him. It didn't matter, though, for he knew Steve wouldn't say a word.

"Wow. You sure blew off some steam. That was good, I think," Steve said, trying to be agreeable. He then tried to change the subject from the camping trip to The Woods again.

"Yeah, like I said, tomorrow I'm going to be busy, so I won't have time to go with you till I return from camp."

Steve looked sad, but Justin could tell his friend was still trying to devise an alternative plan.

Then, Steve let Justin know what he was thinking after a few moments.

"Why don't we sneak out tonight and see what this is all about?"

Immediately, Justin was against this. He did not like the idea that if they did sneak out, it would be lying to Steve's parents. It didn't sit well with him, and he told Steve this.

Their debate lasted about twenty minutes. Justin gave reasons not to go, and Steve seemed to provide more reasons to go.

Finally, Justin gave in. He decided that it would have to be tonight if they were going. The camp was over a month-long, and there was no way he would wait until Steve came home to go back inside.

Justin was very bothered about his decision, so Steve tried to lighten things up.

He went to his closet and took out his duffel bag, which he would take to camp. Quickly, he took out two flashlights.

"Mom doesn't want me to be without a flashlight while I'm

at camp. She is so afraid that I will get up in the middle of the night to pee and lose my way back because I don't have any light to see the path. So, what does she do? She puts two flashlights in my bag. She overcompensates. Crazy huh? I love her. I do!"

Steve was trying his best to sound facetious and to lighten the mood. He sat there waving the flashlights around, making them look like strobe lights.

But Justin was also bothered by something else besides the lying. What if they got caught? Steve might not get to go on his camping trip if they were found out.

"I just don't want you to get caught, Steve! You sure you want to go tonight?"

"Hey, it was my idea. I'm a big boy. I can make up my mind. Yes, let's go. Let's go as soon as possible!" His voice was full of delight.

"I want to see if everything you told me is true and you weren't exaggerating. You have to admit this story of yours does sound a bit on the unbelievable side."

Justin had to agree with Steve on this point. Everything he told him sounded a little farfetched, so the only way he could prove this to his friend was to take him to The Woods. So, they would go to The Woods, even at this time of night.

The Adventure

Half past ten that night, the two of them quietly escaped. Once they knew everyone was asleep, they headed out Steve's bedroom window.

Cautiously, they grabbed the big branch from the tree close to the house.

Now, all they had to do was climb down into the backyard. The two of them had done this so often that it was second nature. They could have done this with their eyes closed.

This time, though, they were on a mission. 'Mission of the Sacred Heart,' Justin named it. He had heard this somewhere in his past, and it stuck with him.

Creeping stealthily into the night, Justin thought about this situation he had created.

How could Justin the Just sneak out after curfew? He knew this was wrong. Lying to Steve's parents was also incorrect. This was not what Justin wanted to do. But he was in this, and apparently, he had to see it through.

Justin told himself that sometimes, you had to do things that didn't seem right, but you had to make it right in the end. He didn't like sneaking around and lying, but in his heart, he felt that it was meant to be.

Plus, something else drew him towards The Woods. Something he couldn't quite understand at this time. But he knew, whatever it was, he would find the answer there in the valley.

Justin had devised a plan just in case they were caught. If caught, he would take all the blame. That way, Steve might still get to go to camp after all.

They both calculated that it would take them around twenty minutes on foot, but it should only take around five or ten if they took the bikes.

So, on the bikes, they went. Both of the boys' hearts were pounding fast. This was going to be fun.

The boys rode in and out of the back streets, trying their best not to be seen by any people or cars. The fear of getting caught drove them on. They knew if they were seen, then their little adventure might be over. Fear and excitement seemed to sweat from their pores as they continued into the night.

The boys only saw one car out at this time of the night. It happened right when they left their neighborhood. They had just made it past all the houses when suddenly headlights appeared. They quickly scurried and hid their bikes behind a trash container.

It was a close call because it was a police car that was out patrolling. They knew they had gotten lucky and hoped their luck stayed with them as they continued their journey.

Reaching the dirt road, the boys headed to the same opening that Justin had been to earlier. They heard a dog barking as they did and instantly knew it had to be old Red.

A full moon made tonight's going a little easier on the boys. Now, away from most of the lights, darkness engulfed them.

They both got off their bikes and looked inside the opening of the trees. It seemed darker inside,

"It was a great idea to bring the flashlights," Justin said to Steve as they entered the forest. Quickly, they turned them on and then proceeded forward.

Sure, they had some reservations about going inside, but their excitement was the catalyst that pushed them onward.

Once they were inside, they covered their bikes with brush and leaves. They knew it was silly, but they did it anyway.

It was slow going at first, but Justin was sure he was on the same path he had been on earlier. The surroundings seemed familiar, almost as if he had been here many times.

Without the flashlights, their progress would have been much slower, not to mention a bit scary. After all, it was very dark in this place, and their imagination seemed to be running away with them. Without the flashlights, the boys would have seen something behind every tree or bush they passed.

A short time later, Justin thought about something that might become a problem. If it was nighttime here in The Woods, would it be in the valley? He knew time was slightly different, for whatever reason, but still, this might impact their little adventure.

As the boys continued, Justin sensed that this was the same path he had taken earlier today, but it took a little longer. Maybe it was because he was anxious, or it might also be that Steve was with him this time.

Whatever the reason, it did not detour the boys from continuing their quest.

A few moments later, when Justin thought they might be on the wrong path, he saw the rock with the moss on it.

Now, up and over the rock, they went. As they climbed, they both got their clothes wet from the moss. Neither boy cared, though, because they were too excited.

Quickly, the boys were over the rock and down on the other side without any trouble.

They were now at the same spot where Justin had heard the noise of the river, and sure enough, there it was again.

A short distance later, they could see the light up ahead. Hopefully, this was the same light Justin had seen the first time here.

Something seemed different, however. It was dimmer. It was so vague that it did not shine to the top of the trees. Justin thought that maybe it was because it was supposed to be dark outside in the valley at this time.

As they got closer, they started to peel back all the growth that was in their way to get through. There seemed to be a lot more foliage this time.

When they pushed the bushes and limbs aside, the light grew brighter. This seemed to answer his earlier thought of the night and day dilemma.

"But it's nighttime on the other side of The Woods, so how could it be light here?"

Justin said this to Steve, knowing that no answer would come.

The boys were glad it was daytime here because this would benefit them. After all, they didn't want to go to a place they didn't know much about and be in total darkness.

The boys then looked at each other and turned their flashlights off simultaneously, realizing they would not be necessary at this time.

As they walked out of the darkness of The Woods to the open area, they could feel their excitement increase.

Justin said to Steve, "Look down there. This is where we must slide down to get to the bottom."

"Yes. It does look too steep to run down," Steve said. "Now, where are those steps you said you used to get back up the first time?"

Justin then walked over to where he thought the steps were. Try as he might, he could not find them. It was almost as if they had disappeared.

"That's strange," he said to Steve. "I could have sworn that those steps were right here. I don't see them now, but I bet they will be here when we return this way!"

Stepping up to the middle of the knoll, Justin let out a "Geronimo" and slid down. Once at the bottom, Justin looked back up at Steve. For some reason, his friend was waiting before he slid. Justin then had to coax Steve into taking that first step.

As Steve stood there debating whether this was a good thing to do, he heard Justin say a few words about him being 'chicken' or something similar.

"Well, chicken is good to eat," he said, "but I'm not one of them."

So, down the hill, he slid. It was faster than he thought it would be and as fun as Justin had promised. Steve was at the bottom in no time.

"I told you it was fun," Justin said as he helped his friend to his feet.

Justin smiled broadly and said, "What were you waiting for, Steve?

Steve had to come up with something, so he quickly answered.

"I was waiting for the right time to slide. The wind wasn't blowing in my direction. As soon as it did, then I slid. You have to know these things because if you don't, you could get hurt. Remember that in the future slides, my friend." Steve tried to sound diplomatic as he said this to Justin.

After some laughter, Justin said, "Come on, let's get moving. We don't know how long we have been here since time seems different, so the longer we chat, the less time we have to explore."

Then, in unison, they looked at their watches. Both watches seemed to have stopped working. If they weren't stopped, they were at least going slower than usual.

Justin then shrugged and said to Steve, "I guess it's just one of the strange and different things that happen here in this valley. I can't explain it or any other things that seem odd."

As they moved on, Justin couldn't help but look over at the weeping willow tree. Try as he might, he could not see the little man he met the first time. He hoped he would meet him again when they returned this way to leave. He never had the chance to thank him for the first time he was here.

With Steve in tow, Justin headed toward the river. When they reached it, Justin bent down and picked some sand up. Like before, the sand quickly melted or sifted through his hands.

Then Steve did the same. He, too, saw the sand melt in his hands.

"How can this be possible? It's almost like the Kinetic sand we used in science class this year."

After a short pause, Steve added, "So far, everything you told me is true, and you want to know something? I like it here! This is fun!"

Steve almost shouted this to Justin as they surveyed the area around the river.

Justin then chimed in. "I like it here, too. It's almost magical in a way. Maybe even enchanted."

Then Steve asked, "Justin? Did you go into the water? Did you try to swim?"

"No, I didn't. I didn't have enough time, or I thought I didn't. Anyway, let's see how the water feels."

Justin bent down and slowly touched the water. He pulled

his hand back quickly as if he had been burned. But there was no reason to. Justin was just a little edgy and overreacted to how it felt on his skin.

The water felt excellent. It wasn't the same cool they were used to, though, but it was still cool to the touch. You could tolerate it. No matter how long you kept your hand in the water, it didn't get any colder.

Justin tried to explain it better but couldn't.

"Go ahead and try it yourself, Steve. That might make it a little easier to understand!"

Steve stood there watching as Justin put his hands in the water. He walked over to the water and did the same thing.

Sure enough, it was just like Justin had described. It was cold, but yet it wasn't. That didn't make much sense, but there was no other way to say it.

They both nodded in disbelief and chalked this one up to another strange thing they had discovered.

Once again, the boys started walking along the river's path. As they did, they noticed that the sky was getting darker. The clouds began changing from their ivory-white texture to pearl black in color. These were dark, ominous-looking clouds, and the boys knew they would have to find shelter if it started to rain.

As if on cue, raindrops started to fall. The only possible shelter was by the side of the mountain. It had a few rocks hanging over, which could block the rain if necessary. The rain wasn't too bad right now, so the boys continued their journey.

There were two paths; one followed the river, and the other went around the mountain.

The boys decided to take the mountain path. They could tell that several people had used this path in the past. Some of the weeds at the side of the path had been stomped down, and there were shoeprints in the dirt.

The boys had now picked up their pace as they followed the path the best they could.

Then, just before the two of them reached the mountain, something caught the corner of their eyes. Both of the boys turned to see what it was.

What they saw was something that appeared shiny, and it seemed to be reflecting in their direction. It looked like it had come from the same area they had entered the valley.

Trying to get a better look at what it might be, both of them stopped walking.

A short time later, the light stopped shining. It was there one moment, then gone the next. But when it did stop, they could see some movement. Whatever or whoever did this was now too far away.

"What was that?" Steve asked Justin with some worry in his voice.

"I don't know, but it's gone now. It looked like someone was trying to signal us with a light!"

"Yeah. I think you may be right," Steve said.

He then added, "Maybe it was someone who was trying to warn us of something? After all, we don't know much about this place yet."

There was a little bit of nervousness attached to Steve's answer. He just wanted them both to keep their guard up in case something happened.

The boys gave one last look and continued walking around the mountain.

The rain started to come down harder as they continued their trek.

Suddenly, breaking through the air, there was a shrill sound. It almost sounded like some bird trying to cry, if possible. It was so loud that it hurt their ears. It also seemed to be very close to them.

Justin quickly told Steve, "I heard something like this the first time I was here, but this one is much louder."

As they covered their ears, they were bewildered about where it came from and why. Then, as quickly as it started, it stopped. The sound had only lasted five or ten seconds at the most.

Now, the boy's pace had quickened even more. Something told Justin that they should get moving and that it might be wise to do this as quickly as possible.

Their walking seemed a little more challenging and a bit slower now. The reason was that they were walking on a slight incline around the mountain.

With Justin leading the way, they finally reached the top.

As the two of them stood there, they noticed another beautiful valley. And there was something else.

They saw a little village with houses next to another part of the river.

Standing there, they realized these houses looked more like thatched-roof huts. Some seemed a little bigger than others, but for the most part, they all looked the same.

The huts' colors seemed to be the same, too. Most of them had green roofs and brown siding.

Strolling down the road, they saw that the river had branched off. One branch passed through the village and was just a slow stream. The other part continued south from where they had entered the valley. There was also a bridge that connected the huts on each side of the river.

The boys could now see beautiful flowers surrounding the huts. But the one thing they had not seen yet was people.

Justin and Steve looked at each other with bewilderment in their eyes. Still, they continued forward.

As they walked down the path toward the village, they could see more and more flowers. They were also beautiful and seemed very colorful and bright at this time of day. Even the grass here seemed to give off a kind of greenish glow.

With all of this, and still, they saw no people.

Someone had to build these homes, maintain them, and take care of the flowers. But who? Who were the people of this little village? Where could they be?

Both the boys realized that the only way to answer these questions was to go down there and find out for themselves. So, continuing down the road, they went.

With their little adventure getting more curious by the minute, they had forgotten about the weather.

The rain was still falling but even harder now. And there was something else. It wasn't just coming down; it was also beginning to hurt when it hit them. The raindrops seemed to be getting bigger.

They were more significant than any drops either boy had seen or heard.

At first, they thought it was hail, but the more they looked at the drops, the more they realized they were raindrops.

Another thing they knew was that the longer they stayed out in this weather, the more likely they were to get hurt by the drops.

Cautiously, they continued toward the huts. They had to find some cover till this storm blew over.

Before they reached the first hut, they could see that the raindrops were now the size of a baseball. They weren't as hard, but they still hurt when they hit you.

Standing under the hut's porch, the boys turned toward the front door. Justin knocked two or three times, but there was no answer.

"Think we should check and see if the door is unlocked?"

Steve asked Justin this as they both began to shiver from a wind that had come with the rain.

"No. I don't think walking into someone's home would be wise. Besides, I think we should be safe here. This overhang isn't too big, but at least we're off the baseball field!"

Justin said this to Steve, all the while trying to sound funny. Both of them had slight grins on their faces when this was said.

They both turned away from the door and looked at the other huts and the rain.

Suddenly, the door opened behind them, and two hands came out. Both boys were grabbed by their shoulders and pulled inside.

The Chase

Rhonda knew they were up to something. She could tell just by how Justin acted when he came over tonight. That is why she listened at her brother's door. She wanted to know exactly what was going on.

She couldn't quite make out what they were saying as she listened, but she knew they were planning to sneak out tonight.

She knew their escape route: out the bedroom window, down the tree limb, and then to the garage to get the bikes.

Rhonda had seen her brother do this many times in the past.

So, she waited.

Then, a little after ten, she heard her brother's window open. She quickly turned off her bedroom light to watch them from her window.

She sprang into action once the boys left the tree and went to the garage. Ronnie grabbed her flashlight and quickly went to her brother's room. Unknown to him, she had a spare key.

Her parents were asleep, so she tried to be as quiet as a mouse. It was late at night, and she knew the slightest sound might awake them.

Climbing down the tree limb would be easy for Ronnie.

Even though she was only twelve, she had done this many times.

Nothing phased her. She was a tomboy at heart. She always liked hanging out with the boys in the neighborhood, for they played sports and did fun stuff.

For her age, Ronnie was a pretty tough little girl. She could hold her own with most of her peers, so following the boys wouldn't be hard.

Ronnie then climbed down the same limb while keeping the boys in sight.

"Where the heck are these two going," she said as she grabbed her bike.

Quickly, she jumped on and pedaled as fast as she could. She only lost sight of them once, when the boys pulled to the side of the street and hid behind a trash bin to avoid a police car.

"So, they must be up to no good; otherwise, they wouldn't have tried so hard to avoid the police," she said with satisfaction.

Thinking about this a little more, she realized that curfew was in effect, so maybe that was why the boys hid from the police. After all, she had done the same thing, hadn't she?

Whatever their reason, she didn't care. She only cared about keeping up with them and not getting caught herself.

As Ronnie followed them, she saw they had reached the

outskirts of town. There was nothing out here for miles except one place. It was a cornfield that was owned by a farmer named Tucker.

She could barely see them now but was thankful there was a full moon, for she would indeed have lost them. The flashlight she had brought did help, but not much. She had only turned it on sparingly, for she did not want the boys to see the light.

Suddenly, the boys took a hard left and headed down a dirt road on Tucker's property. On the left side of the dirt road was Tucker's cornfield; on the right side was the place known as The Woods.

"What could they possibly want in this field," she said as she pedaled faster and faster, all the while trying to stay within shouting distance of them. She hoped they were going to the field, not The Woods. Even she knew that The Woods were an area no one wanted to visit or go inside.

Now, she was around a hundred yards behind them, so she stopped on the side of the road and watched. Ronnie then realized that her fears about them going to The Woods instead of the field were coming true. This was the one thing she dreaded the most.

Ronnie then got off her bike and walked to where the boys had entered the forest.

"Oh no. I'm not about to go in there by myself even if I have a flashlight," she said defiantly.

A short time passed, and she thought about her situation more.

So, what was she going to do? Stay out here and wait for them to come back out? Go home and tell on them for sneaking out?

"I should tell on them, but I won't!"

Ronnie knew deep down she would never tell on her brother unless he made her mad enough. He was just out having fun. She was only angry at him now because he was having fun without her.

It didn't take long for Ronnie to decide what to do. She wasn't about to sit in the dark while the boys were going inside this thicket—not her.

Quickly, she walked her bike inside the hollow while trying her best to stay unnoticed.

As Ronnie moved forward, she found their bikes relatively quickly.

"They sure didn't do a good job hiding the bikes. They must have been in a big hurry."

Sitting on her bike, she could faintly hear them talking. This seemed to help her get the elusive courage to follow them further. Rhonda knew the longer she waited, the farther away the two would be, so she gallantly got off her bike and followed their voices.

"I know I can do this. If Steve and Justin can do it, then I can, too. I'm as tough as they are."

These thoughts of encouragement helped her start walking forward into the darkened trees. Deeper and deeper she went. She followed their footsteps the best she could. It was rough going, but she knew if something did happen, she could yell out to her big brother, and he would save her.

A short time later, as Ronnie continued on the path, she started to get scared again. It was dark, and she hadn't seen or heard the boys in a while. She began feeling that she had lost them, and panic started to sit in.

Just as she was about to give up, she approached a rather large rock. As she looked at the rock, she could see a light that seemed to shine over the top of it.

Ronnie then took her flashlight and inspected the rock. She discovered that footprints had been left behind by the moss that covered it. These footprints showed precisely where to step if you wanted to climb it.

Now, a glimmer of hope resurfaced, for she figured the footprints had to have come from Justin and Steve.

Surveying the rock and the area, she realized that she would have to go up and over it if she wanted to catch up to them.

Getting her courage up again, she quickly climbed the rock while doing her best to step into the previous footholds.

Once down on the other side, she noticed the light she had seen previously. But now, the light seemed to be fading. As she got closer, she turned off her flashlight, which wasn't needed now.

Ronnie then heard the boys up ahead, so she quickly hid inside some bushes just inside the trees. As she watched, she saw them slide down a hill overlooking a big valley. Quietly, she moved forward a few steps.

As she continued to watch, the boys walked over to a river. After a short time there, they headed onto a path that led toward a rather large mountain.

She was relieved she had found them again, even though they were moving away. They were taking a path that seemed to curve around the mountain.

Like the boys, she was in awe that there was sunlight here, and it was dark before she entered this valley. She let this fact go, for she was more in tune with catching up to them than wondering why it was day or night.

As she waited for the right moment to emerge from The Woods, she noticed that the boys had moved further ahead of her again, and she panicked a little.

She then turned her flashlight back on and tried to signal them, hoping they would see it and stop and wait for her.

The flashlight worked when she was in The Woods, but when she stepped outside and into the open, it didn't. All it did was flicker a little and quit.

While waving her flashlight, she noticed that Justin and Steve were almost out of sight and heading around a bend by the mountain. She watched them follow the path around the mountain while trying her best to get their attention.

Ronnie then went back inside the opening and tried her flashlight again. It worked this time, so she started to wave it at the boys.

But it was now too late, for the boys had rounded the bend of the mountain and were out of view.

Now that the boys were out of her sight, anxiety began to take hold. Quickly, she emerged from the trees and ran to where she had seen them slide down.

"I can't believe I waited this long to come out of The Woods. I should have come out when they were at the river. Now, I may never catch up to them."

She slid down the hill without hesitation. Ronnie then started walking on the path around the side of the mountain, praying that she could catch up to them.

A loud noise pierced the air at this time. It was unnerving, but Ronnie kept walking. The noise made her want to catch up to the boys even more.

Then she noticed a slight incline, but something hit her forehead before she got to it. At first, it felt OK. Then, after a few more hit her, they hurt a little. She realized it was raindrops, and they were getting bigger by the minute.

"This sure is a different place," she said, trying to calm her deepening fears. "These raindrops are huge!"

The sky was now completely dark, and a threatening tent was attached. Rhonda was almost to the top of the incline, but a slight fear crept up.

She knew she would have to find some cover as the drops kept coming. Luckily, she spotted a small cave at the side of the mountain. She then ran over to it as quickly as she could. This little cave wasn't too big, just enough to keep her out of the rain.

A short while later, the raindrops got smaller, so she ventured out of the little covering. She then put her hand out so some of them would hit it. They were indeed smaller now, and they didn't hurt her anymore.

Shaking her head in disbelief, she headed to the top of the incline, still searching for her brother and Justin.

Finally, once she reached the top of the incline, she noticed a beautiful valley and some quaint little huts. But her brother and Justin were still nowhere in sight.

Ronnie knew now that she had messed up badly; all she could think about was going home and getting in bed. At this point, she didn't want anything to do with this place.

What was she going to do now? What if she had lost them? How could she get back?

Her eyes began to fill up with tears as she sat down on the ground.

The Village Elder

They fell onto the floor. It was all so sudden that both boys were caught off guard. As they lay there, they could see someone looking down at them.

To Justin, this person looked almost like the man who showed him the steps the other day. But the more he looked, the more he realized it wasn't him. There was just a slight resemblance. The other man at the tree was short, and this fellow was much taller.

As the two boys lay there, they knew that this man had to be the one who pulled them inside the hut. They also noticed that, for some reason, this man was looking at them disgustedly. His arms were crossed, and he was tapping his foot.

Glaring at them, he started to pace around the room.

Stopping before them, he said, "What do the two of you think you were doing out there? Didn't you hear the warning sound?"

Justin and Steve just looked at each other.

Warning sound? Did he mean that awful sound they heard and had to cover their ears? The noise that almost pierced their eardrums?

"You two have got a lot to learn. You don't even know about the warning alarm! If you don't know about that, then you probably don't know much about anything else in this valley."

The man just looked at them, shook his head, and then turned and headed to another room.

As the boys slowly sat up, they glanced at each other with bewilderment.

This guy seemed to be a very odd character. He was medium height and had a long but bushy beard. He looked ancient, and his face was much wrinkled. His feet were small but wide. And his eyes! Both of his eyes had small pupils that were dark in color. Also, his eyelids even looked strange. When he blinked, it looked like his eyelids covered the eyes and then some. They looked as if they were stretched an inch too long.

He wore a wrap-around garment with a little rope around his waist, which he used as a belt. His brown shirt looked to be made of leather or even some type of thread.

This man's shoes looked like they were made of leather, too. They had a brownish tint to them and looked very worn.

Sitting on the floor, Justin looked closer at this fellow as he moved about in another room.

He wore an odd-looking hat. It looked like an old aviator's hat, which Justin had seen in a museum a few years ago. He could also tell that it was made of leather; he was sure of that.

This old man also wore pants that looked like they could have been made of wool or cotton. They seemed to be very loose on him.

A moment or two passed, and they could no longer see the man inside the hut. Justin looked outside the hut's window and saw him looking up at the sky.

The man then turned toward them and motioned to come outside. They noticed the sky was getting brighter and clearing rapidly when they did.

The boys then walked up to the man, and he pointed to two chairs on the front porch.

The chairs seemed to adjust to their size and weight as they sat down on them. After a minute or so, their body structures fit perfectly in them.

The old man was right: Justin and Steve had much to learn about this place.

For a short time, there was silence. Justin decided that it would be him who broke it.

"My name is Justin. This is my friend Steve. A few days ago, I came through The Woods and practically stumbled into this place mostly by accident. I was so impressed with this valley that I told Steve about it, and he wanted to see it for himself, so here we are."

Justin hoped this would break some of the awkwardness between the three of them, and for the most part, it did.

The old man began to speak.

"Let's begin. You two can call me Jib. I am the so-called village elder, or leader, here. Our village has no name, mainly because we never thought there should be a name. Other villages have names but not ours."

Jib went on and on about his village. He then realized that he was talking way too much about it. Shortly, he changed the subject from the village to more important things.

"Anyway, I must ensure everyone is safe when the alarms go off. That noise you heard when you covered your ears was one of the warning signals. It tells us that something is about to happen; in this case, it was the rain. Heed to the warning next time you hear it," Jib commanded.

Justin then realized something. Neither he nor Steve had mentioned to this Jib fellow that they had covered their ears when they heard that awful sound. That seemed strange to him.

But how could this man know that they had covered their ears? They must have said something; otherwise, he could not have known. Or maybe he was outside at the time and saw them do it. This wasn't logical either because they were not yet in sight of the village when the alarm sounded.

Well, whatever the answer was, it didn't matter. The warning sound was over, and hopefully, it would not reoccur.

Jib then stopped a second and looked at the two of them with some concern in his eyes.

"If I hadn't pulled you two into the house, you might have both been hurt badly or even worse." Jib looked serious when he said this to them.

Once again, Justin and Steve looked at each other. Why were they getting a crash course on what to do and what not to do while here?

Sitting listening to Jib, they saw other people coming out of their huts. They came around and nodded to them while Jib continued to lecture.

The villagers didn't pay the boys much attention at all. They just went about their business, which now looked like they were trying to repair a few of the huts damaged in the storm. All of them were now sweeping and cleaning the porches and yards.

"I know that the two of you have not been in our valley very long. From how you are dressed, I can see you just came to visit. Both of you are not prepared for anything. You didn't bring any food or water with you either. You must learn that when you go somewhere, you must prepare for anything! That means never go anyplace without some food and water."

The boys looked a little sheepish, almost like they had done something wrong. After all, they just wanted to come and see what this place was all about, not to move in or become a burden.

But deep down inside, both boys knew he was right. Steve had learned some of these precautions from his camping trip last year.

Justin also knew this to be true because his dad had taught him. In the past, they always brought extra food and water whenever they went hiking or rock climbing. But this time, the boys didn't because they completely forgot. Mostly, they were too excited about going, so it impaired their preparations. Plus, this little adventure of theirs was on the QT.

Jib reached into one of the many pockets attached to his clothing around his waist. He then brought out a food-like substance.

As the boys stared at it, they saw it looked like some form of meat.

"This is called Stringer. You will find them on vines throughout the valley. When we harvest them, they seem to last a long time. They will give you the nourishment that you need. Sure, there are other things to eat, but these are handy when you are on the go and need something quick."

Jib then handed the boys some. They looked at each other to see who would first try it. Once again, Justin took the lead and ate a few bites. Then, shortly after, Steve did the same.

"That's not too bad," Justin said. "I was a little hungry, but this has curbed my appetite. It doesn't taste that bad, either. Thank you, sir."

Jib nodded to each of them and said they were very welcome.

When they all seemed to be done eating, Jib got up and returned to his hut.

A few moments passed, and he returned outside and said, "Let's take a walk if you don't mind." "I think I need to explain some things about this place you two have stumbled into!"

As the three walked along the river, Jib once again told the boys about the valley. They listened intently, and hearing him talk about this place was interesting. They both could tell the old man loved this village and was proud of the people there. Justin hoped this information would be helpful to them as they continued exploring this area.

As Justin listened, his mind began to wander.

This is such a great place. How did it get here? Why has no one ever found it all these years? Somehow, this area was cut off from the rest of the world. They were self-sustained, not needing anything or anyone from the outside.

Justin knew these were good people, but he also felt that if people from the outside found out about this valley, they would somehow ruin it. He almost started to become defensive about this aspect. It was as if he had finally found a place where he felt he belonged, but somehow, he could lose it if he wasn't careful.

"I don't know about you, Steve, but I love it here. I never want to leave. This is such a great place."

You could hear the excitement in his voice as he said this, and his sense of adventure had heightened. Both of their faces were smiling from ear to ear.

"I love it here too, Justin, but forever is a long time. I have things to do back home." Steve suddenly stopped his sentence short.

There was a commotion to their right. It seemed to come from the same direction they had entered the village.

Looking up the road, they saw some town folk helping someone walk into the village. They couldn't tell who it was, but the person looked young.

"Wonder who that is," Steve said to Justin. "They must have lost their way. Or maybe they caused the people who live here some trouble or something."

As they watched the person approaching, Justin realized who it was before Steve did.

He then said to his friend, "No. Not trouble for the villagers. Trouble for us. It's your sister Rhonda!"

"What? How can that be?"

Steve had almost yelled these questions at the top of his lungs.

His face had quite a skeptical look as they stood there watching.

Shortly, he ran toward the person to ensure it was his sister.

"She is supposed to be home and in bed asleep. How can she be here? I don't believe this!" Steve was stunned and almost shouted his reply.

Steve ran to her and helped her to a chair on Jib's front porch. He could tell she had been crying and looked afraid. He put his arms around her to try and settle her nerves.

A few moments passed, and then Ronnie began talking.

"You are in big trouble, Steve. I'm going to tell Mom and Dad when I get home."

As she said this to Steve, she could feel the chair conform to her body as she settled into it.

Now, it was Steve's turn to get tough.

"Yeah, that's right, Ronnie. Deflect the possibility of you getting in trouble and put it on me. You and I both know you won't tell them. You will be in as much trouble as I would if you do. So just shut up and sit there while I try to think of what we will do with you."

Steve was mad. He was angry at her and himself for letting her follow them. He should have been more observant and guessed that she would do this.

But then again, he wasn't just mad; he was worried. Now, he would have to ensure she didn't get into any more trouble until they left for home.

Jib interrupted them at this time. He could tell they all knew each other but tried to be polite.

"Do you know this little creature? Is she one of you?"

"Unfortunately, we know her, and yes, she is one of us. We don't know how she got here, but I must take her home." Steve was very apologetic as he answered Jib.

Jib stood there looking at the three of them. He had a smile on his face as he shook his head in agreement. They all knew that he understood.

Justin looked at Jib and could tell he was a good man. He

seemed to be a trustworthy person and one that wouldn't harm you or anyone else. That is probably why these people elected him to lead their little village.

Steve turned to Justin and said, "I must take her home. We can't go on any further with her here. Maybe you can keep exploring, but I must take her back. It has to be getting late by now, so the sooner I get her home, the less trouble there will be if we are caught."

Steve shook his head in defeat. He couldn't believe that his sister had followed them. She could have gotten hurt or lost. Once he got her out of there, he would give her a piece of his mind.

But Steve was also in awe of his little sister. He didn't think she had the nerve to follow them or even go into The Woods alone, especially at night.

Justin stood there, trying to decide what he was going to do. It didn't take him too long, for he knew the answer. Sheepishly, he turned toward Jib with a slight frown on his face.

"We all have to go home. Please forgive us if we have intruded or caused trouble for any of you. If at all possible, we would like to come back sometime. It's very late in the night where we came from, so we must go!"

Once again, they noticed Jib looking into the sky. The sun

was going down. With all the excitement, the boys never saw this.

"If the three of you are going to leave, then hurrying would be in your best interest. It will get dark here soon, and being out after dark in our valley might not be a good thing. So, hurry now, on your way!"

Then Jib turned to Justin. There was a strange look in his eyes as he walked up to him.

"Justin, you can come back anytime you want. You are welcome."

There was a delay in the old man's voice as he said this to him. It was almost as if he wanted to say more but couldn't.

Justin also sensed that he was saying this to him and not to Steve or Ronnie, but then he added, "You all are welcome. When you get to the hill, the man you met the first time will be there to show you the way up."

The three kids nodded their thanks and headed back up the incline and around the mountain.

Once they reached the river, they could barely see the hill, for the darkness had caught up with them.

"Turn the flashlights on," Justin commanded. All three tried, but none of the lights worked here in the valley.

Rhonda was now getting scared, so Steve picked her up and

carried her the best he could.

They seemed to hear things around them as they continued toward the hill. Maybe it was just their imaginations, but even Justin was slightly unnerved.

Leading the way, Justin kept looking to the sides and behind them just in case someone might be watching or following.

If there was someone, then who could it be? What was Jib talking about when he said it might not be a good idea to be in his valley at night?

Suddenly, over to his right, just beyond the nearby trees, Justin saw something move. Since it was getting darker by the minute, he did not stop to see who or what it was. It looked like a man to him, but it also seemed you could look through it. It almost looked like a specter of some kind.

With no time to lose and figure out what it was, Justin led them onward.

Now they reached the hill, and just as Jib had promised, the little man was there waving and telling them to hurry.

He quickly showed them the steps, and they ran up them as fast as they could. Once at the top, Justin turned to thank the little man, but just like before, he was gone.

Without any hesitation, they hurried into the dark opening.

Something in Justin's mind made him think about trying the flashlights again. When they did, they came on.

Nothing mechanical, like their watches and flashlights, seemed to work in the valley, but now that they were out of that area, they did.

Shortly after arriving at the big rock, all three were up and over without much effort.

Then, like the first time he was in The Woods, he felt like something or someone was watching. Justin was sure he had heard something but wasn't about to stop or let the others know he had.

Quickly, they got through the wooded area without any problems.

Once they reached their bikes, they couldn't have started pedaling fast enough. Home was their refuge, at least for Steve and Rhonda. But not so much for Justin. He was feeling a little homesick for the valley he had just left. Somehow, he knew he would go back, but for now, he would have to wait for the right time. This sneaking out was not what he wanted to do, and he felt troubled by doing it.

They realized they had been fortunate as the three of them headed home. Getting home was their top priority, and not getting caught was also high on their list. If they made it home, then everyone would be none the wiser.

Caught

The kids were only two blocks from Steve's house when the lights and siren came on. All three were shaky and scared as they got off their bikes to talk to the policeman.

After explaining what they were doing, he allowed them to walk their bikes the rest of the way home. The officer followed them to ensure they went home and escorted them. The only good thing about being pulled over was that they knew the police officer.

As the kids waved goodbye to him, they thought this encounter seemed too easy. All they got was just a warning about being out after curfew. They sighed in relief when they saw him leave, but it didn't last long.

Silently, the three of them took their bikes to the garage. With this done, they knew the hard part was about to happen.

Steve then pulled out his house key and, as quietly as he could, unlocked the door without making a sound.

As they tip-toed up the stairs to their bedrooms, they suddenly heard someone clearing their throat.

"OK, out with it? I need an explanation, and I need a great one!"

It was Mr. Williams, and from the sound of his voice, he was not in a very good mood.

The kids just stood there frozen on the spot. Now, they all knew the real reason they had only received a warning.

Justin immediately started with the story he had rehearsed in his mind so many times tonight.

"I'm sorry, Mr. Williams. It was my fault. I should never have got them to go with me. I know of a," but Steve cut off Justin's words.

"Dad," Steve said quickly, "we were just out riding our bikes. None of us could sleep, so we were racing. We just lost track of time, that's all!"

Steve didn't like lying to his father but felt it would be better than telling him the whole truth, at least at this time. It was also the same story Steve had told the officer earlier.

Now, it was Steve's turn to be interrupted. Justin could not let him say these things when he knew in his heart that they were lies.

Justin went on to tell Mr. Williams more, but he did not tell him about the valley or how far they went inside The Woods.

"I'm sorry, Mr. Williams. I should never have let Steve and Ronnie go with me. It is my fault, not theirs."

Mr. Williams was more curious than they thought, and he didn't just let this end, at least not yet.

"So, if that is where you three went, then WHY? What could make you all go out there in the middle of the night?"

Steve chimed in at this point, and it seemed he already had another excuse to say to his dad.

"Dad, I know this looks bad, but we didn't go and do anything wrong. I know we shouldn't have left the house this late, but none of us were tired, so we slipped out. I apologize for my behavior and fibbing. I'm so very sorry."

Steve bowed his head at this time. He looked down at the floor, not daring to look at his father.

Mr. Williams knew there was more to this story. He also knew his son was not telling the whole truth when he did not look him in the eye.

"Fibbing? No, it's a little more than a fib, young man."

Steve hung his head even lower and still could not make eye contact with his father.

The silence was deafening as they waited for Mr. Williams to speak.

Mr. Williams didn't know why they were out tonight, but he knew his kids and Justin, so whatever the reason was, it couldn't have been that bad. He also knew that, in time, he would find out the whole truth.

Steve's dad stood there for a few more moments before he delivered his verdict.

To Justin, Steve's dad was one of the best grownups he knew, besides his mom. He was always fair in his decisions, and Justin hoped this would be another.

"I want to start by saying that I am very disappointed in all three of you. I know you want to take the blame alone, Justin, but that won't happen. Steve and Ronnie are also to be blamed. Steve, more than his sister, because he is older. He should look out for her instead of getting her into trouble."

Mr. Williams then started to pace around the room a bit, trying to devise the best possible punishment.

Shortly, it was delivered.

"Steve and Ronnie will be grounded for one week each. As for you, Justin, I must tell your parents."

He saw the look on Justin's face, so he added, "Only your mother."

Mr. Williams knew about Mark and the so-called stories of how cruel he might be, so telling him was not an option. He thought there was no need to get the boy into serious trouble.

"I don't condone what the three of you did, but I understand it. I was young once if you can believe it, and I did a few things against my parents' perspective. Now, whatever reason the three of you had, it was wrong. Nothing you have said can make me feel otherwise. We will discuss this more in the morning. Now, off to bed!"

Even though they were being grounded, they felt like they had got off easy. Mr. Williams did ground Steve and Ronnie, but they could live with that. As for Justin, Mr. Williams would only inform his mother about their little escapade, not his stepdad.

The more Justin thought about it, the more he knew that Mr. Williams was a fair man indeed.

Mr. Williams knew he was lenient with the kids but trusted them and Justin. None of them were bad kids. That was one of the reasons he wasn't so hard on them tonight.

Another reason was that he had been best friends with Justin's father. Together, Chris and Jim had owned a sporting goods store in town.

Being such good friends with Chris and his family seemed to help with the decision just to tell Justin's mother and no one else.

He also knew some of what was said about Justin's so-called stepdad. If only part of it was genuine, then it was too much. But he wasn't the type to butt into someone else's business. He tried to stay out of it as much as he could.

On the other hand, he still kept a close eye on Justin. He wanted to ensure things didn't go too far with this Mark fellow.

He would always tell Justin that if he needed help, all he had to do was ask. But so far, he never had. The kid was like that, though. Justin never wanted help or to be a bother.

Justin was his son's best friend; the two were almost inseparable. The boys' proximity made it easier for Mr. Williams to keep an eye on Justin.

And as far as this Mark guy, no one liked him and never would. He was too hard to get along with, primarily because of his drinking problem.

He was a leach who had attached himself to Mary and whom she couldn't get rid of.

***

As Justin and Steve went to bed, they were quiet. Neither boy said anything for a while. They were each wrapped up in their thoughts about all that had happened to them earlier, not only getting caught by the cops but also about all they had discovered in the valley.

"Did you notice that when we came out of the valley, our watches and flashlights started to work again? It seems like anything mechanical doesn't work in there. Odd, don't you think, Steve?"

Steve then answered, all the while closing his eyes.

"Yeah. And another thing. When we were in there, it seemed like a couple of hours, but it had only been an hour at the most when we got home. Plus, I was a little tired going there, but once inside, it was like I had caught up on sleep somehow. I wasn't tired at all. But now that we are home, I am so sleepy. Strange. Strange indeed," Steve said.

"I agree. But I don't think the valley is a bad place. We all got a little scared, but I can live with that. And those people, where did they come from? And that valley. It was beautiful and seemed to go on forever. I still want to go back in. I hope I get another chance."

The boys then slowly started to fall off to sleep.

"If you do get a chance to go back, then give me a call," Steve mumbled as he fell asleep.

They both drifted off to sleep, exhausted from all the excitement. They were back in their world of trouble and mean and dishonest people.

One dishonest person came to mind, and Justin knew he had to get his mom away from him somehow. He decided to start working on that problem tomorrow.

Back to the Woods

The day to leave for summer camp arrived. The boys waved goodbye to each other, with Steve going off to camp and Justin returning home.

Once again, Justin didn't get to go to camp, which was no surprise to him. He knew Mark would never let him go.

Mark had once again come up with a lie about something Justin supposedly did. And once again, Justin didn't refute it out of fear for his mom's safety.

"It's ok, though," Justin said to himself. "At least by staying home, I can keep an eye on my mom. Make sure he doesn't hurt her."

This was how the kid always rationalized the bad things that Mark did to him.

It was Saturday morning, and you would think Justin would be happy because of this, but not today. Mark had already told him he was not going away for the weekend.

As Justin's wave of goodbye subsided, he slowly turned for home. He didn't want to go home, but he did, only because his mother was there.

It had been a week since the three of them had been caught coming home that night from The Woods. The school was out for the summer, and Justin, for the most part, would not like this vacation.

He knew that these next three months would be long and miserable. Mark would make sure of that.

The only thing that had gone right for Justin lately was that Mark had not found out about them getting caught out after curfew. Mr. Williams had kept his word and had only told his mother.

As Justin continued walking home, he could feel the lure of The Woods was strong today, but he resisted. He had tried to explain this to his mom about the wooded area but knew she wouldn't understand why he liked going there.

Justin didn't know the complete reason himself. All he knew was that he felt great inside the valley; it was someplace he wanted and needed to be.

Justin had felt so bad about not being completely honest with his mom. He knew he had to make it up to her somehow. If only he had told her he would be going to The Woods that night, he wouldn't have felt so downhearted.

But the more he thought about it, the more he knew it wouldn't have worked. If he had told her, she would never have let him go in the first place. He just shouldn't have gone, and he knew it. They were fortunate that nothing happened to them, especially to

Ronnie. Their time in the valley could have been disastrous.

Justin was only a few houses away from his home when he heard some yelling. From the sound of the voice, he knew that Mark was shouting. He also could tell that he must be yelling at his mom for unknown reasons.

"Hope he hasn't discovered what I did last week over Steve's!"

This thought seemed to echo in the young boy's mind. He then started to pick up his pace and even ran some of the way home.

Entering the house, he went into the kitchen, where he could hear the commotion escalating.

"What's wrong now?" He yelled this to both of them, but mainly to Mark.

Justin quickly stepped in between his mother and Mark as he said this.

Mark stopped yelling and turned to see who it was. Then, realizing it was Justin, a wicked smirk came across his face. He looked straight into Justin's eyes.

"Today is going to be a good day for you, boy. You and I are going to get to know each other a little better. I also have a few tasks for you to do. Now, no backtalk, young man, no backtalk!"

Mark had said this in anticipation of some back talk, but none came.

"It's Saturday, and you have nothing to do or planned, so get ready to go with me. That's final!" Mark then stomped off to the garage.

Justin looked at his mom to make sure she was all right. She shook her head, and he could tell she had been crying.

Now, he felt downhearted. If only there were something he could do or someone to talk to about this predicament he and his mother were in—maybe someone with more knowledge about situations like this. But there were none, at least none, that he knew about.

He knew Mr. Williams said he could talk to him, but Justin didn't want to get him involved.

Suddenly, Mark came bounding back into the kitchen. His chest was pushed out, and his breathing was rapid. Once again, Justin could smell alcohol on his breath.

And that smile just wouldn't go away. It looked so hideous on his unshaven face. A bout of nausea seemed to surface in Justin's throat.

"I wonder what he wants this time," Justin thought. "Well, whatever it is, I can handle it. I can handle anything he can muster up." Justin automatically took a defiant stance.

Mark stood before Justin momentarily, then headed to the

backyard while shaking his head.

"Hopefully, he passes out from all of his drinking," Justin said to himself, all the while knowing that it would never happen.

As he watched Mark in the backyard, he saw him start banging around on a few things.

Justin then turned and looked at his mom. He could see the fear and the hurt coming from her eyes. He knew she didn't want her boy around this man, but for now, there was nothing that she could do.

Then Justin said to his mother, "Whatever you want me to do, no matter what it is, I will do it for you. I am so sorry for acting like I did last week and going to The Woods without your permission. I know I lied, and I know I hurt you very deeply!"

A few tears started to form in his eyes. His voice had also been shaky, but he didn't care. He loved his mother so very much. She was all he had left.

His mother stood there looking at him. Her face was blank, but then it suddenly changed. Her soft and gentle smile appeared.

"You want to know something? Standing here looking at you reminds me of your dad. You are so much like him. He, too, had that yearning for adventure, just like you. He kept it hidden deep inside of him, but still, I saw it. And I see it in you also. That's what I love about you two."

As Justin stood there, he realized what she had said. It made sense. He did have that sense of adventure inside of him.

Most kids his age were socializing with friends, attending parties, or playing sports.

But for Justin, it was different. He always seemed to be looking for an adventure of some kind. Some place he could explore. Maybe that was why he was attracted so much to The Woods.

As he reflected, Justin knew things worsened when Mark came into their lives. Justin was just getting over the loss of his dad, and then a few years later, this man appeared. It was almost too much to take. But he knew he could take anything this Mark guy came up with. He had to, at least for his mom's sake.

A few moments later, Mary turned toward Justin, and with a gentle voice, she said, "Yes. I am still very upset about what you did last week. It is one thing that you do that alone, but it's another thing to involve other people. Someone could have been hurt. I thank God that Steve's dad called me instead of Mark. You would never live this one down in his eyes."

She gazed out the kitchen window to see if Mark was still in sight.

"You don't have to do anything for me son. I know you did

something wrong last week, and I also know I grounded you from any TV. I hope that helped teach you a lesson, but I don't think it did. You never liked watching TV anyway."

She had a slight smile, and she laughed, mostly under her breath. She had to be discrete about punishing Justin for lying, so no TV was all she could come up with. This had to be done without Mark finding out, and so far, it had.

Once again, she looked toward Justin and said, "Now go outside and see what Mark wants!"

There was a worried look on her face as she said this to her son. She knew that this wasn't a good situation for either of them to be in.

Justin could see a few tears rising in her eyes, and his heart sank again. He reached out, put his arms around her, and hugged her. He did not want this hug to end but knew he had to let go and head outside.

There he is, King Mark, standing in all his glory. I wonder what kind of work he has cooked up for me this time. Well, whatever it is, then bring it on, old man!

When Justin walked up to Mark, he could see the answer to his last thought. Some concrete needed to be broken up. Then, it had to be carried to his truck and hauled away. It had been here for some years and had become a daily eye-sore.

"OK. I can do it," he assured himself. It will take me all day, but that's OK, too. I don't care."

Justin then started to look around to see if this was all Mark wanted him to do. This was enough, but knowing his stepdad, he might have hidden more around the side of the house and sprung it on him when he got through with these slabs.

He started by picking the small pieces. They were heavy, but he somehow lifted them. The next step was to get the sledgehammer to help him break the larger pieces up.

Grabbing the hammer, Justin began to swing it the best he could. Time and time again, he smashed it into the concrete. Most of it broke apart easier than he thought, but it took time. He started around 10:30 and didn't stop until almost noon.

Justin then went into the house where his mom had lunch ready. He could tell his mom was still upset, but he didn't let on that he knew.

Lunch came and went far too soon for Justin, so he returned to his task. The next time he looked at his watch, it was almost two o'clock. He was so tired but did his best not to show it.

The sun was beating down with every blow he launched. His arms began to ache, and his shoulders started hurting, but he kept working. He thought about the adage, "It builds character, son," and almost cringed from the proverb.

He worked hour after hour, and every bone in his body hurt. He had been working for over three hours, but thankfully, he was almost finished.

Mark then made an appearance with his proverbial drink, which was anything alcoholic.

"OK, Justin, you can stop now. I have something else for you to do. Now, we are going to the dump. You can throw this concrete off there. Plus, I have a little surprise for you. As I said earlier, you and I are going to get to know each other better." Mark then turned and went into the house.

As Mark walked away, Justin saw that wicked smile reappear on his lips. He also heard that oh-so-distinctive laugh. The laugh that was always filled with contempt and hatred.

Justin was still in the dark as far as knowing what Mark was talking about, but he was sure whatever it was, he wouldn't like it.

A few moments later, Mark returned, walked to his truck, reached behind the seat, and pulled out a rifle.

From what Justin could tell, this rifle was probably the one Mark did all his so-called hunting with.

"It must be the one that he and his buddies used when

searching for big game," Justin thought sarcastically.

Justin never knew what they hunted for, but he could feel Mark's hate and killer instinct permeating his entire being.

He watched him as he held the rifle and pointed it at the sky while pretending to shoot.

Now, Justin could smell a stench of something coming from Mark, and it wasn't from the booze either. It was like a foul odor from all the killing that he had done through the years. It seemed to surround him.

"We're going to go do a little hunting. I know some woods I once hunted in when I was young, and you will go with me. This will make a man out of you, and you will do it whether you like it or not!"

Mark stood there glaring at Justin with that all-too-familiar smirk on his face. Then, he continued with his fragmented speech.

"This way, we can bond. You know, get to know each other better. Yeah, that's what we need: time to bond. Don't you agree, you little runt?"

Justin could feel just how much hatred this man had for him when he said those words. But one thing he wasn't, he wasn't a runt. Justin was as tall as Mark, just not as 'wide,' so hearing those words didn't faze him. Justin knew he could stand up to Mark and protect his mom from this monster in a few years. But till then, he would take whatever Mark dished out, no matter the price.

A few moments passed, and Justin started thinking about this hunting trip he and Mark would go on.

The thought about Mark and him getting to know each other better was a lie. He knew in his heart that he didn't like him and didn't want anything to do with him. It was just some ruse Mark had drummed up in his watered-down mind.

Justin knew he didn't want to go with him no matter where they were going. Mark had been drinking, which was no shock, but he was also about to take them somewhere to hunt.

"This guy is drunk, carrying a loaded weapon, and going to be driving. Yeah, this is going to be fun, loads of fun," Justin said to himself, but with some sarcasm attached.

His mom was likely not at home at this time, or Justin knew she would have already come out and stopped him from going on this so-called hunting expedition.

As they drove down the road, Justin wished for one thing. He hoped that the same cop that caught them last week after curfew would pull Mark over and end this charade. But, like always, there were no cops to be seen.

"It always seems that when you need a cop, they are never

there, but you do one thing wrong, and there are four or five," Justin thought, but with some self-pity attached.

Once they got to the dump, Justin unloaded all the concrete himself. Mark sat in the truck as expected, smiling and sipping another beer.

When Justin was finally done, he jumped back into the truck. Mark then made his big announcement.

"Well, little boy, it's time for you and me to go hunting. It's going to be a lot of fun."

Justin could tell by the scorn in Mark's voice that this would not be fun.

Justin felt odd as they drove away and headed to the area where Mark said they would hunt.

As Justin sat there quietly, a worried look appeared on his face.

"Where did he say we were going hunting? Some woods? There is no way it could be The Woods! No way!"

But before Justin knew it, they were driving to the wooded area. It wasn't the exact spot where Justin went in, but it was still The Woods.

From what Justin could tell, this area was about a mile north of where he had entered. There were several ways to go into the wooded area; apparently, Mark knew one of them.

Justin felt his anxiety increasing once again.

As they continued driving, Justin looked bewildered. He couldn't understand why Mark wanted to hunt inside these woods. No one he knew had ever gone hunting in this area.

The so-called hunters went to places much farther away. Some even went out of state, depending on the type of game they were hunting.

A worried look came over Justin as he thought about the people in the village.

"What if somehow Mark found his way to the valley and the village? This might turn into some real trouble for the villagers. I can't let that happen."

This thought unnerved Justin somewhat, and he could feel his heart racing.

Now Justin started to worry. He thought one of the villagers might be inside this area, and Mark might mistake them for an animal and shoot them.

"I'm going to have to keep a sharp eye out for anyone or anything when we go in there," Justin said but under his breath.

Justin didn't like this predicament one bit. All he wanted was to go home.

But then, another thought came to mind. This one seemed to be a good thing.

"Maybe he'll go in there and get lost," Justin quietly said to himself with a smile. "Mark might get lost and never find his way back home. Wouldn't that be great? Or maybe he'll go in there, slip, and shoot himself. Yeah, that might happen."

However, Justin knew none of what he thought would happen because things hadn't been going his way lately.

"If anything bad happened, it would probably happen to me. Maybe that is the real reason we came out here!"

Another worried look came over Justin as he thought about this possibility. He knew Mark didn't like him, but even he wouldn't sink that low. Would he?

As he considered this possibility more, the young lad's mind wandered. He would have to ensure things didn't get out of hand once they reached their destination.

Upon arriving, Justin felt an ominous feeling come over him. He could almost tell that something terrible was going to happen. He hoped he was wrong, but this foreboding feeling wouldn't go away.

After parking the truck off the paved road, they approached The Woods. Once at the entrance, Justin prayed that something would stop them from entering. He did not want Mark to go in and start shooting. He didn't want Mark anywhere near The Woods or at home. He just wanted Mark to get out of their lives once and for all.

Now, standing at the edge of the trees, Mark motioned for the two of them to go inside. He had his rifle ready for anything that might come into view.

As they started to enter, Mark suddenly stopped. There in the bushes, off to his right, something moved. It had been quick and elusive, but still, somehow, Mark saw it.

At first glance, it looked like a rabbit, but upon further inspection, they realized it wasn't. This little animal had ears, but no fur was on them. The ears also looked too short, and they pointed slightly outwards.

Justin sighed in relief because he knew that at least it wasn't one of the villagers.

The two of them looked at the little creature with bewilderment. As they did, they also noticed something about this area. It was now eerily quiet. Nothing seemed to move, not even the wind.

But the silence didn't last too long. Suddenly, a shot rang out. Mark had taken dead aim at the little animal but somehow missed.

"How the heck did I miss that thing?"

He had said this out loud, but a few curse words were attached.

"I won't miss this time," he swore as he raised his rifle again and focused on the target still in range.

Just as he started to pull the trigger, Justin let out a loud cough, which seemed to throw Mark's aim off. The bullet missed by several feet.

Mark then quickly turned toward Justin. Once again, his face was full of hate and disdain.

"You think you're cute, don't you, smart guy? You coughed so I would miss my kill. OK, big boy, it's your turn now. Let's see what kind of man you are!"

Justin stood there for a few seconds, just looking at the weapon. Shooting this rifle was the last thing that he wanted to do at this moment.

Standing before Mark, Justin finally said, "I don't know how to shoot it. I've never shot one, and you can't make me either."

Justin was bold in his answer on this matter and refused to budge. He wasn't about to shoot the creature that was in this area. For all he knew, it might belong to someone inside. He wouldn't shoot any animal in or out of The Woods, and that was final.

"Oh, you're not going to shoot the rifle?"

Mark had asked this question in such a condescending way.

"Maybe I'll bring your mother out here next time. She can learn to shoot the rifle. It's just her and me out here in these woods alone. I hope everything works out when she comes here. But she'll be OK with me, don't you think, Justin?"

There was that awful, wicked, and gut-wrenching smile again. Justin knew that Mark had brought him here to belittle and scare him, and as far as Justin was concerned, he was doing just that.

Mark never missed an opportunity to put Justin or his mom down, but this seemed to be going too far.

Justin realized what he had to do. He had to give in to this crazy man's demands and shoot the rifle. No way did he want his mom coming out here with this drunkard.

"Give me the gun. I will shoot it after all. I can't promise that I'll hit anything, though. Just don't be mad if I miss it. That's all I ask!" Justin was almost pleading with him now.

Justin grabbed the rifle and put it on his shoulder. He then got the creature in his sights but lowered the gun at the last second. Then he pulled the trigger. He missed his target by at least ten yards.

Then, for good measure, he shot at the animal two more times. And, like the first shot, he missed the animal by several yards.

Justin could see Mark getting a big kick when he missed the animal.

"Glad I could brighten up your day, Mark," Justin said, but with much contempt behind it.

Mark returned with, "You're the worst shooter I have ever seen. You don't just need practice; you need another set of eyes. What the heck is wrong with you? You're nothing but a blind little idiot. You're going to grow up just like your worthless dad. He ran away and up and died on you two. Now I'm stuck with a couple of real losers!"

Justin was mad now. Mark should never have said anything about his parents. After all, he still had the rifle in his hands, didn't he?

But it didn't matter because there was no way Justin would use it on him. He was just mad at this moment. The thought did cross his mind, though, but that's all. He gently handed the gun back to Mark.

"Let me show you how a real man takes care of things. I'll show you how I can get us dinner for tonight."

Mark now had something else in his sights. It wasn't the same creature as before, though. Whatever this was, it made Mark lower his rifle and take a step closer to it.

Now, he was at the very edge of The Woods. Still, Mark was not inside; he was just outside the first line of trees.

Quickly, the little creature moved further away from them. It probably did this to get more cover or a better hiding place in the bushes and trees.

As they took a few steps closer, Justin saw the creature again. This animal was not a rabbit or any other animal he had ever seen. Its fur was long and straight and bluish-colored.

Mark then moved even closer to the trees. Still, he did not venture entirely inside. He was trying to get the best possible spot to ensure he got the kill this time.

Suddenly, the creature moved. When it did, its color seemed to change with its immediate surroundings, almost like a chameleon. But yet, it wasn't a lizard.

This area was primarily green and brown, which was exactly what color the little animal appeared to be now.

The two also noticed that this animal walked on its hind legs but ran on all fours.

"What the heck is that thing? I have never seen an animal do that. Walking on its hind legs! Well, no matter, it's still going to die."

Mark almost sounded unnerved as he said this but still

pointed the rifle at the animal.

Without hesitation, he put the rifle sight on the animal's head. Pulling the trigger without any hesitation, he got the round-off.

And once again, Justin came to the rescue. As Mark started to pull the trigger, Justin gave him a slight nudge.

At first, Mark wasn't sure he had hit his target. They would have to go inside and check, but Mark needed to say a few choice words again before they did.

"You must be the most bumbling kid I have ever seen. You're a disgrace to society. You can't even stand upright without falling. It looks like you might have been the one who was drinking, not me."

Once again, Justin saw that this last barrage of insults made Mark laugh again. He laughed so hard and loud that Justin thought Mark might throw up from all his bellowing.

A few moments later, Mark had stopped laughing and regained his composure somewhat.

"Come on. Let's see if I hit it. I want to know what it is." His voice was full of anticipation and glee when he announced this.

However, the kid did not move from his spot, which made Mark continue his insults.

"What's the matter now? Are you scared to go into the big

dark forest? You don't have your mommy and daddy with you, so now you're going to cry. Come on, cry for me, you baby. Cry!"

Mark had said this in an almost whiny, baby-like voice. He wanted to ensure Justin knew he was making fun of him.

Still, Justin held his ground. He didn't want to go in there to get the creature. He didn't want to see if it was dead. He felt somehow that he had let the little animal down by not pushing Mark harder when he took the shot.

Justin also felt that the longer he hesitated, the more this might give the little creature time to scamper away if it could.

Plus, Justin didn't want to be the first to enter The Woods. Not that he was afraid, no, far from it. He didn't want Mark behind him with a loaded weapon. No telling what might happen. Mark could trip or fall, and the gun could go off, or that was what he would tell everyone occurred.

So, Justin stood his ground, not budging one inch unless Mark moved first. But that didn't happen either. Mark just stood there with a worried look on his face.

Justin caught onto this but didn't let Mark know, at least not now.

Still, the insults just kept coming. Mark was on a roll now and wouldn't let up any time soon. He moved just a foot inside the trees but went no further.

Why? Could it be that he was the one who was scared of the darkened forest? No. Not big bad, Mark. No way! He was way too tough to be scared to go inside.

But he hesitated. It almost looked like he tried to go inside, but something kept him from entering. To make matters worse, the kid knew it was time for him to chime in.

"What's wrong, Mark? You're not scared, are you? How could that be? Go on in and find your trophy. You deserve it. You probably shot whatever it was. It should be good eating at supper time, don't you think?"

When Justin said this, he was very disdainful with his question. He wanted to make sure Mark knew he was mocking his hunting attributes.

"Yes, I sure got him on that one," Justin thought, smiling at Mark. I don't care if he beats me again; it was worth it."

Then Mark spoke up. But when he did, there was a slight shakiness in his voice.

"No. That's not it. We have to get back. Your mom is expecting us for dinner, and she said not to be late."

Then Justin retaliated, "That's funny; I thought you would get us dinner tonight! Guess things have changed in the last five minutes or so."

He was being facetious towards Mark, and it felt good.

Now, when in the world did Mark ever listen to his mom? Justin knew this was all just a lie and that for some strange unknown reason, Mark didn't want to go into The Woods, at least not by himself.

All Justin wanted was for them to leave, and that was what was happening.

"Come on, let's go home. Fishing is more my sport anyway. This is too much work for me."

Mark turned and went to the truck. He was in quite a hurry, it seemed.

Reaching the truck, he quickly opened another beer and drank it without taking a breath.

"He must have needed that one," Justin said under his breath.

As Justin looked back to the wooded area, he wondered about the little animal there. He wanted to see if it had been hit so he could tell Jib and maybe get the animal some help.

Justin was sure this animal had to have come from the valley, for it was so strange-looking. No animal he had ever seen looked and acted like this little creature. So, Justin would try to get some help somehow.

With Mark at the wheel and getting drunk by the minute,

they headed home. It was good that these woods weren't that far from their house because the more Mark drove, the worse he got.

When they finally arrived home, Justin exited the truck and almost kissed the ground. He was so thankful for making it home safely. Mark had driven in and out of oncoming traffic most of the way.

"That guy should not be behind the wheel. Someday, he will kill someone," Justin thought as they headed into the house.

Once inside, Justin went and took a shower. His mind drifted back to the little animal.

Justin was thinking that if he ever got the chance to go back inside, he would let Jib know about this incident. He was hoping that Jib might be able to help the little animal.

He was also going to tell him exactly what happened. He wanted to ensure that Jib knew it wasn't his idea to go into The Woods and hunt.

"Sure, hope he believes me," he said as he cleaned up.

After his shower, Justin prepared for dinner and tried to forget about this awful day. He was so tired from all his work, and every bone in his body seemed to ache. At least he knew he would sleep well tonight.

Still, he could not stop thinking about that little creature. If it had been hit, it would have more than likely died.

But, as we know by now, that would never satisfy Justin. He had to make sure if it had died or not.

So, when he got the chance to go back in, he was going to try to check up on the animal. He had to make this right, to make it up to the villagers if this little creature was indeed one of theirs.

Helping

As he lay in bed, there was a knock on his door that evening. He knew by the soft sound that it was his mother. She quietly entered his room and sat down beside him.

"Where did you two go this afternoon? Is everything OK?"

Mary was a little nervous, and her voice seemed shaky when speaking. She was upset because she discovered her son had been in the truck with Mark.

Mark had not told her that they were going to the dump or that he would take Justin hunting. If she had known, she would have stopped this.

Mary was furious, but what could she do? She knew if she stood up to Mark, he would somehow get back at her. She didn't care about that, though. What she cared about was that he might hurt Justin. Now, that was the one thing she would not stand for. So, at this point, discretion was the better part of valor.

As she looked at her son, she knew he didn't have to answer. Mark had gleefully told her where they had gone earlier. That was the reason she had come upstairs to talk to her son. She wanted to make sure he was safe.

Wherever they had gone didn't matter to her at this time. All that mattered was that Justin was home. But as for Mark, she would make sure that this was the last time he drove her son anywhere while drinking.

Mary considered telling Mark off but quickly changed her mind, realizing that doing so would do no good and would only make matters worse.

Thinking back, she questioned herself. How did she ever get into this mess? What did she ever see in this so-called man? If only her husband Chris hadn't gotten sick and passed away! Things would have been so different, that's for sure.

But all of this was a moot point now. She was in this mess, and there was no easy way out yet. Somehow, she would have to find an answer for all her and her son's troubles.

Mark had been nothing but a hardship for her and Justin. Mary was afraid that if she didn't get Justin away from him, then he might hurt him.

After talking a little to her son, Mary went downstairs only to get there in time to watch Mark stumble into the house, say a few choice words about Justin, and then stumble into bed. A short time later, she heard him snoring away.

Mark always seemed to come between them. For some odd reason, he tried to keep them apart. It was as if he didn't like the attention that Mary gave her son.

"Oh well," she thought, "he just better get used to it because there is no way I will ever give up on my son."

Mary wanted so much for Justin. She wanted him to grow up and do the right things, like go to college, marry, and have a family. There was nothing wrong with that. But by how things were going lately, this didn't look like it would ever happen.

Standing back and looking at her son, she saw Chris in him. Chris had been the so-called adventurer. She could tell that Justin would be one, too.

As she reflected, she remembered more about Chris. On the day that he had left to seek a cure for his disease, she was sure that to him, it was just another adventure he was on. She knew that he saw it as a quest of some kind. She also knew that if he had found a cure, he would have returned for the two of them.

But apparently, it didn't turn out that way. He had gone away, and a short time later, she received that letter that had broken her heart. It was from the clinic that had taken him in and had done the so-called experimental treatments on him.

A lot of secrecy was involved, but being in such distress then, she didn't question much of it. Time had made her accept it. She had to admit that Chris wasn't ever going to return.

So here she was with her son. She did not know which way to turn or who to turn to.

She had checked a few things for Mark in the past few months. It was counseling and AA meetings. When she mentioned this to Mark, he clarified that he didn't want anything to do with these meetings. He had even told her that he didn't have alcoholism and for her not to mention it again.

She also talked to a couple of officers in town about her situation. They told her that there wasn't much they could do for her at this point. She would have to prove that he had hurt her or Justin.

Getting evidence would be the hard part for her. Sure, she had seen a few marks on the back of her son's legs, but when questioned, all Justin ever said was that he got hurt in some activities at school.

But Mary knew that Mark had hurt her son. Even if she couldn't prove he hurt Justin physically, she knew he hurt him verbally. She realized that this couldn't go on much longer.

So here she sat, waiting and wondering what she could do about this situation she had put her son in.

"I've let him down. I failed my son," she told herself. "But somehow, I'm going to make it up to him! This I promise!"

Mary did have some sort of plan, and it involved selling the house. Mark knew about this, and he was quick to tell Justin. What he didn't realize was that once Mary sold the house, she and Justin would move away, but not him.

To her, this seemed like the only chance they had to get away from this monster.

Still, it would take time to sell the house. In the meantime, she would have to do her best to keep Justin out of harm's way.

***

Nighttime had arrived, and Mark was still passed out from all the alcohol he had consumed. Somehow, he had moved downstairs to the couch.

"Good," Justin heard himself say. "Maybe he will stay passed out all night. That way, I won't worry so much about my mom."

Even though he was tired from all his work that day, Justin quietly headed to the garage. There, he found his bike with a flat. He then aired the tire up and quickly sneaked out the side door, all the while without making a sound.

After walking his bike until he was out of sight of his house, he jumped on and slipped out into the darkness.

He knew he would have to pedal fast and keep a lookout for anyone who might see him.

Once again, he disobeyed his mom, but he had made up his mind. He felt he needed to return and check on that little animal.

This time, though, he left a note. If his mom found out he was gone, the message would clarify where, when, and why he left.

"Maybe she won't worry so much if she finds it," Justin thought.

Justin wanted to return to The Woods to ensure the little animal was okay. Maybe he could take it somewhere to get help if it needed any.

The kid felt he had to do this, and although it was unnecessary, he was willing to take the chance.

The creature was strange-looking, and Justin could tell it was young, which seemed to increase the urgency of finding the animal.

When he first saw the little animal, it resembled two or three different animals rolled into one. To Justin, it looked like a kangaroo and a wolf. But when it ran on all four legs, it resembled a horse.

It was not your ordinary creature, that's for sure. Even its color would change with its surroundings. Its skin looked smooth, and its eyes seemed round but with slits in its pupils. Plus, it could rear up and stand almost vertically. Also, when it did stand up, it could walk.

It was a strange animal, indeed. But no matter. All Justin knew was that this creature was harmless. He could tell that it didn't want to hurt anyone or do any harm whatsoever.

Justin also felt that it had only wanted to get away, and with some luck, it may have done just that.

Passing farmer Tucker's field, Justin couldn't help but look at the farmhouse. As he pedaled by, he saw a light on the back porch. Even from this distance, Justin could see Tucker and Red. Tucker was rocking in his chair, and his faithful dog was beside him.

There always seemed to be something different about the old farmer and his sidekick. They were both friendly but in an odd sort of way. Never once did Tucker object to him or Steve going to the hollow from his property. And he and his dog always seemed to have an eye on everything that went on in this area.

"If only I could go in from this part of the hollow, it wouldn't take long, and I could return quicker."

This last thought was quickly dashed, for he was already past Tuckers and was approaching a turnoff he would have to take to the other part of The Woods.

Once arriving at the other entry, he got off his bike and walked inside as silently as possible. He then hid his bike the best he could, although he was in quite a hurry.

As Justin entered, he noticed something immediately. Even though it was the middle of the night, there seemed to be more noise.

These sounds seemed to come from everywhere. It was almost as if the noises were coming from some of the animals in the area. It kind of sounded like something, or someone was moaning. Or maybe he was exaggerating, thinking that some harm had come to the little creature and the animals were angry.

Justin then moved deeper into the trees. He had never been to this area before, so finding his way around took him longer.

It was dark inside, so he quickly flipped on the flashlight he had brought.

As he kept searching for the animal, the sounds of The Woods seemed to grow louder and louder. Justin almost felt that the creatures in this area were upset about something.

Could they be angry with him? If they were, he would have to try and find this creature and make things right.

When Justin walked inside, he started looking in all the bushes and behind the trees. He felt his search would probably end without finding this animal, but he still had to try.

Suddenly, he saw something up ahead. Some movement came from a bush on the side of the path.

An animal appeared and momentarily startled Justin. Looking at the little creature, Justin could tell that this one looked like the other one that Mark had taken a shot at today.

The animal slowly started to move away from Justin. Strangely, it didn't run or hide.

As he continued to follow the animal, he saw some blood on the ground. Now, he knew that one of the little creatures had been shot.

Walking behind the animal, Justin did his best not to spook it. When he had almost caught up to it, he saw it disappear into some thick bushes and leaves that had fallen recently from a giant tree.

As Justin approached the leaves, he started to push and move them aside. There, hidden by all the leaves and limbs, was a light and an opening. This was almost like the one he went into on the other part of The Wood's, but it was more hidden.

This opening was tiny, and it seemed that the more Justin tried to get through, the harder it became. A few short moments later, he finally reached the other side.

As he stood up, he saw the animal he had been following. It had stopped a few steps ahead of him. It appeared that the little animal had waited for him to catch up.

When Justin looked around, he noticed that this river must be the same as the one in the other part of the valley—the same river, just in a different location. He also realized that this part of the river was above where he had come in the first time.

As he watched the river flow, he noticed a waterfall. It, too, seemed to come right out of the side of the mountain, just like the first one he saw.

Looking up, he realized that it was daylight here. He then shut his flashlight off because he knew it wasn't working.

Justin then continued his journey. He was putting a lot of hope in finding this animal. Not just seeing it but helping it if at all possible.

Walking beside the river, he found a path. He then thought about the other time he was in the valley and the village.

That Jib fellow seemed like a nice enough person. The whole village was great. He wanted to go back to the little town so badly now. Justin wanted to get to know them and learn about their history and way of life.

A short time later, he heard that moaning sound again. It was the same sound he had first heard in The Woods. This time, it sounded closer to him, though. He was sure he was supposed to hear whatever it was.

He was almost to the waterfall and had now reached a bend in the river. When he walked a little further, he saw the creature. It indeed had been shot. Slowly, Justin walked up to it.

Justin gingerly sat down by the little animal. Suddenly, out of the foliage came more of its kind. They all gathered around the hurt animal, which was now lying on its side and unable to sit up.

Once again, Justin thought about how different this animal was. Not only was its color ever-changing, but it also had seven toe-like appendages on its front paws.

As Justin sat down, he noticed just how bad the situation was. Where the animal had been shot, there was an opening that blood was spewing out of. Justin could tell that things didn't look good for the little creature.

Justin then tried to move closer, but some of the other ones crowded in his way. To Justin, it seemed as if they were trying to protect the hurt animal.

Suddenly, a noise came from the underbrush to the left where the animal was lying. All of the creatures stepped back. It was almost as if they knew what was headed their way.

"Whatever it is, it must be big," Justin thought.

There was so much noise that even Justin took a step backward in case this situation worsened.

He could hear many branches snapping and some brush being moved aside.

Then it appeared. Standing before them now was a more enormous creature than the hurt one. Justin could tell it was fully grown by its size. The other smaller animals seemed to part in the middle and let the larger one through.

His earlier assumption about these creatures looking like they were a cross between a horse, kangaroo, and wolf was correct. Their legs weren't as long as a horse, and they didn't have hoofs.

The creature then surveyed the situation, or so it appeared. He looked the hurt one over and over. Then, it bent down and dropped something from one of its appendages. It landed just out of reach. The giant animal then pushed it to the mouth of the bleeding animal.

The wounded animal did his best to try and chew whatever was given to him.

The bleeding seemed to slow down shortly after he chewed

it. Even the animal looked better.

Then, after a few more moments, the injured animal stood gently on its four legs. Then it reared up and stood on two of them.

Justin then moved closer for a better look. Try as he might, he could not see the wound that had been bleeding profusely a short time ago. The animal was now completely healed.

So, whatever this was that the large animal gave to the hurt one, it had stopped the bleeding and cured it in about an hour.

"That must be one heck of an herb," Justin said as he stood there, thinking how incredible some things were here in the valley.

Then, his mind took another course altogether.

"What if this herb worked on humans also? If indeed it does, then it would be a big benefit to the outside world."

Even though he knew people needed it outside of The Woods, he knew it somehow shouldn't leave this valley. Justin was torn between these issues as he continued watching the little creature.

The others began to disperse shortly after knowing the injured animal had been cured.

Another sound was heard, and it seemed to be coming from the south of where Justin had entered. All the animals seemed to be getting ready for whoever it was.

Soon, Justin could tell it was a person coming towards them. Once the person was in view, he knew exactly who it was. It was Jib.

As Jib approached the cured animal, he shook his head in agreement. He knew that the little creature had been saved somehow.

Quickly, the larger animal looked over at Jib, then turned away and left. The rest of his kind did the same.

"Yes indeed, Justin, many things in this valley differ from yours."

Jib looked at Justin for a moment or two and seemed to want to tell Justin some more things. Shortly, he did.

"I think it might be time that I filled you in on some things that happen here in our valley. Those animals are called Nampo. They are very useful here. You could say that they are our guards. They scout around our borders to see if people have made it into our valley and are coming this way."

"Wow. Now that is strange," Justin thought. "This guy seems to have answered some of my questions. The strange thing is that I never said these out loud."

Justin's bewilderment was at an all-time high as he continued to listen more.

Jib stopped for a second and looked in the direction that the Nampo went.

"We hope that the things that are different here are different in a good way. But as you have guessed, some things should only be used here, not out there where you come from. Like the plant that the hurt one ate. It must always stay in our valley."

Jib had now stopped talking and started heading in the same direction he had come from. He motioned to Justin, letting him know that if he wanted to follow, then it was okay.

A few short steps later, Jib continued his conversation.

"We call this plant Rapha. If this plant left our land and went outside, others might come and look for more. It is very scarce. There is a chance that this plant may dry up, and then we would have to do without. So, if others took it, our valley would be in jeopardy of becoming extinct. It is one of the few herbs that help some of us when we get hurt or sick. We don't know all that could happen to the plant, so we closely monitor it. We must."

Justin understood this completely. If he were in their place, he would do the same.

Learning something like this made Justin want to know more about this land. He felt this area had to be one of the best places to live.

Then, his imagination began to run away with him again.

What if he told his mother about this place? Maybe she would want to come, and then the two of them could build a life in this valley—that way, they would be rid of Mark once and for all.

After thinking about this, Justin shook his head. He knew that this would never happen. He felt living here in this valley would be too hard for his mom. She was used to her world and likely couldn't adapt as well as Justin had.

As the two of them continued to walk along the river, Justin felt like he didn't have a care in the world for a moment or two. He didn't even know where they were going, nor did it matter. He was glad that the animal was cured and that things seemed to be in order again.

Jib then said to Justin, "You came back! I'm glad that you did. I had a feeling that you would. But what about the other two with you the last time?"

Justin spoke up at this moment.

"Steve wanted to, but he left for summer camp this morning.

And his sister is too young. We all got in trouble the last time we were here. Steve would have been grounded, but his parents had already paid for the camp, so they said they would deal with him when he got home. Now, I, too, got lucky. My stepdad didn't learn about me getting in trouble. Only my mom knows, and she kind of understands."

Jib listened intently to Justin's story even though he didn't understand most of the things he was hearing. After all, he was not from their side of The Woods.

"Sorry to hear you all got into trouble, but how about now? Are you in trouble again for coming here?"

"If they find out that I left, I probably will be. I don't care what my stepdad thinks, but my mom I do. I don't like sneaking behind her back, but she wouldn't understand this now. I had to get back here to see if the animal was OK. I did not hurt the animal; it was my stepdad."

Justin felt so relieved now that he told Jib precisely what had happened to the little animal.

As the two of them continued walking, some things started to look familiar to him. He then realized they were approaching the same area where he had first entered the valley.

He could see the little hill he had slid down and the weeping willow tree beside it. The river they were walking beside disappeared underneath the slope he had slid down. It then reappeared like the waterfall that he had seen the first time.

As he looked past the waterfall and to the left of the river, he saw something that he didn't see the first time he was there. It was a small bridge that was a little further down the path. It had two weeping willow trees on each side of it. This bridge seemed to enhance this area somewhat.

The bridge crossed the river to the path that continued further on. Justin might want to explore where it led sometime in the future.

He shook his head with wonder. It seemed like each time he came back, he found something different. Most of these things were exciting and quite a sight to behold. How anyone could not love this place was beyond this young man's comprehension.

Justin was in deep thought as they continued on the path around the mountain. To him, this place seemed to be one of the most excellent places he had ever seen or gone to. A place where someone could spend the rest of their life. And hopefully, that someone was him.

Suddenly, Justin was brought out of his daydream.

"You know Justin," Jib said, "you are welcome here anytime you want to come, but we would like this place to stay secret. That way, we won't worry much about the plants and other valuable things. If you do go back, do me a favor. Please tell the other two to try and do their best not to tell anyone about this place. It would be hard for people to find this area, but some might, and we don't like certain strangers in our valley."

Jib stopped for a moment to try and gather his thoughts. There was so much he wanted to tell Justin. Strangely, it almost seemed there wasn't enough time to do so.

Continuing his conversation, Jib said, "Too many people may not be good for our valley or our way of life. I don't want to be judgmental, but from what you have told me about your stepfather, it would not be good for him to come here. He doesn't belong."

There was a worried look on Jib's face as he finished his sentence.

Justin agreed with Jib on this matter. He didn't want Mark anywhere around here or back home, for that matter. Justin knew that if he did come here, somehow, he would mess this place up. He might even try to shoot some of the Nampo's just for sport.

As they entered the village, they walked up to Jib's hut. Jib invited Justin inside.

Justin didn't have a chance to look at the place the first time he was here. But things seemed a little more relaxed this time, so he looked closer at some of the items in Jib's dwelling.

As Justin glanced around, Jib asked him if he would like to sit for a while and talk.

Jib then pointed to a chair for Justin to sit in.

As far as he could tell, this chair wasn't wood or plastic. It seemed to be made out of cloth or possibly feathers. It was very soft when he sat down. He even seemed to sink into the chair a little. It felt good to sit in and wasn't hard like most chairs.

Jib had entered another part of the hut and was now back with two glasses. These were funny-looking, almost oval. You still could drink out of them, though. When he did, he noticed that the so-called water he was offered tasted cleaner, even smoother than any water he had ever drunk.

Jib had been sitting in his chair, rocking back and forth, thinking about Justin.

"So, how long do you plan on staying here this time, Justin the Just?"

Jib stopped for a second or two so that what he had just said to Justin would sink in.

"That's what they call you, isn't it?"

Jib saw the surprise in Justin's eyes as he said this to him.

Justin was taken aback. He hadn't heard that phrase from anyone in a long time. Steve was the only one now that ever called him that. To say that he was caught off guard hearing this from Jib was quite an understatement.

"Yes. That is what some people used to call me. My dad coined that phrase on me years ago, and it seemed to stick. I don't think anyone calls me that much anymore except Steve. The answer to your other question is that I can't stay here much longer. I have to get back home. I just came to check on the hurt Nampo."

Justin finished his drink and looked around the room some more. It had a comfortable feeling attached to it—even the way it smelled made you feel at home.

He could see the kitchen area and a simple wooden table inside. However, there were no modern appliances.

I wonder how they keep their food fresh. How do they keep it from spoiling? These were just two questions Justin had, but he was sure many more would follow.

From where Justin was sitting, he could see into another room. There was a bed in it, and as far as he could tell, it was the same as any other bed. So, some things were the same, he thought to himself.

While sitting there, he suddenly realized that this hut lacked something. So far, he hadn't seen any televisions, phones, or radios. There were no communication devices at all.

No TV? What did these people do in the evenings without TV?

"We sit around and talk to one another. We love the gift of gab. It keeps everyone closer. We stay in touch with each other better that way!"

Justin sat there, seemingly a little stunned.

Now, what in the heck is going on? How did this Jib fellow know what I was thinking? He seemed to know what I was about to say or ask a couple of other times, too.

Justin then sat back in his chair and looked bewildered again. He was hoping to get some answers to these questions.

Jib then cleared his throat several times as if preparing to speak. A short time later, he did just that.

"I'm sorry, Justin. Let me explain. As the elder of this village, I have this unique ability to read people's thoughts here in this valley. Not all, and not all of the time. It is useful most of the time, though. Also, it can be rude when I do that, so please forgive me for doing this."

Justin was excited to see Jib do his little mind-reading trick.

He thought this could be one of the most intriguing things he had learned here in the valley.

Jib knew this and realized that Justin was still curious, so he told him more details to enlighten him on this ability.

"As I stated earlier, I can read some thoughts, some of the time. Very few of the other villagers can do this, though. It's like a gift that is given to the village elders. Somehow, it just comes to them when they are elected."

Jib stood there, hoping that his answer was enough and appropriate.

"And, as you probably know, as the elder, I'm responsible for my people here in the village. I have to make sure everything is going along smoothly. When outsiders find their way in, it seems that things don't run quite as they should for a while. Plus, I can…" a screeching sound suddenly drowned out his voice.

It was like the sound they heard when the rain came. Justin looked out the window to the sky, but no clouds were lurking.

As he continued to look outside, Justin saw the people of the village start to run. They began to pick up some of their things to hide or protect. Jib then motioned to Justin to follow him.

The two of them began to trot up the little hill and into some bushes behind two or three big rocks. The whole village seemed to be running and hiding from something or someone.

What was that noise? It must be the alarm, but what were they all running from? What were they afraid of?

A short time later, the villagers were entirely out of sight. What they were hiding from would soon be revealed.

The Black Intruders

As he unpacked his clothes, Steve stood there and started talking to the other boys in his group. He knew in his heart that this summer at camp would not be as fun as last year.

He came here for the first time last year, which was exciting and new. But this time, he knew it wouldn't be the same.

Something had changed, and deep down inside, he knew the answer. It was because Justin and he had found what was inside The Woods.

That place was so much better than here. These woods were not bad, but the real Woods were different and exciting, especially with the valley they had discovered inside.

Continuing to unpack and straighten up his area, Steve remembered when they entered the valley.

"Wow. And to think that valley has been there for years and years, and nobody found it. Oh well, that's their loss."

Steve said this to himself in a low tone so no one nearby could hear him.

A short time later, the boys that shared his room headed out for roll call, leaving Steve alone. This gave him some more time to think about the valley.

Steve was already feeling homesick. He wanted to go back home so much now. But if he did get to go home, Steve knew that his grounding punishment would begin. That was the only bad thing that could happen if he left camp early.

"No, that wouldn't be much fun at all," he said without thinking. "But going back into the valley would be fun, at least more fun than this place."

A slight smile was on his face when he realized what he had just said.

"I bet no one has ever said those words here in camp." He quickly turned and headed out the door to join the other boys.

Yes, Justin only found it a short time ago, and Steve had only been there once, but still, it was great. There was so much to see and learn from that valley and its inhabitants. The possibilities were endless. He knew he couldn't wait till camp was over.

Standing there waiting to introduce yourself was a monotonous procedure. One kid after another would tell everyone who they were and where they came from.

After about the seventh boy had spoken, Steve zoned out. He started thinking of ways to get kicked out of camp.

"Maybe I'll tell them I am a serial killer, and they will send me home. Or maybe I'll just lie down in the grass and start crying. Then they might let me go. They will probably think I've had a nervous breakdown or something of that nature. They will have to let me go home then."

As Steve was thinking about these things, he was nodding his head in agreement with the possibilities of each one.

"Whether I get to go home or not, one thing Justin better not do is take Ronnie with him when he returns inside. If he does, then I will not be his best friend anymore. I swear it!"

Thinking about his sister, he realized he hadn't talked to her about their little adventure since they had been caught. It didn't matter, though, for he knew she liked it too. Anyone in their right mind couldn't help but like it.

Then, it came time for Steve to give his name and background.

"My name is Steve Williams. I'm from Orchard Park over in Golden County. This is going to be my second time here. I had a great time last year, so I came back."

Oh, how he wanted to add, "But not this time. This place pales compared to what my friend Justin the Just has found. What he found makes this place look like an outhouse. Sorry!"

But he didn't. He held his tongue. There was no way he would tell anyone about The Woods.

Once the formalities were over, Steve headed back to his cabin. He shared this with three other boys who were about his age.

As Steve sat in his cabin, he thought about his roommates. He hoped one of them would know of a surefire way to get him kicked out of camp because there was no way he would stay here for a month and a half. He wanted to go home to the actual woods.

He was in deep thought as he crashed down on his bunk, trying to relax.

Steve knew that he wouldn't leave camp, though. His dad had already paid for this outing, and it wouldn't be right if he left early. Leaving would cause Justin's dad to lose all the money that it cost to get him in this camp in the first place. That was the only reason they let him go. If they hadn't paid in advance, then he would have had to stay home, get grounded, and probably be made to go to summer school with Ronnie.

Suddenly, a new thought came to him. Steve realized that he and Ronnie had cell phones. He could call her, and she could keep him posted. Plus, he could call Justin and beg him not to take anyone else into the valley, at least not without him.

Quickly, Steve took his phone out and tried to call Justin. To his dismay, his cell phone wasn't working at this time.

Steve's face showed a defeated look. He was so mad that he reared back and started to throw his phone, but at the last second, he recanted.

Right before he let loose his phone, he remembered what they had told him at the general meeting when he arrived. Cell service was unavailable this far inside the forest, but there was a phone booth at the cafeteria.

"Now, that is something you don't see every day: a phone booth. Well, I guess that will have to do, but for now, I better try to get used to my situation until I can go home."

Steve knew there had to be a way for him to get out of there. It wasn't that he was homesick; no, not at all. It was mainly because of the valley they had discovered. Like Justin, he wanted to return inside as soon as possible.

He then lay back and drifted off to sleep, thinking of the possibilities awaiting them when they returned inside.

***

The warning noise had stopped, which relieved Justin's ears. He was still in the dark about who or what they were all hiding from. Everyone seemed to know exactly where to hide because even Justin couldn't see them.

Jib then motioned to him to keep down and not move. They were safe where they were, but Jib knew that might change if they didn't keep still and quiet.

Suddenly, there was a sound. It almost sounded like thunder or a stampede of horses coming their way. Whatever it was, it was getting closer and louder by the second.

Off in the distance, Justin could see smoke. As the smoke crept up to the village, he could see it wasn't smoke. It was dust, and it came from hordes of animals. The dust came from them, stirring it up as they came closer and closer to the village.

Justin tried to gauge how many there were, but it was useless. His guess was around twenty or more.

Now that they were closing in on the village, Justin could see that there were riders on these animals. The more he looked at the animals, the clearer it became what they were. These people were riding the Nampo.

The riders also looked like they were all male. Most had their shirts off, making them look dirty from all the dust they stirred up while they rode. A few of them also had long hair. Plus, their faces were hairy and unshaven. Their skin seemed well-tanned and dirty, mainly from the dirt and dust.

This valley was primarily green with lush vegetation. But the direction from which the riders came lacked any green foliage or trees. It was barren to some degree. They rode in on an old dirt road adjacent to the mountain.

Then, as Justin continued watching the riders, he saw something that looked like a weapon on their side. This object was also hooked to their pants. Even with limited knowledge of weaponry, Justin could see that these, indeed, were weapons. They looked like boomerangs, in a way. They were even V-shaped like one.

Justin knew they were weapons because of how these people carried them. It was almost as if they were ready to throw them at any moment or anything that might move.

Then, as fate would have it, something did move. Off to the left and down the hill, one of the villagers started to run. He must have panicked and run out of his hiding place.

As soon as some riders saw the movement, they threw their weapons. It did look and fly like a boomerang, but in this case, it didn't come back to the person who threw it. And, to top it off, a net came out and entangled the villager.

Whatever it was, it was accurate. The hairy creatures had turned sharply and thrown their weapons without hesitation. They hit their intended target in two or three seconds.

The victim immediately went down and hit the ground. It almost looked like it had even killed the man because he didn't move for a short time.

Two riders then picked him up and took him with them. Each held him under his arms and carried him to a Nampo.

A few moments later, Justin saw the man move. He started to struggle with the other two, but it was futile. These men were too big and strong for him to get away.

Off the two of them went with their prey. The speed at which they entered the village was equaled when they left. Carrying someone didn't seem to slow them down one bit.

A few other men went into several huts and seemed to search for things they might want or need.

Then, as suddenly as they came, they were gone.

But before they did leave, one of them looked back. He, too, had long, thick, matted hair on his face and head. The others listened and cowered to this man; one could tell he was their leader. He was the first one in the village and the last one to leave.

As he started to ride away, he stopped and turned almost in the same direction as Jib and Justin. His ears seemed to perk up, and he even seemed to snort. Justin realized this man was trying to see or hear if more people were in this area.

And then a strange thing happened. His wicked smile changed. It disappeared from his face altogether. It even looked as if he bowed his head. There seemed to be some sort of sadness in his facial expression as he looked toward the ground.

Maybe Justin was way off on his assumption, but it did look like the man, if you could call him that, showed some empathy for what they had done to their captive and the village.

Only for a moment. One second, he looked sorrowful, then the next, his evil smirk was back on his face. He then emitted a loud and sadistic laugh.

Turning his Nampo around, the man shouted something, but they were too far away to understand. Quickly, they all rode out of the village.

Once again, there was a loud noise, but this time, it was pleasant and soothing to the ears. As it sounded a few more tones, the villagers came out of the brush or wherever they were hiding.

Justin and Jib ventured out of their hiding place cautiously. Slowly, they headed back to the village to check up on the town and its inhabitants.

As far as they could tell, everyone was OK except for one lady who was crying. She had a couple of children by her side, and they seemed to be trying to comfort her.

"Yes, those are her children," Jib said but caught himself. "I'm sorry, Justin. I read your mind. I will try not to do that anymore. It's just so easy sometimes. Forgive me, I beg of you!"

"No forgiveness is needed. It is something you have, and it is helpful. I envy you in many ways," Justin said with a smile.

Once they checked on the villagers, Jib turned toward Justin. He wanted to clarify and tell him more about what had transpired.

"I know you have some more questions, so I will do my best to answer them. Please let us walk a bit so we can chat!"

As the two of them started walking, others followed. Some of the villagers still seemed afraid of what had happened.

"You might have guessed by now that the people who came here are our enemies. Yes, it's true, even we have enemies. We are a generous village, but others want to take what we have, and they take it without asking. Over the years, groups or clans, as you might call them, have grown stronger and ruthless."

The two of them reentered the village and headed toward Jib's hut. All the other villagers went back to their huts to inspect them. They needed to see if anything had been taken or damage had been done. They also wanted to make sure that all their loved ones were safe.

Then Jib went to check on his hut. One glance is all he gave, nothing more.

Justin could tell that Jib didn't care much for any materialistic items that he might have. The whole village seemed to be that way. All they seemed to care about was their family and friends. If they were safe, then that was all that mattered.

They were a peaceful village and didn't seem to want much. All they seemed to want was to live their lives and go about their business, not hurting anyone or anything.

Shortly after, Jib told Justin more about their enemy and what they had done.

"These enemies of ours are called the Black Intruders. They normally raid villages for supplies or men and women. They need these people to work for them. Today, they captured one of our men. You saw his wife and children crying. He will be working in their fields tomorrow. Their fields consist of vegetables and fruit-bearing trees. I'm sure people work in the fields where you come from."

"Yes, but where I come from, the workers get paid for it and are not forced to work. That is one drawback I see here in this valley, at least from the Black Intruders."

Jib stopped talking momentarily, went into his kitchen area, and made them some kind of herb drink. He handed it to Justin, and then both of them drank. It tasted like some type of tea and had a pleasing aroma.

They sat there in silence while sipping their drinks. Jib was in deep thought, and Justin could tell that there were more things that he wanted to talk with him about.

"Yes, our valley isn't that different from yours. But there are some differences; you will learn them all in time. One different thing is the Stringer you saw earlier. I'm sure you don't have that where you come from. Another thing that we have are some herbs that you saw being used earlier. They can cure some things rather quickly."

Stopping once again, Jib took a swig from his cup. Shaking his head in agreement with the taste of his drink, he smiled.

"There are some good things and some bad things. You will learn them all in due time—that is, if you choose to stay with us!"

There was a question on Jib's face, and his eyebrow rose when he spoke these last words.

Stay with them? How could he do that? Sure, he wanted to, but what about his mom? What would she do without him there to protect her from Mark?

Now, with the thought of his mom on his mind, he stood up quickly.

Justin couldn't stay, at least not this time. He had to get back to her. He knew she would be worried if she found out he was gone.

Shortly, Justin told Jib that it was time for him to go home.

They both put down their cups simultaneously and headed out the door. Back up the incline they went. Jib followed Justin to the top because he knew it was time for the lad to return home. He then nodded his head, and Justin did likewise.

Justin then looked down at the little village. He could almost see some villagers looking at him, and maybe even a few waved; he couldn't quite tell from this distance.

"This isn't fair," he said to Jib. "I should stay here with all of you forever!"

Jib smiled and nodded to Justin in agreement. Quickly, he turned and headed back toward his village.

As Justin turned, he started to run as fast as he could. He wanted to get to the hill to get out of there and back home.

Upon reaching the river, he quickly headed toward the hill with the hidden steps. But this time, the steps weren't hidden. They were in plain sight.

Justin was almost to the top when he turned and saw the guardian look up at him and wave. Justin waved back.

Then he discovered something. As the little man returned to the branches that hung from the weeping willow tree, a rock moved, and the guardian went inside. It seemed to move when he put his hand on it.

"So that's how the little man disappears so quickly," Justin said with amazement.

This last thought quickly faded. He began to run as fast as he could through the opening. He knew the consequences could be dire if he didn't get home soon and his stepdad found out he was gone.

But, just like before, once he came out of The Woods, it had only been a short time since he had entered. Justin was having difficulty getting used to this aspect of the valley.

As Justin kept running, he felt as if something wasn't right. At first, he couldn't figure it out.

Suddenly, it dawned on him. He didn't come into The Woods from this point. It was almost a mile away in another direction. Plus, he had ridden his bike, and it was at the other entrance.

He had been so hurried to get home that he had utterly

forgotten where he came into The Woods. Now, he would have to do double time to get home before anyone found out he was gone.

As he reached the top of the dirt road by farmer Tucker's field, he heard an old hound dog bark again. He was so glad to listen to his barking, even at this time of night.

Justin could also see the light was still on the farmhouse's back porch. Underneath the porch light, he saw old farmer Tucker still rocking back and forth in his chair.

Leaving the cornfield, Justin started running north. It was about a mile from the cornfield, but being a youngster, it didn't take him that long to get there.

Reaching the area he had entered earlier, Justin quickly jumped onto his bike and pedaled for home. The only thing that could stop him now was if someone caught him. But finally, luck was on his side. Justin was once again fortunate, for there were no cars or people out at this time of night, at least none in his area.

A short time later, Justin passed farmer Tucker's field but didn't hear or see Red this time. He knew that even if the old dog was out in the cornfield, he could not have seen him because he was pedaling way too fast, and the darkness shielded him somewhat.

Reaching home, he quietly hid his bike on the side of the garage. Silently, he crept into the house and slowly walked up the stairs to his room.

Once he locked his bedroom door, he knew he was safe, at least for now. He stood with his back against the door because it seemed like this act would somehow keep a certain someone from coming into his room.

One thing he knew for sure was that if it weren't for his mom, he would have stayed there with the villagers. That was where he felt he belonged. Deep in his heart, though, he knew he would never leave her behind.

Justin also knew that he hated his so-called stepdad, but at the same time, he felt sorry for him. He was sad that he couldn't stop drinking and that it consumed him every day.

"The guy might not be so bad if he didn't have this problem," Justin said to himself as he prepared for bed.

Then reality hit him. This guy was bad news; that was all there was to it. Justin felt that he couldn't take much more. He was getting fed up with Mark.

As Justin got into bed, he knew that things had to change, and they had to change soon. He was tired of Mark treating his mom and him wrongly.

As far as Justin was concerned, it was time for Mark to move on.

Wishing and hoping

The next couple of weeks went by relatively fast. So fast that it almost seemed like a blur. The reason was that Justin didn't have any spare time. Mark had so much work for him to do around the house. And it didn't look like he would ever let up on the kid.

Mark had Justin split firewood, wash the cars, and mow lawns. It didn't matter what it was, just as long as it was manual labor.

But Justin didn't mind; he could take anything Mark dished out. He couldn't care less what his stepdad came up with or what he made him do.

It had been over two weeks since Justin had been inside the valley. However, he had received a few calls from a girl named Ronnie, which he refused to answer. He knew what she wanted, but he felt she was too young to go back inside. Plus, he didn't want to worry about her when visiting the valley.

Steve had also called and wanted to know when Justin would return to The Woods and the valley.

All Justin told him was that he didn't know and had too much to do around the house right now. But he then told Steve that they might have a chance to go back in when he came home from camp.

Justin knew that Steve and Ronnie wanted to return inside, and he couldn't blame them either. But he also knew they didn't seem to belong there; even Jib seemed to agree.

While washing his mom's car, Justin could not stop thinking about the valley and what might have happened when they were inside.

What bothered Justin the most was thinking about Ronnie when she followed them. What if she had gotten lost or hurt while she was in there? No one knew she had followed the boys, so if she had gotten lost, no one would have known when or where she went. They may have never even known that she was in there at all. This last thought sent shivers down his spine.

They had been lucky for the most part. He knew he did not want to take this chance again, and it would be better if he went alone.

But still, deep down inside, Justin knew he would give in and take Steve with him when he returned from camp. After all, he had promised him he would, and Justin was not the kind of kid to go back on a promise.

It seemed that the longer he stayed away from the valley, the more he missed it. He longed for the world inside and knew that if things went as he hoped, he could call that place home someday.

***

Yes, she got grounded. Her parents had scolded her well, and Ronnie knew this summer would be slow and long. She was grounded for one whole week and wouldn't be able to go anywhere until that time had passed.

At first, she didn't think it was fair that her brother got to go to camp and not be grounded. Then, she found out he would be punished once he returned. Now, it seemed fair, sort of.

The only thing she would get to do was the dreaded summer school. She couldn't stand it and wasn't sure why they made her go.

As Ronnie started to put away some of her washed clothes, she started thinking about everything she wanted to do. Then, as some twelve-year-olds do, she started wishing.

"Wish they would have let me go to camp. I wish they would let me stay home and not go to school. I wish I could go back to that forest. Wish we hadn't got caught!"

This last wish was the one she wanted the most. If they hadn't gotten caught, everything would have been different.

"I hope Justin takes me with him next time he goes to The Woods," she said with conviction. "My brother and Justin think I'm too young to go in there, but I'm not, I tell you! I'm not!"

Walking over to her bed, she lay down and started thinking about the valley and the little village. Once again, she started talking out loud to herself.

"That place is incredible. I can't believe it's real. One thing I will not do is tell anyone about it. Justin told me not to, and I will keep my promise. Well, unless they try to keep me from going next time. Then I might tell on them. They have got to realize that I want to go and have fun, too. Soon, Steve will be back, and they will return to The Woods. Then they will go and explore some more without me. It's just not fair. Not fair at all."

Ronnie's mind now drifted to when, if ever, she could go back inside the valley.

While lying on her bed, she started twirling her long red hair through her fingers, which helped her relax and think more clearly.

As she thought more and more about going back in, her excitement about the adventure seemed to escalate.

"Once I'm off from being grounded, I can hopefully slip away and go back in. I will call Justin up and see if he has gone back inside. I bet he has because I know I would have by now," she said with certainty.

As she lay there, she knew that the valley held many adventures. She liked being inside there. The sky was beautiful, the huts were quant and clean, and even the river seemed to sparkle somewhat.

Yes, indeed, she loved every aspect of that place. Even the people there were friendly. She hadn't talked to many of them, but she could tell they were good people.

She had only been inside briefly, but she could tell Justin seemed to belong there.

"Yes, indeed. That is a great place. It is where someone could go and spend the rest of their lives."

Somewhere in her mind, she knew exactly who that someone was. She also knew that Justin was probably thinking the same thing.

Back home

Since Justin had been caught that night with his friends, Mark seemed to keep a closer eye on him.

He even went as far as entering Justin's bedroom at night to ensure he was asleep.

This was bothering Justin. He didn't think things could get any worse with Mark, but somehow, they had.

"Why does he suddenly check up on me? Does he know when I slipped out and went to The Woods? If he does, then wouldn't he let the beatings begin?"

Things had worsened since that fateful night, or so it seemed. Mark started treating Justin even worse than before, if that was possible. He gave him more chores and less time off, making it almost impossible to do anything or go anywhere.

But that was OK because Justin knew Mark was on the wagon. Or was it off the wagon? Justin shook his head because he didn't know, and he didn't care. All he cared about was that when Mark wasn't drinking, he was a little nicer to his mom, and that was all that mattered.

Suddenly, in the dead of the night, there were footsteps. It was the footsteps he dreaded to hear. They were coming from the stairs.

Justin could hear Mark clambering up the stairs one step at a time until he reached the top. He heard some more footsteps and knew they were heading towards his room.

Then, there was a slow creak in the bedroom door as it opened. Once again, he could smell that familiar stench floating across the room.

"Well, so much for being on the wagon or off," Justin thought as he did his best not to move or make a sound.

He knew that if he did move, then it might give Mark a reason to yell at him, so being still and quiet is what he would do. Justin knew anything could set him off, with Mark drinking again.

Shortly, sensing that Mark had left his room, Justin got out of bed and went to his bedroom door. As quietly as possible, he turned the knob. Peering out into the darkened hallway, Justin tried his best to listen.

What he was listening for was a sound of alarm. If someone was there, he could jump into action and start running if necessary.

But there was nothing—only the deep-seated darkness of the hallway.

"Mark must have gone to bed and passed out," Justin thought as he closed his door in relief.

How much longer can my mom put up with this guy? This man was almost too much for anyone to handle.

Justin knew his mom had tried to get Mark help, but he said he didn't need it and didn't want to hear any more about it.

What Justin had found out about this disease was that the person with it had to want to get help. You couldn't make them go and do it.

It was sad to see, but the worst part was that his mom had to put up with this guy daily.

Justin then turned around and returned to bed now that the danger was over.

As he drifted off to sleep, though, there was another sound. Not the sound of someone coming into his room. No, this seemed to come from outside of the house.

"Maybe Mark was packing his bags and moving to greener pastures," Justin thought with hope and glee. But he knew that there wasn't a chance in heck that this would happen.

Thinking that he had imagined this slight noise, Justin laid back on his bed to try and go to sleep.

"I must have been dreaming," he thought as he tried to determine whether the noise was real.

Then suddenly, he heard it again.

This time, it sounded like a rock or a pebble hitting the side of the house or even his window.

He thought it was more than likely just the wind as he tried to close his eyes again, but curiosity had him now.

Justin quietly slipped out of bed and crawled over to the window. Slowly looking up and over the edge of the window sill, he looked outside.

As he peered into the dark, he still did not see anything. He did this for about a minute, but there was nothing. There were no more noises or movements from the outside. He only saw the darkness and a few lights from some neighborhood houses.

It must have been a dream, he said with a smile as he got up and returned to bed.

But he didn't make it back to his bed. Another sound stopped him abruptly.

As he turned, he knew now that the sound had come from the outside. It wasn't loud at all. Whoever made the sound did not want anyone else in the house to hear it, only him. He was sure of that.

Justin then turned and walked back to the window. This time, he did not hide but looked outside and into the shadows. After a few short moments, he slowly opened his window.

Suddenly, he saw a dark figure standing in his backyard. Once the figure saw him, it quickly moved into some bushes by the garage.

Silently, Justin stood there watching and waiting. Waiting for whoever it was to make their next move.

A few moments later, the figure did just that. It moved out of the bushes and back into the dim light from the side porch. Justin could tell that it was indeed a person in his backyard.

As he stood there, he started to imagine all sorts of possibilities. Could it be that Jib had found him and needed help? Or did one of the villagers need him to return for whatever reason? Or could it be someone trying to break in?

None of these things seemed logical right now. Even the one about someone wanting to break in was way off the mark.

Why would someone want to break in and throw pebbles at his window in the night? Justin knew that this was a crazy thought and almost chuckled.

Then, before Justin could develop any more theories, the shadow spoke.

In a soft and quiet voice, it said, "Justin, it's me, Steve. I need to talk to you. I came home early."

At first, Justin couldn't quite place the voice to the person. He knew the voice sounded like Steve, but he also knew he was at camp.

A few moments passed, and things began to make sense to him.

The more he thought about it, the more he realized it had to be Steve. He then leaned slightly out the window to get a better look.

Suddenly, the shadow spoke again. "Come on down so we can talk. I will fill you in on why I'm here."

Justin quickly got dressed and, as quietly as he could, crept out of his bedroom. Down the stairs he went, all the while trying to be as invisible as possible.

Reaching the bottom of the stairs, Justin silently walked over to the side door and turned the knob that went to the backyard.

Now that Justin was outside, he could tell it was Steve. The two boys then moved back into the shadows and further away from the house so that Mark wouldn't catch them if he were awake.

It didn't take Steve very long to start talking. He seemed more than willing to tell Justin why he was here at night.

"I came home early from camp. I just got back today. Can you guess what my parents did? They grounded me. Go figure!"

Deep down inside, Justin knew what the next question would be. He could tell Steve came home early because he wanted to return to the valley.

However, knowing this, Justin wanted Steve to wait a little longer, so he interrupted and asked him something, but he put sarcasm into the question.

"So, you skipped out of camp early, huh? Why did you come back so soon? Did they find out that you were a girl?" Justin let out a small laugh but quietly.

"Hilarious, Justin. No. It just wasn't the same this year. It was no fun at all. The friends I made last year didn't come this time. I told my parents I was sick, so they let me come home. Anyway, I found out that my dad could get some of the money he paid for me to go to the camp. It might not be a total loss." Steve stood there shrugging his shoulders.

"Besides, you know exactly why I came back early! I want to go back inside. And I was afraid you might take someone else next time. Maybe even Ronnie."

Justin started shaking his head. He wasn't about to take Ronnie with them next time or any other time.

"No. No way. She almost got lost last time; we might not have gotten caught if she hadn't gone. She's also too much to worry about. We need to leave her out of this."

Justin then stopped briefly, trying to think of something more to say.

"You didn't tell anyone about what we found inside, did you? I asked you not to! It's essential not to let anyone know about that place."

Justin's face was filled with deep concern when he said this. He was so worried that he almost got sick, fearing one of them might say something. Keeping a secret about the place beyond The Woods was crucial.

"NO! I didn't tell anyone, and I never will. You can trust me with this secret. But if you decide to return inside, please take me with you. That's all I ask."

Listening to Steve, Justin could tell that he was telling the truth. His voice hurt when he answered.

Changing the conversation, Justin then decided to tell Steve where he and Mark had gone and what had happened.

"I have something to tell you, Steve. For some crazy reason, Mark took me out to hunt last week. I don't know why he did, but he did. He said he was trying to make a man out of me or something like that. Anyway, we went shooting in The Woods. I couldn't believe it. We drove right up to them. It was a different location, but it was still The Woods."

Justin stopped for a second and looked at the house to ensure no one was awake and listening.

Then he continued. "When we got there, he started shooting into the forest. He seemed to shoot at anything that moved. Then, shortly, he shot one of the little creatures inside The Woods."

He then filled Steve in on all that had happened in The Woods with Mark. He even told him about Mark not wanting to go completely inside, at least not alone.

"Mark would not go without me going first. It was almost as if he were scared."

Justin then continued, "We never went completely inside. Mark could not bring himself to go and check out his kill. It seemed something kept him from going in, so we left. When we got home, Mark passed out as usual. I once again did the unthinkable. I snuck out later that night and went back."

Justin then went on to tell Steve all about what happened and what he had learned from the village. Steve listened with keen interest.

After filling his friend in on what had happened to him, he could tell that this didn't detour Steve. If anything, it made him want to go inside even more.

"So, when do you think we can go back? I want to go as soon as possible, don't you?"

As Justin stood there, he saw the genuine excitement coming from Steve when he asked him this question. His friend's face and voice showed Justin that he truly loved the valley they had discovered. Justin knew that keeping him away from it would be wrong.

After a few moments, Justin started thinking about when they could return inside. He then began to formulate a plan.

First, they would have to go there better prepared. Jib had told them last time that they should always be prepared. He told them to bring some food and water next time. Justin also felt it might be wise to get an extra set of clothes if needed.

One thing he didn't want to tell Steve was that the other time he was in there, he got the impression that Steve and Ronnie might not be all that welcome. It wasn't to say that Jib and the villagers didn't like them; it was just that he knew they didn't want too many strangers in their hidden valley. They tried to keep their little paradise to themselves, and Justin didn't blame them either.

Justin wanted to be diplomatic about his answers, so he told Steve, "I was thinking about returning soon. It depends on how my stepdad acts. We can go if he leaves, as always, on the weekend. When we do go back, we must be better prepared. We should take food and water, just like Jib said."

Justin stopped talking for a few seconds. He wanted to ensure that Steve knew they had to be more careful the next time they went in.

After a short pause, Justin continued his conversation.

"I just don't want to get caught when we do go back. That is priority one!"

This was not the answer Steve was hoping to hear. He felt he had waited too long already and told Justin so.

"Look, I snuck out of my house to find out when we could return inside. The least you could do is to tell me when we could go. I promise I won't bring my little sister next time or let her follow us."

Steve stopped talking briefly to give Justin a little while to think about everything he had told him.

Then Steve continued," Why don't we go now? We can stop at the store and get whatever we might need. Your parents are asleep; mine don't know I snuck out again. So, let's go now?"

Justin wanted to tell Steve not to beg, that it was beneath him, but all he could think of was that he didn't like sneaking out all the time.

"Oh no. I'm not going to take that kind of a chance again. We were fortunate the last time. I have done it twice now, and that is enough. I don't want to go inside if we have to sneak in. That way, we won't have to worry so much about coming back too quickly or getting into trouble."

Finally, Justin told Steve they might have a chance to go soon and that he should be patient a little longer.

Justin could see that his friend was feeling down and needed to think of something else to soothe him.

"Didn't you just tell me that you are grounded? Doesn't that go on for a whole week?"

"Oh yeah. I forgot about that. Yes. I am still grounded, but I thought we could go again tonight like last time."

Justin started shaking his head in disbelief at his friend and his thought process. He was only thinking about going back inside and nothing else.

Once again, Justin answered him but stayed firm.

"No. I'm afraid we can't go right now. I have too much to do and don't want to lie to my mom again. Besides, I'm sure once you're off being grounded, we can find a time to return to the valley."

Steve had a sad look, but he knew Justin was right. He also knew how Justin felt. He was true blue and didn't like doing anything wrong or getting in trouble. After all, that's why they called him Justin the Just, right?

Justin then said goodnight and headed inside his house. Steve, with his head down, waved goodbye and headed for home.

It was tough for Steve, but he knew it was right not to go to the valley tonight. He would have to wait a little longer, and the two of them would get to go back.

As Steve headed home, his thoughts once again turned towards The Woods. He knew he could go into them alone, but something just told him he shouldn't do this without Justin. After all, Justin had initially found the valley. It wouldn't seem right if he went without him.

At least now, he was convinced that his friend would not take anyone else without him, so waiting for the right time was what Steve would have to do.

Dilemma

A little over a week had passed, and for the most part, things were looking up for the kid. His stepdad had already left for the weekend, and all his chores were done. The next thing he had to do was call Steve to see if he could go to The Woods today. Steve said he could and would be over in about thirty minutes.

Something in the back of Justin's mind told him that Steve would be over much sooner than that, and he was right.

Fifteen minutes later, Justin opened his door, and Steve stood there. His excitement seemed to be spewing out of his pores. It almost looked as if Steve couldn't stand still for very long. Justin knew that it was because of the excitement of going back inside.

Justin then turned to his mom and told her where they were going and not to expect them for lunch.

Mary didn't like him going off into that area, but after all, he was growing up, and she knew she couldn't keep him home all the time.

"Just be careful," she told them as she watched them jump on their bikes and head down the road.

Both boys had been to this place a few times before, so she thought this shouldn't be unusual as the boys headed out.

When they arrived at The Woods, they hid their bikes just inside. But this time, they sat and waited. What they were waiting for was to make sure that a certain little someone hadn't followed them. They got lucky last time and didn't want to repeat that ordeal if they could prevent it.

As they waited, they noticed old farmer Tucker working in his field. There, for a second, it looked as if Tucker glanced over in their direction. If he had, then it was only for a few seconds.

A short time passed, and as far as they could tell, no one was following them this time. Still, they waited. The longer they waited, the more their excitement grew.

Finally, they realized it had been long enough, so the boys turned and headed into the dark woods.

Quickly, Justin strapped his backpack on, for it had all the supplies. There was food, water, and two small blankets. This may or may not be needed, but Justin wanted to ensure they had something just in case.

Both boys were excited and couldn't wait to see Jib and the others in the village.

Following the same path as before, the boys went up and over the rock as usual, but when they reached the ground, they had difficulty finding the opening. It took them a little while to see it, and both boys sighed relief when they did.

From what the boys could tell, the opening was being blocked by all the trees and bushes. As the brush and trees grew, the opening got smaller, making it harder to find. It seemed to alarm the boys at first, but their excitement outweighed the risk of not being able to go inside anymore.

Luckily, the light got brighter as they pulled and pushed the brush to the side, helping them reach the other side of the opening. Upon coming out of The Woods, they realized they had arrived in the daytime.

Once they were standing on the plateau, they did the same thing they had done the previous time. They slid down the hill, followed the river, and then around the bend on the side of the mountain that overlooked the village.

As they peered into the valley, they both realized nothing had changed. Everything seemed to be just like they remembered.

Shortly, the two of them reached the village. Suddenly, one of the villagers came out to greet them. The man approached the boys, shook their hands, and introduced himself to them. This man, like Jib, appeared to be an older gentleman. He had a bushy white beard and almost the same attire as Jib. The only difference was that this man had long hair, and Jib didn't.

"My name is Hebo. I am second in command of the village while Jib is away. So that should answer your first question!"

When he said this to them, he told them he had read their thoughts. Justin had earlier told Steve about Jib and his mind-reading ability, so it wasn't something his friend didn't know or was shocked to find out.

"Jib is away at this time. He is in another region. He had a pressing matter to take care of. Jib went to try to get the man that the Intruders had taken. He has gone to see if he is OK and try to get him back if possible."

Hebo's face looked lost as he said this. Justin felt the man taken was a friend of his.

"Is this man that was captured a friend of yours?" Justin asked Hebo with sincerity.

"Yes. He is my brother. His name is Lebo. He is a good man, a good husband, and a good father to his family."

As Justin thought about the last time he was here, he remembered seeing a lady crying after the man had been abducted.

He also remembered that Jib had told him that the lady crying was the wife of the captured man. Now, it all seemed to come together for Justin.

"Is there anything that we might be able to do to help you get him back safely?"

"I don't know," Hebo said, "but when Jib returns, maybe you can ask him. He will know more."

Hebo stopped a moment and shook his head. Anyone could see that this man cared deeply for his brother.

"It is a sad time in our village, and if we don't seem too hospitable, please forgive us."

The boys then told him that it was understandable and that they didn't expect anything from them. They had just returned to visit this village and the surrounding valley.

Justin then looked at Hebo and asked, "Is there anything we could help you with around your village? I know the Intruders left a mess when they attacked. Maybe there might be something Steve and I can help you fix!"

Hebo touched his old bearded chin and thought for a second. Then he answered.

"You know, when the Intruders came, they destroyed parts of our water system. It needs some repairs. Maybe you two can help us with that!"

They both agreed and asked him to lead the way. Hebo then

took them to a part of the water line that some villagers tried to repair.

To the boys, it looked like a straightforward water system. It seemed to be made out of bamboo, but it did look very sturdy. It was also very primitive, something you might have seen long ago. But it still worked for the village, so that was all that mattered.

They could see exactly what had to be done as they examined it more closely. Hebo then brought some repair parts he thought they might need.

He then showed the boys some plaster that they had. This plaster was made out of plants and soil. It was then used to smooth over some parts of the water system that were busted and leaked.

The plaster dried very quickly, and it did indeed stop the leaks. When the plaster dried, it seemed to turn into concrete. It was rugged and sturdy, and it did the job.

The only part of the repair job they could have considered problematic was that the bamboo pipes weighed quite a bit. Several villagers and the boys took pipes to each part of the broken water system. They repaired all of the busted pipes without any trouble.

For some reason, these villagers were not very good at repairing things; that is what it looked like to the boys. The only tools they had here were brooms, rakes, and shovels. There didn't seem to be metal tools like wrenches, screwdrivers, picks, or anything else.

These villagers were advanced in some areas but seemed far behind in other ways. It seemed odd to Justin, but he didn't want to question it. He enjoyed being able to help them, and he could tell that Steve did, too.

As the three of them headed back to the village, Hebo told the boys some history about the valley.

"Our village never had a well or a watering system. In the past, we only got water from the river that ran through our town. And then, one day, someone came into our village and changed a few things—but only for the good."

Hebo then took out his pipe and started to smoke some of the weed that was inside. It had a pleasing aroma, which seemed to relax him a bit.

He then continued. "What happened was that one day, a stranger came and built this water system for us. He had come here, made the system, then moved on or disappeared. Legend had it that he had just left one day and never returned."

Hebo paused briefly, moved over to a bench, and sat down.

"This man did more than just build the water system. He also came up with the early warning alarm. That is the noise you will hear when strangers are approaching or if something bad is about to happen, like weather or Intruders. We have some large birds in our valley, and they will make a loud screeching sound, as you can attest."

Hebo stopped for a second and looked down. It almost looked as if he was bowing his head for a moment. Justin figured that he was once again thinking about his brother. The boys could tell that Hebo missed him, and he hoped that Jib could somehow get him back home where he belonged.

Justin could also see that Hebo and the others thought highly of the so-called stranger who had come here and helped them.

A short time passed, and Hebo continued his story.

"This stranger had figured out that if you feed the birds the Stringer, they will make the warning sound. When you give them more, then they get louder. They seem to like the Stringer, but the funny thing is, they won't eat it unless someone feeds it to them."

Hebo then took a few puffs on his pipe before he continued his story.

"So anytime someone comes into our valley from The Woods, the Nampo let us know, and then the guardian of the birds feeds them. The Nampo's will begin to act strangely and run in circles. Then, the guardian will feed the Stringer to the giant birds. If bad rain comes, the guardian will feed them more. That's why sometimes the alarm you hear is louder or quieter, depending on what is about to happen."

Hebo sat there with a slight smile while shaking his head. Shortly after, he stood up and had the boys follow him to the center of the village. He then pointed to the well in the middle of the town and told them more about what the stranger did to help them.

"This is another thing the stranger did for us. He dug this well for all the village to use. This made it easier for us to get water. This way, we didn't have to use the river for our water as much. It has been very beneficial. Now we don't have to do without water at all. Our water system is used mainly for watering our crops, bathing, and cleaning up. Our well is used for drinking and other things. It has helped our village immensely."

It was plain to see that this stranger had been a friend to these villagers. But the good thing was that everything the man did for them didn't change their way of life or their village. It just seemed to make their lives easier in specific ways.

A few moments later, Hebo said, "Please forgive me, for I have been rude. Let me offer you two some food!"

They entered Hebo's hut and sat at a neatly decorated table.

There, they ate vegetables, some fruit, and some bread with a honey taste.

The villagers knew these two had earned their keep, so they were welcome to stay longer. Hebo asked them this, and Justin, speaking for Steve, answered yes.

"Yes. We do have more time this visit. We just came here to explore more of the valley. This is such a beautiful place. There is so much to see and learn here."

After their meal, the three started walking to another part of the village.

When the boys first saw this place, it seemed very small. But now that they were taking a little tour, they could see it was much larger than they had first thought.

As they walked about, Justin noticed some old buildings. They were not like the huts that the villagers lived in. These buildings looked like ones used in towns and cities outside the valley.

The old buildings were set apart from the huts. The boys could tell that these were not used as huts to live in but possibly places one might work or use as storage.

Most of the buildings were built against the side of a hill.

Over the years, trees and bushes had grown over some of them. They were not hidden, just camouflaged somewhat. Also, the foliage seemed to give the buildings an antique look. It made them look older than they probably were.

Hebo then explained that the buildings housed books written long ago by people from the valley. Thousands of old books were stored here for safekeeping.

Justin figured that these buildings were equivalent to a library. He also felt that if he had the time, he might be able to read them and learn more about this area and its history.

After walking some more, the boys thought they had come to the end of the village but noticed even more huts along the river. However, these huts were spaced further apart and seemed smaller than the ones in the town.

Once again, they noticed more green trees and shrubs. There were so many that they hid many of the huts. Plus, there were more flowers in this part of the village. What seemed a little different was that the flowers seemed brighter and illuminating, almost fluorescent. This fact seemed to put the awe back into their adventure.

A few short steps further, Justin continued with his observations.

"See how the bridges are evenly spaced through the village. They seem to have huts on both sides of the river. The river winds a little, and it flows gently by their village. Each hut is close to the river. Some canals go in front of the huts, and a small channel runs on the side of every hut so they can use that water for whatever reason."

Justin could tell that the channel was used to prevent the contamination of the other water flowing further down the stream.

This little village had achieved quite an endeavor, which almost made Justin proud of what he had seen.

Steve was also impressed with what they discovered and the scenery they were taking in. It was mesmerizing.

Steve knew he would love to stay here forever, but something in his mind told him he should go when it was time to leave.

On the other hand, somehow, he knew that Justin should stay because he seemed to fit in with this valley and the people.

Looking at the village, Justin had the same thing on his mind as Steve. Justin wanted to stay here forever. This feeling was intense and seemed to get stronger each time he returned.

"I could live here and earn my keep by doing things for the

villagers," he theorized.

Then he came back to reality. He knew that would never happen. There was too much on the outside holding him back.

Justin was then brought out of his daydream by Hebo saying something to him.

"Look! Up ahead, it's Jib. He has returned from Danton."

As he said this, he saw the puzzled look on each boy's face, so he explained what he meant.

"Danton is the region that we think the Intruders took my brother Lebo. I hope Jib has returned with good news!"

Hebo quickly headed down the road to greet Jib, who was just getting off his Nampo. Jib had dust all over his outer clothing. As he dismounted, Justin could see how old and tired he looked.

As Jib walked up to them, he looked worried.

"So! Justin the Just has returned to us. That is a good thing. We may need all the help we can get soon." Jib's words seemed to trail off, most likely from being tired.

Slowly, their little group walked back to the village and into Jib's hut. Jib looked over at Steve and seemed to scowl. It was almost as if to say he wished he hadn't returned.

Steve caught the look and seemed to be offended by it.

Unbeknownst to Steve, Jib looked at Justin and gave a wink, letting Justin know that he was just kidding around.

Once inside, they all sat in a semi-circle, with Hebo sitting the closest to Jib. This was so he could hear all of the information, if any, Jib may have found out.

"I have good news and bad news for you, Hebo. Your brother Lebo is alive, but he has been taken to Danton as we feared. He is indeed being made to work their fields, though."

Jib then looked at the boys and decided to fill them in on Danton and other regions here.

"Danton used to be an amiable village long ago. It was the largest of its kind. It takes us about a day and a half to get there by cart. The journey is very bumpy, for the roads are not that smooth. There was always much trade in the town, which might be why it was so vulnerable and taken over so easily. As you might have guessed, it was taken over by the Black Intruders group."

Jib stopped for a moment as if trying to gather his thoughts. He seemed to be reflecting on something in his past. It almost seemed he was trying to figure out something that had bothered him for a long time.

"These so-called Intruders lived so far away that we never really had to worry about them hurting us or doing anything to our village. They also never really seemed too bright. But then something happened that changed this clan. From what he had discovered, this clan had acquired a new leader. This new man somehow made this group smarter, especially fighting."

Justin interrupted at this point.

"You said it is a day and a half from their village to yours. What change made it easier for them to come to the other villages?"

Jib then answered Justin's question.

"This new leader showed his men how to ride the Nampo. Most people didn't know how to ride them, nor did they want to. When the leader taught them, getting to other villages was quicker. It cut the time down by quite a bit. When they ventured here, they raided us for our food supplies and men and women. These people can be very ruthless at times. Their leader is a very cunning man who is in total control over his men."

Jib then stopped and let out a long sigh. His tiredness was showing now, but he continued with more news.

"They have no feelings for us or anyone else for that matter. They will do whatever it takes to get what they want and need. They will cut down anything or anyone that stands in their way!"

Jib stopped his speech and went into the kitchen. Shortly, he was back with some cool water for all of them to drink. Since no refrigerators were here, Justin wondered how they kept the water cool.

The water tasted good, and Jib continued his information after a few moments.

"As I stated before, Danton is one of the largest villages around, and it was also one of the friendliest until the Intruders took over. Now, it is ruled with an iron grip. And it is now quicker to get to our village because of what the Intruders have learned. We are always vulnerable to attack, so the early warning alarm is useful. But one thing is for sure: we can't go on living like this much longer. Soon, they will want to take us over. We will all be their captives, and I, for one, will not live that way. I'm old, so that wouldn't be much of a loss. But for the children here, if they had to be enslaved and lose their freedom, well, that just won't do, no way! They will never live like that and shouldn't have to."

Jib stopped for a second, then said, "We do, however, have a few options to consider!" He then stopped talking and lit a pipe he had pulled out of his pocket. The aroma from it was delightful and soothing. Justin could tell it was the same weed that Hebo had smoked earlier.

"One option is to go on like we are and hope they don't take us completely over, or we could take flight and run. We can go deeper into the valley until we find a haven for our villagers."

Jib then stopped talking for a second so he could catch his breath. Shortly, he continued.

"Or, we could fight back!"

Memories

He knew the kid was up to something. He could feel it in his bones. Well, whatever it was, he was bound and determined to find it out.

Just before Mark told them he was leaving for the weekend, he heard Justin asking his mom if he and his buddy could go exploring today. This alerted Mark that something might be up with this kid, so he changed his plans.

At this time, Mark told Mary that he was leaving and left the house. Then he went to the outskirts of town. Keeping a low profile, Mark hid where no one could see him. It was off the main road, but one that Justin would have to use to get to wherever he was going.

"I'm not going to wait much longer. I have a lot of drinking to do. But that kid is up to no good. I'm sure of it."

As he sat back in his truck, he opened yet another beer. His drinking had consumed him lately. He loved it, and he loved wasting his time doing it. The only thing he loved better was to give Justin a hard time.

A little while later, the time he had wasted was rewarded.

Just when Mark was thinking about giving up and returning to Mary's house, he saw two boys riding past on bikes. He could tell they were in a big hurry from their speed. He also could tell that one of them was Justin.

"Where the heck are they going?" he said aloud. "It doesn't matter. I got you now, you little disobedient punk."

An evil smile came across his lips as he surveyed this situation. He was almost foaming at the mouth, thinking about everything he would do to Justin when he caught up to him. This time, he was going to make it hurt. He might even make his mom hurt for having such an unruly child. He was going to teach this little weasel a lesson. One that he would never forget.

Then, after a short pause, he slowly pulled his truck back onto the road and cautiously stayed behind them. He kept a reasonable distance away so they wouldn't see him.

Suddenly, he saw the boys turn down a dirt road next to an old cornfield. Mark noticed that The Woods were adjacent to the field.

"Well, that answers one question. Now, why are these boys going down this dirt road?"

Mark was very perplexed about what might be going on now. Still, he wanted an answer.

He then parked his truck and got out. Quickly, he surveyed

the area the best he could.

Hiding in some bushes at the dirt road entrance, he watched the boys as they sat down just inside the hollow trees. They did this for about five minutes, then finally disappeared inside the thicket.

Now, a low gurgling sound came from Mark's throat. It sounded like a grunt but had a wicked noise attached.

While he stood there thinking about his next move, he was happy with himself. He was pleased because he had come up with that lie about going away for the weekend. He knew the little snot-nose brat was up to something, and now his waiting and lying were paying off for him.

One thing Mark didn't want was for the boys to see him too soon. If they did, then his little surprise would be spoiled.

What had changed his plans about going away for the weekend was that a few weeks earlier, Mark had heard a rumor from a friend at the police station. His friend said three kids had gotten in trouble for being out too late one night. The friend couldn't give Mark their names, but from the description of the kids and the area where they were caught, he was pretty sure it was Justin and his buddies.

This was the same time Mark had stepped up his so-called surveillance on Justin. He wasn't letting him do hardly anything.

The kid was not getting to go out and play or go with his friends anywhere. All he made him do was stay home and work.

Still, Mark had not caught the kid doing anything wrong—nothing whatsoever—well, at least until now, or so it appeared.

Mark felt nobody could be this perfect, so he closely watched Justin. He figured that sooner or later, the kid would mess up. In Mark's mind, it seemed sooner had finally arrived.

Pulling his truck to the entrance, Mark heard a dog barking. The more he listened to the bark, the more he felt it might be directed toward him.

"Bark all you want, but I will still catch those two. Justin is going to pay dearly this time.''

Mark drove his truck to the same area that he saw the boys go in. He then got out and slowly walked over to The Woods.

Leaving caution to the wind, Mark crept up to the thicket. Slowly, he looked inside the wooded area. He walked into the hollow when he was sure the boys were not around.

As his eyes became accustomed to the dark, he spotted their bikes. Scanning the area, he searched for the boys, but they were nowhere in sight.

Talking out loud to himself, he said, "Getting their bikes will keep someone from stealing them. I'll put them in my truck, and they should be safe. You see, I am a good guy, after all."

Mark couldn't help but start laughing out loud at his last thought. It seemed so funny to him to take their bikes.

He then grabbed the bikes, for they were only a few feet inside the trees. Then he took them to his truck and put them in the back.

Suddenly, a slight nervousness came upon him. Not only was he nervous, but he also started to sweat profusely. Something hidden in the back of his mind for so many years seemed to resurface.

What he had forgotten about was his 'fear.' The alcohol he consumed daily always seemed to keep it at bay. But now, as he looked inside this darkened area, his false bravado seemed to escape him. And to think that it only took a few steps inside this hollow to rekindle his long-lost phobia.

Yes, he had forgotten about this fear, but now it was back and with a vengeance. This fright haunted him and even mocked him even after all this time. It was so strong that it stopped him from going further into The Woods.

Then it hit him like a head rush. All his childhood memories about this area and these woods came flooding back.

He was nine years old, and his dad had brought him to this forest.

His dad had been drinking pretty heavily that day, but that wasn't the fear that gripped him. The fear that made him sweat and shake was from The Woods itself.

On the day he came here, his dad told him he wanted him to learn how to shoot and kill animals. This was almost like what Mark tried to do with Justin a few weeks ago.

As Mark remembered that fateful time in his youth, he tried his best to recall exactly what had transpired on that day so long ago.

When he and his father went inside, it was eerily quiet. A few moments later, his dad announced that he spotted something ahead.

At first, Mark could not see where his dad was pointing. The movement had been swift and elusive. The creature had now adapted to its immediate surroundings. Neither one of them could see precisely where it went. But that didn't matter to them because whatever it was, or wherever it went, it would be dead when it got within their range.

Suddenly, Mark saw something else move. It had two red eyes that seemed to shine at them and sharp teeth that looked like they could cut you even from this distance. This animal was unlike anything either one of them had ever seen.

Mark could hear the animal snarl at them. Somehow, it knew the two of them had come here to kill it.

His dad quickly pointed the rifle at the animal and took two shots. This seemed to shatter the stillness of the forest.

Just before his dad took the shot, though, Mark heard a loud noise that seemed to be coming from some of the foliage in this area. It was almost like a warning of some kind.

Could another animal have tried to warn the one that Mark's dad shot at? Were these creatures that smart?

Mark didn't know, and he didn't care. All he knew was that sound, whatever it was, scared him quite a bit, and he was rooted to the ground. He felt that if he moved, one of the creatures might try to hurt him.

To Mark, these last thoughts enhanced his terror. Now, other noises seemed to escape through the overgrowth. The silence was no more.

As Mark continued his search, he saw many eyes that seemed to peer out of the bushes. Eyes that penetrated and watched his every move. They seemed to be all around him, almost as if they were trying to encircle him so he wouldn't have a way to escape.

His dad looked at him and could tell that his son was scared. To his father, it was a sign of weakness.

"You're nothing but a little sissy, aren't you?" his dad accusingly said.

"Look at the little sissy boy," his dad screamed. "Well, little sissy boy, guess what you're going to do now? You're going to shoot the rifle."

He then handed it to Mark, who took it willingly. He would do anything to make his dad stop calling him names, so shooting the rifle was what he needed to do.

Surprisingly enough, when Mark held the rifle, it felt good in his hands. It almost gave him a sense of power—a false sense, but power, just the same.

As he steadied the rifle, the creature made a move. Quickly, Mark aimed and delivered the bullet. And just like in the movies, he hit his target, or at least thought he did.

"Not bad for a nine-year-old," is what he wanted to hear his father say, but no accolades came. No Atta boys were coming from him, either.

Whatever that creature was, it took off deeper into the trees. As far as he knew, the animal may have gone to find a place to die.

"It deserved to die," thought Mark. It had made him look like a coward in front of his dad.

"It better die," he said under his breath with a slightly wicked smile.

This was the same smile he would always have whenever he saw something hurt or someone needing help.

"Go and find the animal, son. Well, unless you're a fancy lad. Are you a fancy lad?"

His dad asked this question but had attached a rather loud and sarcastic tone to it. Then he started emitting a bellowing laugh.

"Don't worry; I will be behind you once I get a cigarette. Now go inside and find your kill."

Mark handed the rifle to his dad and started heading toward where he last saw the animal enter the thicket.

He was so pleased at this moment. He felt he had done something good, or at least something his dad would be proud of.

But now, as he pushed forward into the trees, he felt vulnerable without the rifle. Still, he kept walking to avoid giving his dad a reason to start repeating things. He didn't want to hear his dad call him any more names. He wouldn't be able to stand much more of it.

Mark imagined hearing the bushes and trees talking to him as he entered. Also, those eyes were back, and they watched his every move. They almost appeared to want him to go deeper inside the forest.

After a short time had passed, Mark felt something wasn't quite right. So slowly, he turned around. He was all alone. His dad was nowhere in sight. His father lied to him and did not follow him.

He was a nine-year-old boy, and his worthless father had left him alone in The Woods for some morbid reason.

What possessed an adult to do such a thing to a young lad? It was hard to imagine, but his dad had done this very thing.

To this day, Mark still fears being lost inside The Woods. No matter how old he got, it never left him. It didn't matter how much he tried to drink it away; it always seemed to catch up to him.

As Mark approached the bushes and trees where Justin and his friend entered, he grabbed another beer and cigarette. As he stood there trying to regain some courage, he started once again thinking about his younger days.

The one thing he remembered from so long ago was that he had been unable to find his way out for so long.

Also, the noises seemed to be getting louder and louder.

They seemed to surround him, not wanting to let him leave. The howling sounds told him he had done something terrible and should be punished.

Continuing to look for a way out, every path seemed to lead to a dead end. It almost appeared hopeless at times, which brought on more anxiety for Mark.

Then he remembered something else. He was so scared that he started to cry and whimper.

Then he started yelling for his dad. "Dad, where are you?" He yelled this command repeatedly but to no avail, for there was no answer.

Mark was so scared that he would have done almost anything to escape this place. But there was no escape. At times, it seemed nearly futile.

Then he ran as fast as he could. Mark went in every direction. Panic followed, making his situation worse.

Suddenly, the trees and bushes seemed to be closing in on him again. He could feel the creatures of The Woods watching him, wanting to hurt him like he had hurt the animal.

In this young boy's mind, he was sure that what he was seeing was real.

He promised he would never return inside if he escaped this alive.

Shortly, Mark lit another cigarette and drank yet another beer. He was now trying to regain some nerve he had lost in the last few moments.

Taking a few more drags on his cigarette and guzzling down his beer, he continued with his so-called reminiscing.

What he remembered about his first visit to The Woods was very embarrassing. When he got scared, he would wet his pants, and this was one of those times—not once but twice—but he didn't care by this time. All he wanted was to leave this forest and never return.

Then, finally, after what seemed to be hours of running, he found the way out.

As he continued to reflect on his first time in The Woods, he was still shaken from the experience.

"To think, after all these years, I am still afraid to go in there." He had said this last sentence while shaking his head in disbelief.

"I was just a young boy then, and my imagination had just run away." He tried to convince himself that what he had heard and seen years ago wasn't real.

But what was real was that when he finally did escape, his dad was at the truck and started laughing at him. Then, to make matters worse, his dad saw that his son had wet his pants. This made his dad laugh even more and louder.

It was so hurtful to Mark that it made him cry even more. It is sad to say that he has never gotten over this incident.

Finally, after all of his thoughts and memories had resurfaced and revealed, he reached into the back of his truck and brought out his rifle and a knife.

"Yeah, I'm going back in. There is nothing in there that can hurt me. I'm locked and loaded and ready for anything."

Once again, he said this out loud, trying to sound convincing and find that ever-elusive courage again.

He needed to go back in there. Not just to find the delinquents but also to prove to himself that he wasn't a sissy boy. He wanted to prove that his dad had been wrong all these years.

Even though his dad had passed away several years ago, it still mattered to Mark. He still needed to prove that he was a man and could go into The Woods alone.

Nothing was going to stop him from going and getting those kids out. He was going to make Justin pay this time.

With his rifle in one hand and a knife in the other, he stood there defiantly.

But he felt he needed more encouragement before going in, so he grabbed another beer and a cigarette.

Then, when he was finished, he bravely ventured into The Woods.

"Keep Down, Keep Quiet, And Don't Move."

The boys stood there looking dumbfounded. "What did Jib mean when he said they could fight back?"

As far as the boys could tell, this little village didn't have that many inhabitants, and none of them seemed like soldiers.

Also, they hadn't seen any artillery or weaponry of any kind. No guns, ammo, knives, or even bows and arrows existed. And, by the look of it, the four couldn't fight anyone hand-to-hand either.

Maybe he meant something else. Perhaps he meant they would outsmart these Intruders and possibly set traps for them. Yeah, that was what Jib meant; it had to be.

"You are correct, Justin." Then Jib stopped abruptly. "Sorry," Jib said to Justin.

Justin knew precisely why Jib had apologized. He had read his mind once again.

Jib was now in his chair, staring at the fire he had started in his fireplace when they first entered the hut. The fireplace looked so eloquent. It almost seemed too lovely for this simple hut of his.

"What we need is some defense for our village. We have our early warning alarm, but we need more. We need to set some traps. Something that will make the Intruders think twice about returning this way!"

Jib sat back in his chair and looked at the boys, but mostly, he looked at Justin.

As Justin looked at Jib, he wondered if he wanted him to devise a plan.

Justin and Steve were just young boys, so what would they know about fighting battles or making any traps? Justin was at a total loss. He wanted to help them so much, and he knew if he could, he would.

Suddenly, breaking through the silence, there was a screeching sound. It sounded like the alarm Justin had heard the first time he came into the valley. But this one seemed a little different.

Both boys looked directly at Jib. They waited to see if he would tell them to hide or defend themselves, but he did nothing. All Jib did was slowly get up out of his chair and go over to the fireplace. He then turned the log to burn on the other side.

"No need to be alarmed," Jib finally said as he turned away from the fire. "That is another one of our alarms, but it is quite different. It just tells us that someone has entered The Woods. It went off when you came here the first time. It is only used when they feel a threat coming our way or into our valley. This one lets us know that someone is coming that might be harmful. We hate to judge so quickly, but over the years, we have learned that we are right about whoever has come here most of the time."

Justin stood there wondering how they could determine that the person entering the valley was harmful. Maybe it was their actions or what they brought—possibly weapons or tools.

Shortly, Jib continued his speech.

"Now for the person coming into our valley from The Woods. It would be nearly impossible for them to find their way into our valley unless they saw the light that showed the point of entry. We like it that way, but some occasionally find their way in and present problems. This person found the way, and he will be watched closely."

Jib had stopped talking for a second to let the boys think about what he had told them. Shortly, he continued his talk.

"When you came in, you came here on your own. You were lucky. Something must have helped you find the opening. You were kind of let in the second time you came with Steve. The point of entry was still available. We felt that we knew you by then, so any friend of yours was a friend of ours."

Jib then explained more, especially when Ronnie came into the valley.

"Your sister," Jib said to them but mainly to Steve, "got

inside because she was close behind you two. The opening was still there, making it easy for her to see. But now, we have been trying to make it impossible for anyone else to get in. Shortly, the entry point will be concealed forever, and there will be no way in or out. We are still working on it, though."

There was a smile on Jib's face as he stared at Justin. There was also something else, but Justin couldn't quite understand it. It was how he looked at him when he said this last sentence.

"Sure, you all found the way in, but most people wouldn't. The opening would be disguised, and the hill that overlooks the valley would not be assessable for the most part."

Jib seemed pretty sure of what he told them, and when Justin thought about it some more, it seemed easy to come here the first time. He had just been lucky to see the light that led him to the opening and the valley.

"We don't want just anyone coming into our little domain. We can keep out just about everyone. But as stated earlier, once in a while, some do slip through. When they do, we feel that fate led them this way. Still, they can't get in most of the time, which is good."

Jib then walked back into the kitchen but stopped for a moment. It seemed he had forgotten what he had come in there for.

Then, suddenly, he picked up something and brought it to the front room.

As he handed it to them, Justin saw it looked like jerky. Jib broke a few pieces off, gave some to the boys, and ate it.

"Go ahead, eat. I can hear your stomachs from across the room." Jib's smile was reassuring.

As they ate, they realized that the taste and texture of the food tasted like jerky but unlike any they had ever had.

Shortly after their snack, they all walked to the front porch for a breath of fresh air.

Suddenly, cutting through the air was another alarm. Even the boys could tell it was different from the first alarm this time.

Jib jumped up as quickly as he could. He motioned to the boys to follow him. This time, they did not go up the road but rather to an area close to the old buildings across the bridge that divided the village.

To Justin, it was just like the first time he and Jib hid from the Black Intruders.

Now they could see that all the town folk were running and hiding as fast as they could. It seemed that this had happened a lot in the past, for Justin could see how organized they all seemed to be in finding hiding places.

From where Justin and Steve were, they could not see much of what, if any, was going on in the village. All they knew was what they were told. Keep down, keep quiet, and don't move.

Justin knew that something terrible was going to happen. It was almost as if he had a sixth sense about this situation. He didn't realize how bad things would get for him and Steve, but in a short time, he would.

Silken

Something about this last raid seemed to bother the leader of the Black Intruders. He could not figure out what it was at first. The more he thought about it, the more it became clear though. There was something about the two people hiding behind the foliage and the rocks.

There was an older man and a young one. The older man was the village leader; he was sure of that. But the young lad he knew nothing about. He had not encountered this person before, but he could tell by how this person smelt that he was young and new to the area.

As he was known to his clansman, Hess could almost see the two people hiding from him, not literally, but still, he could sense them in a way. He could practically see right through things at times. He had acquired this trait from eating some of the plants in the valley, at least from what he could remember.

His men had gone out searching for food, water, and workers. They had acquired all three in such a short period.

This had been a good hunt; he told his fellow clansman. Soon, they would have enough to hold them over for quite some time. Then, they would be able to enjoy the fruits they had confiscated.

As Hess sat there, he once again thought about the young person who had been in hiding. For some strange reason, one that he couldn't quite understand, he was repelled by him. It was almost as if this young man was sitting in judgment of him.

Yet how could that be? Hess didn't sit in judgment from anyone. He could care less what anyone or anything thought about him or his actions. He was the leader, and that was final.

Casting these thoughts aside, the leader sat back in his chair. He was now alone in his domain, enjoying the meal he and his men had stolen.

The area that Hess called his home was just a cave. This cave housed him and a few of his men. Some of his other men, the weaker ones, would live outside in their little huts. They would be his first line of defense if anyone came to harm them.

The funny thing is that no one ever came this way. No one ventured into their neck of the valley, at least not into his area. It was as if everyone in this land had decided not to enter their territory. Word must have gone around that the leader was ruthless. He was a leader who would kill or enslave anyone who ever got in his way.

The cave itself was a slight distance away from the village, but still Hess was in charge. From this advantage point, he could control everything in the town of Danton. No one dared cross his path. He was the leader, and all the inhabitants in this quaint little town knew it. They never gave Hess any trouble whatsoever. If they tried anything that Hess didn't like, he would send a few of his men to correct any problem that may have come up.

Most people who lived in the valley weren't harmful—they never had been and never would be. Hess was sure of that. This made it easy for him and his clansman to take whatever they needed or wanted.

Sure, once in a while, his group would come upon some resistance, but nothing they couldn't take care of so far. Mostly, people in this valley were quiet, friendly, and reserved. They were easily controlled, and that's the way Hess liked it.

A short time later, while sitting back and relaxing from his so-called work, the leader was joined by his right-hand man, Cam. Their conversation quickly turned toward who and when they would attack next.

Cam was the next in line should anything happen to Hess. He would then take his place and be in charge of the clan and the village.

So far, the two of them had been able to 'get along,' but tensions seemed to rise for no apparent reason.

To Hess, it seemed that Cam didn't want to wait for him to step down from his position of leader. Cam wanted to be the leader right now.

Stepping down was how things were done in this clan, but Hess knew that if Cam wanted to be the leader right now instead of waiting, that wouldn't happen.

This had now brought mistrust toward Cam, not only toward Cam but also toward some of Cam's followers. He had persuaded some clansmen to side with him, not Hess.

Hess knew that someday, they would have to settle this little dispute between themselves, and the title would go to the victor. That would be the natural and proper way to do things.

But for now, Hess was still in charge. So, whatever he said, the clan would do, at least most of the time.

That was the real reason Hess was now smiling. He had produced a plan to capture another worker for their fields. Plus, they had stolen supplies and food.

His men were easier to get along with when their bellies were full. But when times were hard, then Hess could almost smell rebellion in the air.

After their talk, Cam left the cave, and Hess was alone.

Walking to the cave entrance, Hess looked out upon his valley. It was indeed a lovely site, he thought as he puffed on his pipe, which was full of some of the weed they harvested.

This weed was one of the reasons they needed workers. The workers would be made to cultivate the fields, then pick the weed from the vines that grew the strange leafy material used for their smoke.

They harvested other things, too. One was the strange and eatable Stringers. It was one item that everyone in this land loved to eat. It provided nourishment, and it was very filling to his men. This crop was plentiful, and hoarding it was what Hess made his workers do.

Now, yet another crop was harvested. Many in this valley did not use this crop, as the yield was not plentiful, and its benefits were few.

The name of this crop was Silken. Some say it got its name from the texture of the plant itself. It was soft, almost like silk; hence, the name was acquired.

Most of the villagers didn't ingest this plant. Hardly anyone liked the way it tasted. And they didn't like what it did to some of the unfortunate people who ate it. The side effects from ingesting it were sometimes devastating to whoever partook of the plant.

When some people ate this plant, they experienced strange and terrible things. It made some sick, throw up, or weak, and it also caused others to lose their minds for a while.

Mostly, this Silken was something no one wanted to mess with.

Another plant that the Intruders harvested was called 'Old Ale.' This plant was enjoyed by most of the villagers, for when it was fermented, it turned into a great drink they all liked. This drink gave most people a happy feeling.

But the Old Ale was unlike the Silken. The Silken plant was more potent. Some who used it would turn violent, stronger, and ruthless.

One person that Silken did affect this way was Hess himself. He enjoyed eating Silken. He enjoyed it so much that it seemed he couldn't do without it. This plant also gave Hess unusual strength. This helped him keep his 'King' status in the clan.

Another bad thing it did to Hess was that it made him forget things. Sometimes, he would forget some of his men or places they had attacked.

To some, Silken was a harmful plant that shouldn't be ingested at any cost, but not for Hess. He loved it and the way it made him feel.

For some reason, this plant affected him more than anyone else. When it did, sometimes it wasn't a good idea to be around the leader. He would slash out unexpectedly over anything, mainly for no reason. Most of his clan members knew that it was the Silken doing it to Hess, but no one here wanted to tell him, at least not to his face.

So, he led his group with an iron fist. That was how he liked it and would keep it, at least as long as the Silken was around.

Once again, he stood there and looked out into the dark of the night. He could now see beautiful stars and the moon, which had crept up over the hills that guarded this part of the valley.

Yes, everything was good in the valley tonight. Everything was in its place, and there was nothing to bother him.

Except for that young stranger hiding in the bushes and behind those rocks.

What could it be? Why was this last encounter constantly on his mind? Try as he might, he couldn't get it out of his head.

To help him forget, he reached down, took some Silken out, and chewed on it for a while. This always seemed to make him forget things, and that was precisely what he needed right now.

It's Back

Slowly, with his fear diminishing, Mark crept forward. Now, he had his rifle in his right hand and his knife in his left. Cautiously, he moved inside the first line of trees.

Somehow, he had found some courage, which helped him forget his fear. He then noticed that the longer he was inside these woods, the less anxiety he had.

As his eyes grew accustomed to the darkness, he ventured on. At first, he felt there would be no way to catch up to them, but his hatred for Justin drove him onward. He vowed not to give up until he found them, no matter who or what got in his way.

Then, after what seemed to be about half an hour, Mark sat down and took a break.

He was trying to convince himself that he was not lost and not to give up. He would prove to himself that he wasn't the little sissy boy his father said he was.

"If only my worthless dad were here! He would see that I'm not afraid to come inside The Woods. He would see that I am a man after all."

He was now yelling at all the trees and bushes around him. There was no one here, but still, he rambled on.

"I did it, Dad! I'm inside The Woods without your help. I don't need your help, and I never did." Mark was yelling this at the top of his lungs, almost screaming.

He almost felt vindicated. He was alone inside these woods and was not afraid like his dad thought he would always be.

Finally, he stood up and began to look around at his current surroundings. As he did, he noticed that he had sat down on part of a large rock.

Mark then looked closely at the rock and saw that it was steep. He noticed that each side of the stone had many trees and bushes—so many that he realized there was no way around it.

"Well, I know one thing for sure: those boys didn't come this way because there is no way to get by this rock."

Then, he took a few steps back to try and capture the whole area. As he did, he noticed a light coming from the other side at the top of the rock.

"Surely that light can't be coming from someone that lives deep inside these woods, could it?"

He said this last sentence as he surveyed the rock some more. He also began to shake his head, mainly from the predicament that he felt he was in.

Then, his thought process changed.

"I bet the boys have some special little friend that lives inside this place. That has got to be the answer."

Even though it was dark in this area, Mark looked closer at the rock. His eyes had now adjusted to the dark to see the rock better. He then noticed some muddy footprints leading up to the top. Now he realized that the boys didn't go around the stone. They climbed it.

Examining the rock some more, he finally spotted a solid foothold. Mark knew now that nothing could stop him from climbing the rock and seeing what was on the other side. He was bound and determined to see this through.

Quickly, he put his knife in his pocket, and his rifle swung around his neck. This would make both of his hands accessible so he could climb. He then started by putting his shoe in the foothold and began to climb.

Once he was down on the ground and the other side, Mark could see the light coming from up ahead. The closer he got to the light, the more it faded.

Suddenly, he stopped as if he were frozen to the ground. He heard someone talking ahead and knew it had to be the boys.

Quickly, he hid behind a tree and some bushes off to the side of the path.

A few moments later, when he was sure they hadn't seen him, he continued forward. Mark cautiously made his way toward the dimming light. He was convinced that this was where he heard them talking a few moments earlier.

"Now I've got you, you little disobedient rat," Mark said quietly to himself.

Mark's face was filled with joy as he continued walking. He had caught them, and they didn't even know it. It seemed so funny to him now.

Walking faster and closing in on the light, Mark left caution behind. With the light beginning to fade, he started to pick up his pace.

There was no way he was going to turn back now. He still needed to catch up and didn't want them to get out of sight.

As he approached the fading light, he saw it was coming from an opening in the trees. He then peeled back some of the brush and weeds that were beginning to hide the gap.

Mark slowly peaked out from behind the trees so that if the boys were still there, they would not be able to see him.

Once he was sure the boys were not near the opening, he stepped out of the trees. As he stood there, he cast his eyes over a beautiful valley.

Staring at his surroundings, Mark lost sight of most of the beauty since he didn't care about nature, its beauty, or mystery. All he cared about was finding Justin. Once that was done, he would take him back home and show Justin's mother how disobedient he was and that you could never trust this kid.

The boys were not in sight at this moment, though. They were more than likely way ahead of him. He felt he had delayed too long and let them get too far ahead.

As Mark continued to look out over the valley, he seemed very bewildered about this valley he had stumbled into.

"Where the heck am I?" he asked, peering again over the valley.

"I didn't know there was any place like this inside The Woods! What the heck is going on?" He was very perplexed by his current situation.

"I know that little brat and his friend came this way. I bet they are hiding out there somewhere in this valley. They are probably laughing at me now. If they are, I will show them a thing or two."

Surveying the area more closely, he noticed he was on level ground. Large rocks were on each side of this plateau-like area.

At this moment, he figured out what he had to do. He would have to slide down the open area before he could get off this hill. It was steep, but he figured that was what the boys had probably done. He could tell that someone had slid down earlier because he could see some indentions on the foliage left behind.

"The boys must have slid down this hill and gone to that path by the river. Well, I guess it's my turn now."

But before he could slide down the hill, a loud noise cut through the silence. It scared Mark somewhat, and it caused him to lose his balance and trip. He started to tumble head-first to the bottom of the little hill.

Once down, he quickly stood up and checked himself to ensure he was not hurt.

Realizing he was okay, he turned and looked back up the hill. He now felt lucky he hadn't broken anything in the fall.

Quickly, he began to search for his rifle and knife. Upon finding them, he ensured the gun remained intact and could shoot.

"I bet Justin put something up there to make sure I fell. He probably knows I'm after him. I bet he thought it would be funny to see me fall. My first hunch was right; they were probably out there somewhere watching me and laughing. I know they are."

Mark shook his head in agreement with this last assumption. His hatred for the kid seemed to rise even more now.

Shortly, he headed over to the river. He was almost bewildered by seeing it.

"Where the heck did this river come from?"

With astonishment, he said this last thought, for he knew no rivers were in this part of the county. He had fished almost all of them in the surrounding area, but this one was not on any map.

Mark was mesmerized by the river and the fish he saw in it. He then went over for a closer look. Standing there, he reached down and took his shoes and socks off. Cautiously, he waded into the water.

"Wow. This feels good. I like this river. It looks like there are a lot of fish here, too. I think I will come back sometime and do a little fishing. I know a lot of friends who would love to go fishing in this river. Of course, they will have to pay me to bring them."

Mark started to laugh out loud.

It almost seemed strange, but there, for a moment, he felt young again without any fears or problems.

But it was just a fleeting thought; once it was over, he stepped out of the water, and his old self returned to him.

Still, for some reason, he felt content. But he knew one thing: he wouldn't want to stay here much longer. This place seemed way too laid back for him. He would only stay long enough to find the boys and return them home.

Once out of the water, he went to a nearby tree. Feeling slightly tired from this adventure, he lay in the shade.

"I guess I'm tired from all of the booze I drank earlier," he said to himself with sort of a laugh.

He felt good at this time, and for a moment, he forgot about all the hate inside his heart. It wasn't long before he fell asleep.

A short time passed, and Mark woke up. At first, he didn't know where he was. Suddenly, he realized where and what had happened. Quickly, he put his shoes and socks back on and headed out onto the path.

He didn't know where the boys might be and felt slightly confused.

"I can't believe I fell asleep. Now, those two could be just about anywhere. I don't care; I will still find and bring them back."

He was mad at himself for falling asleep and letting the boys get far ahead.

"I guess that's what I get for drinking so much."

Shaking his head in disbelief, Mark ventured on. He figured he would take the path and follow it wherever it went, hoping the boys had done the same thing.

He realized it led him around the mountain as he continued on the path. When he reached the top of the slight incline, he looked out to another beautiful valley.

Once again, the beauty of this place eluded him. All he could think of was finding Justin and getting them out of this place.

Now, he noticed something else. He saw some huts, or they looked like huts from this distance.

He could also see that the river flowed through this little village, splitting it into. Small bridges connected both sides of the river so that the villagers could get across for whatever reason they might have.

"How quaint!" Mark said sarcastically. He could care less about who lived in this little village.

As he started walking toward the village, the huts were clearer. He also saw a cobbled stone walkway. This walkway's floor was such a beautiful color, which, once again, was lost on Mark.

The area in the center of their village was round. To Mark, it looked like an area where the people met or sat and talked.

"It looks like this place is very boring. There doesn't look like much to do here or any excitement, either."

Mark looked down on the little village with a disgusted look. He realized that this just wasn't his type of lifestyle.

Then, his demented mind once again turned toward Justin.

"I know for sure now that the little runt came this way. He probably has a friend who lives here. He must. What other reason would he have for coming to this crappy little village?"

As he continued his walk, he was suddenly startled. To his left, he heard a rustling. It seemed to come from some bushes and rocks on the side of the road.

Standing there, he realized that the sound seemed familiar but ancient. He was sure he had heard it before.

Quickly, he raised his rifle just in case it was needed. He then put his knife in his pocket so that he had both hands on the gun. This way, he would be ready to shoot if needed.

Then he heard another sound imprinted in his mind for so many years. He heard the sound when he shot that animal in The Woods as a kid.

He still could remember the way the animal cried. The way it seemed to plead for him not to shoot. But he still remembered how he felt when he hit it. He felt good. He thought it might satisfy his dad if he brought the creature down, so he pulled the trigger.

Oh, how he had wanted to kill the 'thing.' He tried to take the life out of it and give it to his father. That would show him that he wasn't a sissy boy, or so he hoped.

But as it turned out, nothing proved that to his father. His father was nothing more than a wicked man who hated all things and hated his offspring even more.

Standing on the path leading to the village, Mark froze. The fear that he had conquered a while back was rekindled.

"What if it is the same animal? What if it's coming to get me?" As he thought this, he slowly inched his way backward.

"How could this be? The creature should be dead by now!"

Now, there was panic in his thought process.

Then, to make matters worse, another sound pierced the air. It was almost like the same sound he heard when he first entered the valley.

At this moment, panic hit him. As he tripped on some stones in his way, he thought about his next move.

"The creature is coming to get me! It's payback time. I know it is."

Mark was now ranting and raving out loud. He didn't care if anyone heard him. All he cared about was getting away from whatever that sound was.

Now, the noise was all around him. It seemed there was no way to escape it, but he ran anyway. He ran back the same way that he came in. He tried his best to run up the incline, but it was hard. It seemed as if the more he ran away from that sound, the more it trapped him.

Fear now had him and wouldn't let go.

Captured

With her window slightly open, she could feel the heat of summer approaching. Ronnie was sitting on her bed and thinking how boring this summer would be. In a way, she was glad her brother was back from camp, though. This would give her time to convince him to let her go with him and Justin the next time they went to The Woods.

Their grounding punishments were up, and she could go to a few places. Mostly, it was just to summer school or a friend's house.

Now, these things seemed so dull at this point in her life. She knew the reason why, though; it was because they had discovered the valley. Ronnie wanted to go back inside the valley and was willing to do just about anything.

She knew another thing that seemed very important. Her brother had gone to Justin's house today, and she figured they would go to The Woods later. This would be the first real chance for them to go back in since they had been caught that night.

Once again, her brother told her he did not want her tagging along and to stop bothering him about going with them. And once again, she acted like she had listened to him.

But we know by now that this wasn't going to happen. She was too curious to stay home and let them go inside without her. She didn't care if she got in trouble again because, to her, the risk outweighed the price to pay if they got caught.

What made her mad was that the boys could run around all over town, and she had to stay home like a good girl.

Well, she wasn't going to let them get away with this. She was bound and determined to find them again, especially if they went to the valley. If it meant she had to go alone, then so be it.

As Ronnie walked into the kitchen, she started trying to act nonchalant. Her mother was doing some of the dishes left from lunch.

Striking up a conversation, she began asking her mother a few questions. While she did, she even helped her do some of them. Ronnie hoped she could learn where Justin and her brother had gone. But deep down, she knew where they went. She just wanted to make sure.

After her short interrogation, Ronnie discovered that Steve had gone to Justin's house and would be home later in the afternoon.

Once again, trying to act uninterested, Ronnie quickly dried some dishes. A plan started to formulate in her head.

Now the dishes were dried, so she quickly turned and told her mom she had to go and get something upstairs in her room.

Heading upstairs, she searched for something Steve had

brought back from camp that he had given her as a present. It was an ornament with the name and logo of the camp he had attended. It wasn't much, but she liked the thought.

Ronnie then took the pine cone off the top of it and made it look like it was broken.

She then ran downstairs and told her mom that she had to talk to Steve and tell him the gift he had brought back for her had broken. Ronnie said she wanted to show him so he could maybe get it fixed.

She then added that she might stay with him for a little while. If the boys were not there, she would just hang out, talk to Justin's mom, and then come home.

Her mom agreed but told her to call when she got to Justin's house. She wanted to talk to Mary, too.

Great. Her plan was beginning to work. At least now she wouldn't have to sit home all day with nothing to do. And who knows, the boys might not return inside the valley after all.

Ronnie sort of laughed, for she knew that the boys would be going inside sometime today. Steve had been too secretive when she asked him what they would do later. A smile was on her face as she headed out the door.

It didn't take her very long to get to Justin's house. One

reason was that Justin only lived a few blocks away. The other reason was that she was so excited that she pedaled too fast. So fast that she almost lost control and crashed into a bush in Justin's front yard.

Ronnie then went inside and talked to Justin's mother. She asked her to call her mom and tell her she had arrived safely.

Once she did, Ronnie asked her where the boys had gone, all the while knowing the answer.

Finding this out, Ronnie wanted to leave quickly but decided to try and act like she didn't care and that she would go back home once she left.

After about five minutes, Ronnie told Mary she would leave and go back home.

Mary had just finished talking with Ronnie's mother, so this was the opportune time for her to leave.

Ronnie knew that her mom hadn't expected her home for a little while, and Justin's mom thought she was headed home. Great, this was perfect timing.

Her little plan began taking shape as she headed out the door and onto her bike. She was bound and determined that the boys would not have fun without her. Not this time.

Once Ronnie took off on her bike, she waved goodbye to

Mary and then headed back toward her house. It was in the opposite direction of The Woods. She did this just in case Mary was watching her leave. This way, if she were, she would think Ronnie was going home after all.

Shortly, Ronnie looked back over her shoulder. She was now out of sight of Justin's house. She then turned sharply and headed north toward farmer Tucker's field.

Arriving at the field, she saw something very strange. A truck was parked outside where she had followed the boys into the hollow that night. What seemed odd about this was that it looked a lot like Justin's stepdad's truck.

She found that peculiar, for she knew Justin didn't like him. In fact, no one liked him as far as she knew. So, seeing his truck here was a little unnerving.

As Ronnie silently approached the truck, she peered into the truck bed. For some strange reason, the boy's bikes were inside.

She then started to figure out what was happening with Mark being here with the boys.

"Maybe the boys had come here with Justin's stepdad. Once they were all here, they all three went inside."

At least, this is what appeared to her to have happened. It didn't add up, but she still walked to the opening.

Suddenly, just before she went inside, there was a movement from some bushes. Ronnie quickly took a few steps backward in case she might have to run.

Then, a moment later, a dog came running out. It was Red. He had been inside the thicket. More than likely, Ronnie thought he was chasing some rabbits as she bent down to pet him.

Red was one of the most lovable hounds she knew. If he liked you, he would rub up against you and lick you constantly. If he didn't, he would howl and howl until you left. He wasn't much of a watchdog, but he still looked the part.

"So now even Red gets to go into The Woods. More people get to go into this area, but not me. That's just great," she said, knowing this would not do.

She would not let this go, for she felt she should be able to go inside if everybody else could. After all, she would be thirteen years old this year. Being thirteen, she should be old enough to make her own decisions, or so she hoped.

She then told Red to go home, and he obeyed. Ronnie hid her bike in the brush as she watched the dog leave.

Ronnie had no fear this time. She felt exhilarated to be in here. Once again, she had brought her flashlight and quickly turned it on. It was no time at all before she found the rock.

Once she climbed it, she headed to the light from the opening. This time, though, the opening seemed smaller to her. There seemed to be more brush and trees in the way.

Now, she stood on the side of the hill and smiled. Ronnie was glad to be back in the valley. She was so happy that she even forgot about how mad her mom would be if she found out that she disobeyed her again. She didn't like not telling her mom where she was going, but she knew she would never let her go alone.

Ronnie promised herself that she would stay here a little while and head home when she found the boys.

Sliding down the hill was fun, and once she was on solid ground, she quickly headed toward the river.

Suddenly, the leaves started parting in the weeping willow tree. The little man, the guardian of the Tree and Hill, came running out towards her. There was an apprehensive look on his face.

"Please. It would be best if you came inside. Hurry, there is danger," he said with a pleading tone.

The little man was standing there waving his arms at her. He was begging her to hurry and follow him.

Knowing this was the same man who showed them the steps the first time she was here, she quickly listened to him.

Suddenly, there was a piercing sound. An alarm had now

sounded. Ronnie was scared but went inside the tree limbs as fast as possible.

It didn't take long till she saw what the little man was trying to tell her. Three men on some animals rode right past the tree they were hiding in. Luckily, it was almost like they were invisible to the riders. She had just barely got inside the tree area in time. A few seconds later, they would have seen her and the guardian.

As she watched them go past the river and around the bend, she turned to the little man and asked, "What are those men doing here?"

The little man said, "They might be here to capture more men to work for them or to steal more supplies. All I know is that these men are bad people."

Now, panic started to sink in. Ronnie was so afraid that maybe these men might capture Steve and Justin. If they did, then what would she do? She quickly decided that she would have to try to warn the boys that these men were here and they all could be in harm's way.

Ronnie quickly asked the little man, "Do you know if Justin and my brother came in here today?"

"Yes. Yes, they did," the man said. "They should be somewhere safe by now, though. You must try and wait a little longer before leaving the safety of the Tree."

That didn't sit too well with Ronnie, and she said, "I have to go find my brother and Justin. I can't just stay here. These men may capture them."

"I know you're scared, but please try and wait a little longer. That way, these men may be gone, and you will have a better chance of finding them."

The guardian was worried for Ronnie's safety. By the look in her eyes; he could tell she would not wait much longer.

A short time passed, and Ronnie indeed did just that. She left the safety of the weeping willow tree and ran in the same direction the riders had gone, around the mountain and toward the village.

As Ronnie reached the top of the incline, she saw some riders throw something at a man trying to run away from them.

The man running looked familiar. After a few moments, Ronnie realized it was Justin's stepdad. They had captured him and were now turning around.

Quickly, Ronnie tried to hide, but it was too late. The men had seen her and rode toward her. She started to run, but it was useless. They threw a weapon at her, and she was captured alongside Mark.

It had all happened so fast that she didn't even have time to scream. The riders put both of them on their animals and headed out of the area as quickly as possible.

Now Ronnie knew she had messed up badly. She was so scared now that she had been abducted, but there was nothing she could do at this time.

*****

When they heard the alarm, the people in the village hid the best they could. Everyone was so relieved when the alarm stopped.

Some of the villagers quickly ran over to Jib and told him that they saw three Black Intruders capture two people.

As they all stood listening to the villagers, they looked up the incline and saw someone running toward them. When he got closer, they could see it was the guardian of the Hill and Tree.

When he approached them, they could tell he was disturbed about something. Even from this distance, they realized this was not good.

He then told them that the little girl who was here before had been captured along with a man who had followed the boys earlier.

Steve was almost in tears, for he knew it was his sister. The other person caught sounded familiar to them, at least from the guardian's description.

As the guardian of the Tree continued describing the captured people, Justin figured out who the other person was. It was

Mark.

But how did he find his way in here? And why?

Justin knew the answer to these last two questions. Mark had followed them and wanted to punish him some more. He didn't go away for the weekend after all.

Once again, Mark had lied to them. That was just the way he was. But this time, his lies had caught up to him. His lies had now caused him trouble. The kind of trouble that he may never get out of.

Justin was so afraid for Ronnie. What would they do to her? How could they get her back? He was so upset now, and so was Steve. Once again, he wished he had never told them about this place.

Now, with Ronnie captured, they would have to go and try to find help to save them. And if they did go outside to get help, it would likely destroy this valley and their way of life.

"This is all my fault," Justin said, holding back tears. Once again, I messed up, and it could cost Ronnie her life, not to mention the lives of the people in this valley."

Things had gotten out of hand, but somehow, Justin would have to fix it. And he knew that he had to fix it soon, or things may never be the same here in the valley.

Preparing

"Now we have no choice. We must fight back. Not only do we have to try and get Lebo back, but your stepdad and Steve's sister have been taken away also. We must come up with something soon. Something that can get them all back and protect our village?"

When Justin first met Jib, he knew he was an old man—old, but not the kind of man who was stressed.

But now, looking at him, Justin could tell he was very stressed. These recent events had taken their toll on him, and now that was another thing Justin could blame himself for.

Jib then got up and walked over to the window for a moment. He was in deep thought. Jib was very worried about the girl and man that had been captured.

Yet there seemed as if there might be something else he was worried about, something he had not told them but was about to.

A few moments later, Justin's last thought was answered.

"When I went and checked out Danton to see if I could get Lebo back, I noticed a few very distressing details. This village is large, and it is well guarded."

Everyone sitting around listening to Jib could now tell that things did not look good for them. They could see in his eyes that trouble was in the future.

A moment later, Jib continued with his speech.

"Now we have no choice but to try to get the three out. We will need more help. Not just people that will help us sneak into the Intruder's camp, but also people that can fight if it comes down to that."

Once again, Jib was silent. Then came that all too familiar faraway look in his eyes. This was the same look Justin had seen from him many times before. This look was as if Jib knew something everyone else didn't.

Then, after a short pause, Jib continued with his conversation. He had now sat in a chair and looked down at the floor when he began speaking.

"I have a brother. His name is Dar. He is the head of another village. The name of his village is called Catton. It is a little bigger than our village, but much more secure. They have more defenses than we do. They also know how to fight. Our village never thought we would need to learn any of these things. And that is one reason my brother and I have not talked to each other for over five years."

This last sentence seemed to catch the boys off guard a little. They looked at each other with disbelief on their faces.

"Anyway, we are only a little over eight hours from Catton, so I think we should go there and talk to him and see if he can help us with our problem. I'm sure he will if he wants to. We can leave there and go to Danton whether they help us or not."

A few of Justin's questions had been answered. Now, he knew why Jib seemed so much more stressed. It wasn't just trying to get the three people back but also asking his brother for help.

The evening was approaching fast in the valley. Jib felt it was too late for the boys to try making it to the opening. He told them they could stay in his hut till the morning.

Jib then politely asked them if they wanted to accompany him on the journey instead of leaving the valley. Reading their minds was unnecessary, for he knew their answer.

The boys agreed and turned in for the night, but Jib drew them aside and said he needed to talk to them before they did.

Jib looked more stressed as the three of them sat down. He also seemed to bow his head before he spoke.

"I know the two of you are worried about your relatives. I also know you want to return to your home and get help. I would want the same thing if I were you. If you do that, it could cause some serious trouble for our valley. That's why I need you to try and trust me to get them back. My plan to go to Catton and talk to my brother may work. He is very skilled. If he doesn't help, you can go outside and get some help if possible."

Jib knew things could get terrible for the people and this valley if the boys didn't give this plan a chance. If the outside world discovered their place, nothing good would become of it. Going on this journey with Jib and his group was their only recourse. If it worked, then maybe, just maybe, things could be set right again.

Justin prayed that Jib's plan would work somehow. He also figured they might still have time before their parents began worrying about them. So, the sooner they got the three captives back, the sooner they could go home.

The difference in time between here and where they came from always seemed a distraction. Time in the valley was different for some odd reason. Outside of the valley, time seemed to slow down somehow. Naturally, this time difference made the boys think they still had time to pull this off. How much was still the big question?

***

It was now two o'clock in the afternoon, and Mary was getting a little worried about Justin. He had not come home yet and had missed lunch.

With a bit of worry creeping up, she called the Williams to see if the boys had returned from their outing.

Mrs. Williams told her that the boys were still not home. She then told Mary that when they did return, she would send Justin home.

This seemed to raise an alarm with Mary. It was not like Justin to disobey her.

Sure, he had said he wouldn't be home for lunch, but Mary thought the boys should be home by now.

Something was wrong; she could feel it. Maybe it was a mother's intuition, but she somehow knew trouble was lurking around her again.

Then Mrs. Williams asked Mary if Ronnie was still over at her house. Mary told her she had left right after the two of them had finished talking.

Now, it was Mrs. Williams's turn to worry. It had been thirty to forty minutes since the two had talked on the phone. All this time, she had thought Ronnie was still there with Mary.

Realizing what had happened, both of them started to panic. They knew exactly what was going on and where Ronnie more than likely went: The Woods.

Quickly, Mary went over to the Williams house. Mr. Williams was waiting, so they jumped into his car and drove to farmer Tucker's field.

From the description Justin gave his mom, Mary knew the

area to go. Not seeing anyone at the farm, they went down the dirt road and over to The Woods.

When they arrived, they saw Mark's pickup truck. Mary knew beyond a shadow of a doubt that something was wrong. There was no way anything good could come of this with Mark and the kids in The Woods together.

As they looked in the back of the pickup truck, they saw that the boys' bikes were there. This, too, didn't seem right to any of the parents.

As they entered the thicket, they discovered Ronnie's bike. Now they figured all three were with Mark for some strange reason.

This was not a good thing. They all knew about Mark's drinking problem, so time was imperative.

Quickly, they headed into the trees while calling out their children's names as loud as possible.

After an hour or two passed, the three of them decided to head back home just in case they showed up there. Plus, Mr. Williams said he would call a friend who was a policeman.

Luckily, he was the same officer who caught the kid's breaking curfew that night a few weeks ago. Mr. Williams knew he would know what to do and how to handle this situation best.

***

She was now standing inside a cave-like dwelling. Ronnie felt that wherever this place was, it would take an act of God to get her out of there and back with her parents.

Ronnie saw a rather large man pacing around the room. He had long hair, and his body was hairy, too. Plus, he was unshaven.

She could also tell that this man was in a very foul mood. She could hear him saying things to himself, but it was too low for her to understand. It was probably good that she couldn't hear him because it sounded like some terrible language.

Then the man spoke to Ronnie.

"My name is Hess. I am the leader of this clan and this village. You are young, much too young for our use. We need strong, older people who can work in our fields all day."

In a way, this seemed to give Ronnie some hope. She thought that she might get to go home since they couldn't use her.

At this moment, Hess heard some people coming into the cave, so he turned toward them as they arrived.

A moment later, the men who kidnapped her and Mark came into the cave. Being dragged behind was Mark, all the while whimpering as he lumbered into the cave.

These men then left, but one stayed behind. This man seemed to be the boss of the two who had left, for they said things to each other under their breaths that she or Hess could not hear.

The man who had brought Mark in quickly handed the rifle and knife to the leader.

Hess was now pacing the floor again. His face was dark and threatening as he turned toward the other man. Anyone could see that he was very irritated at this moment.

While Ronnie stood there, she tried her best to listen to the two men's conversation.

"What have we here?" said Hess.

Hess started to point the rifle and even aimed it at some of the things on the cave walls.

"Who are these people, Cam? Where did you get this weapon?"

Clearing his throat, the Cam fellow tried his best to answer.

To Ronnie, it seemed that the man named Cam didn't want to look at Hess, almost as if he were afraid of him. Somehow, he managed to squeak out a few words.

"Two men and I went hunting again and caught these two. They were in the same village that we raided recently. And this tool I gave you belonged to this man." He then pointed to Mark.

Ronnie then noticed how the leader looked at Cam. She

could tell he was distraught with him and could feel their tension.

She realized now that she had gotten into something she would regret for some time. Still, she tried her best to remain calm and listen to them as they continued to talk and pace the floor.

Ronnie hoped they would let her go. The leader said she was too young to work in their fields, so they might take her back to where they had captured her. She didn't belong here, and being alone without her brother was almost too much to handle.

Another thought came to her mind.

"Steve has got to come and save me. He and Justin must know by now that I was kidnapped."

All these things were on her mind as she waited for the leader to speak.

Suddenly, Hess looked toward Ronnie and said, "We cannot let you go. You still could be useful to our clan. You can still do cleanup work and help in the fields somewhat."

A moment of tension passed, and another man came into the cave. Hess instructed the man to take the little girl away and to put her in a hut they already had waiting for her.

As Ronnie was ushered out of the cave, things seemed to worsen. All she could think of was getting out of there as fast as she could. She needed to escape somehow, but from what she had seen so far, this looked impossible.

When she arrived at her hut, she noticed a man guarding it, and the door was locked behind her.

Regret started to engulf her.

Why did she follow her brother this last time? How would she ever get out of here and back home where she belonged?

"Does Steve and Justin even know that I was captured? Hopefully, the old man in the willow tree will tell them."

Laying down on one of the cots that were in this hut, she started crying again.

She then looked around the hut and noticed some other ladies were with her. They, too, looked scared and sad.

One of the ladies came over and tried to console her, but it seemed nothing at this moment would do that. Ronnie had messed things up, and her future was in peril.

She knew at least one thing for sure: these men had not caught Steve or Justin yet, for she hadn't seen either. This seemed to give her some hope. With the boys out there somewhere, they might still figure out where she was and be able to save her.

As she lay there trying to find sleep, she decided that tomorrow, she would try talking to some of the ladies in her hut and see if there was some way to escape.

She knew things wouldn't change immediately, but she wasn't about to give up hope on getting out of there. If there were some way out, then she would find it.

***

Hess was very disturbed by all that had developed recently. He had told his men not to go out without clearing it with him first.

Cam had disobeyed him again. Hess could feel that the time for him and his second in command was ending. He also knew that the two would fight for the clan's leadership, and the winner would be the clan's leader.

Hess now looked at Mark and the weapon. He knew what it was called—a rifle, he was sure of that. He wanted to see how this guy acquired the rifle and where he was from.

"My name is Hess. I am the leader of this clan. I need to know a few things from you, and please do not lie to me."

Hess was straightforward with his message and wanted to ensure this fellow knew what he was asking.

As Hess looked at Mark, he could tell he was not from around here. His clothes and mannerisms were different from the people in the valley. Hess was sure that this man had come from beyond The Woods.

To the people in the valley, it was well-known that there was life beyond the trees. The problem was that from this valley, there were no pathways to the outside, at least none that anyone knew of.

Also, why go? Everyone here seemed very content. Even if people could leave, more than likely, they wouldn't. This valley was such a lovely place to live. It seemed to be sort of a utopia or a Shangri-La.

Still, Hess thought this little man might be helpful to him, so asking a few questions might help.

As Mark stood there in front of Hess, he started feeling like he might need to pee, and he was sure that he didn't want to do it in his pants, especially in front of this man.

Hess then started the questioning. "I need to know where you came from and where you got this rifle."

These questions made Mark feel slightly at ease, for he knew this man needed something from him. They were just answers, but this might lead to some kind of swap between them. Mark would only tell this Hess fellow the answers if he let him go.

Mark was gaining some courage and even tried to come up with some sort of a plan.

"So, you want to know where I come from, and you want to know where I got this rifle?"

Now, there was a slight smug look on Mark's face. He even

started to walk around the cave a little, almost as if he owned the place.

But then, suddenly, this courage he had developed was quickly dashed.

"Stop right there!" Hess had yelled this at Mark. It was forceful and to the point.

"There will be no negotiations. There will be no exchange of information where you get something in return. Just the fact that I have not gutted you yet should be enough for you. Now answer my questions immediately."

This message was announced in a thunderous tone, which somewhat scared Mark. The courage he had found was quick and fleeting. Now, he had stopped walking around the room, was glued to the floor, and started spilling his guts.

"My name is Mark. I come from Orchard Park in Golden County. This is my rifle, and I went into The Woods to search for my stepson and his friend."

Mark could not have spoken these words any faster, even if he were getting paid by the speed at which he delivered them. In another life, he would have made a great auctioneer.

He was so scared of Hess that he would have told him anything as long as it meant that he would not hurt or kill him.

Hess then took a long look at Mark. He could tell that this man was a spineless little weasel. He had sung like a canary; getting information from him didn't take much.

"Such a weak little man," Hess thought to himself. Now, there was disdain on his face as he glared at Mark.

"You will be working in the fields that we have here. Maybe by working them, you will learn to become a real man."

Mark knew what the leader meant and didn't like how he said it. But what could he do? This guy was in charge, and by the looks of him, there was no way he could outfight him either.

"Well, not unless I can get my rifle back," Mark said quietly.

At this moment, another man came into the cave. Hess then told Cam and the other man to take Mark to the hut they had for him.

But before Cam left, Hess had a few choice words for his second in command.

"You should not have gone out hunting without my approval. It was wrong. The next time, I will punish you and your so-called followers. You will not appreciate this discipline very much."

It was straight and to the point. Cam understood exactly what Hess meant. As he turned and left, he looked worried.

Hess was now alone again in the cave. As he reflected on

some of the events that had just transpired, he knew that time was just about up for Cam. He was so upset with what Cam had done. Hess felt that there was no way to get around this problem that had been created.

Another problem that Hess had was with this hunt Cam had gone on. They did this without Hess's permission, which would not be tolerated anymore.

Hess knew that doing things this spontaneously could start upheaval within his clan. Also, there was only room for one leader: him. And it would always be him until he felt it was time to step down.

But, as far as Hess was concerned, that wasn't in the stars yet. He still wanted to be the leader around here.

He then stood up and looked out over his village. Darkness had sunk in, and he could see a few campfires burning at this time. Things were still good as of now. Yet he could feel rebellion was on its way.

If Cam wanted a fight, then he would get a fight. But Cam would not win. There was no way that Hess would give up this clan and the village. He would never give up being the King of his domain.

*****

Sunlight awakened the boys from their restless slumber. Neither boy slept much because of the situation they were in.

Still, they were up and ready to go within a few minutes. Jib then handed them some of the Stringers. He told them they had a long day ahead and wouldn't have time to eat much.

The boys didn't care. They were anxious to get going and try and get Lebo and Ronnie back. It didn't matter to Justin if Mark returned, but Ronnie and Lebo needed to be rescued.

The sooner they got to Catton, the sooner they could formulate a plan to free them. Hopefully, they could get help from Jib's brother and his people.

Jib had arranged for Nampo's to carry them and some supplies on this journey. They were easy to ride, but it was slow since they had to take a few carts and some of the men from the village. The men would be needed in case it came down to actual fighting.

They were all praying that it wouldn't come down to that. None of them were warriors, or fighters, for that matter. Most of the men and women in Jibs village were peaceful and never really wanted much, nor had much.

Jib's brother was a little different. He was more into fighting and protecting his village. This was one of the things that Jib and

Dar had argued about.

Dar wanted more defense for the village, but Jib tried to keep it peaceful and open to all who could enter. It seemed too simple of an idea to argue about, but it caused quite a rift between the brothers—so much so that it had been a long time since the two had spoken to one another. They disagreed on more things, but that was the main dispute.

Jib thought it would be good to see Dar again as they continued toward Catton. He missed him dearly. His wish was that if Dar wouldn't help them, they could at least reconcile and end their differences. If that happened, then this journey wouldn't be a complete loss.

Getting to his brother's village would take at least eight hours, giving them time to consider what was in store.

Jib seemed to be coming around to the fact that he would be seeing his brother again, and that seemed to be a good thing.

The group needed this to work out between the brothers, for they were all in a bit of a plight. They knew that things didn't look good for them and any help would be appreciated and needed.

Still, he knew that they needed to get these people back. It would help keep things in their rightful order here in this valley.

As they continued their trek, Jib felt it was time to fill Justin in on some history about the valley. Since it would take a while to get to his brother's village, Jib knew he would have time to tell him a few things. He then led off with a simple story…….

One day, a little man was fishing in the river by the Hill. He was having such a wonderful time. Catching all the fish he wanted seemed easy.

Once he had caught enough, he slowly walked over to a nearby large tree—a weeping willow tree. This tree was also close to a slight hill with a grassy knoll leading straight up to a plateau.

As he looked up the knoll, he noticed an opening. It was dark and small.

Still, the little man was curious about this dark area. He tried climbing the knoll, but it was always too slippery. There were rocks on each side of the slippery slope, and they were also covered with moss. No one could climb these rocks, so the little man devised something else.

The man then realized he would have to build steps leading to the top. He also admitted that he should maybe try to hide the steps somewhat. After all, he didn't want just anyone to reach this opening.

So, hide the steps he did. Only he knew that they were there, at least for now.

Reaching the top of the knoll, he walked over to the darkened area. As he peered inside, he waited until his eyes grew accustomed to the dark. Shortly, they did, and he started to follow a path. This path led to a rather large rock.

As he searched for the path to continue, he realized it had ended before the large rock. Not wanting his journey to end, he decided to climb the rock.

Once down on the other side, he found the path again. This area was tranquil and seemed unnerving to him.

Shortly afterward, he saw a sort of light coming from an opening. He quickly reached it and looked outside the little hollow he was in.

What he saw was a cornfield and a house. Moving outside of The Woods, the little man walked up a dirt road leading to another. This road was black. He had never seen a black road, only dirt ones. Still, he stepped onto the road.

Suddenly, a loud noise came, and a wagon approached him. For some reason, it almost hit him. The noise scared him somewhat, and he moved out of the way of the oncoming wagon. The person driving the wagon yelled something at him but kept on going.

Things here didn't seem as lovely as the place he was from. The air and sky didn't seem as clean, either. Plus, it appeared nosier here on this side of The Woods. The noise seemed to come from more moving gadgets that seemed very fast. What was strange about these contraptions was that although they did have four wheels, they were not like the wooden ones he was used to. They were all different colors, it seemed.

The little man didn't care much about what he had seen outside the hollow. Sure, he hadn't taken much time to look, but he could feel that this place outside of The Woods would not be safe for him or any other villagers.

So, at this time, he took it upon himself to return to the valley and not tell anyone about this so-called life on the other side of The Woods. He felt that it was not a very good place to live.

The only one he would tell was the elder of the village he was from. The elder would know more about what to do with this discovery of the darkened opening and life outside their valley.

Everyone in this valley knew that life was on the other side of The Woods. Legend had that if you could somehow find your way through an opening, you could find your way to the outside. But there never was an opening, at least not until now.

It was funny, but people tried to cut down or pave a way through the trees in the past, but nothing worked. It seemed that the trees and bushes would just grow back quicker when they did. There was no chance to get out if that was what they wanted to do. But none of them wanted to leave this paradise anyway. Things were just too peaceful here.

Well, it's not entirely peaceful. There was still that creature that would lurk around at night. He had been here for as long as anyone could remember. He was someone you did not want to get to know or be around. He was dangerous.

Also, the Black Intruders were in this valley. They had made this area quite unpleasant these past few years, especially with this new leader they had acquired. The old leader was peaceful and helped the villagers of Danton. But the new one was the opposite. He, like the specter creature, was dangerous to be around.

So now there was an opening, but it was beginning to close every day for some reason. No one knew why it had appeared in the first place.

Still, if there was a way out, there was a way in. This wouldn't do, at least as far as the little man was concerned. He also knew that most of the villagers felt the same. They loved their valley and wanted it to stay as it was forever.

So, the little man became the guardian of the Hill, the Steps, and the Tree. He was so cunning that he even figured out how to move a large rock inside the weeping willow tree. It was just leverage, but it worked for him. He was almost a genius at using leverage to his advantage.

Now, it had been many years later, and still, the opening was assessable, for the most part. But it seemed to be closing up for one reason or another. With it closing, they wouldn't have to worry so much about people coming or going. That might be a good thing, the little man thought to himself.

From what the guardian could tell, The Woods was closing the opening. It was doing this with the help of all the foliage and trees in this area, which were growing faster than before. The trees and bushes were also getting stronger. This way, no one could enter or go outside once it closed completely.

But now Justin was here with his friends and family. With the opening seemingly closing up, it would not be suitable for the valley if they had to stay here and not get home. That is why getting them back safely from the Black Intruders was paramount. They needed to get them out of the valley before it was too late.

The little man at the Hill also knew this. He knew he could keep it open, but for how long, he couldn't say. He would just do his best.

Continuing on the road, Justin was thankful that Jib had told him about this valley's history. It seemed to take his mind off the trouble they all were in.

Justin was distraught that this had happened. He never meant to cause any trouble for these people, but he had. Things just seem to get out of hand. He couldn't imagine what they would do next if their rescue effort were unsuccessful.

The Search

The kids had only been missing a few hours, so there wasn't much the parents could do now. They couldn't even put out a missing child report yet. They were told that they would have to wait 24 hours to do this.

However, the police officer, a friend of Mr. Williams, said this wouldn't stop him and others from starting a search party.

A search party was then organized. The group felt it was best to start looking in The Woods first. They seemed very determined and prepared to search all night if needed. There must have been seventy-five to a hundred people searching. It gave hope to the parents of the lost kids.

Mary could not stay home, so she and the Williams family helped in the search. They left a friend at each of their houses just in case the kids might call or come home while they were out looking for them.

As Mary continued to search, it gave her time to reflect on her current situation.

She had so many regrets to live with. She regretted ever meeting Mark. She regretted not listening to her son more and not paying any attention to him when he told her about the wooded area. These things bore on her mind as she searched into the night.

How could she have been so blind to everything that had happened? She swore right then and there that this was the end of her relationship with Mark.

She planned to sell the house, and she and Justin would be moving away, but Mark would not join them. That was the one part she left out from him.

Then, more regret sank in.

"I should have put the house up for sale sooner, then none of this might ever have happened."

But it had, and there seemed to be no easy or quick way out of this trouble.

Her mind began to think about another possibility. Could Mark have figured that they were moving away without him? She knew there was no way he could have, but the fear of this lingered in her mind.

After five or six hours, Mary and the Williams came out of The Woods and rested awhile.

Equipment had been donated to help in the search, so they started passing it out. Flashlights and even blankets were donated for the searchers to use. Food was also brought in for the volunteers.

Mary was sitting and resting just outside the trees when her eye caught a glimpse of old farmer Tucker and his dog Red. Even from this distance, she could see him watching as the search party continued.

She knew the police had questioned him, and he even permitted them to enter his property to search for the missing kids.

He told the police that he saw the boys enter the hollow first. Then, a short time later, he saw the man pull up in his truck and enter. He saw the girl take her bike inside the trees a little later.

He also said he had seen the boys here before, so it didn't seem that unusual. When the other two went inside, it did seem a little odd.

The old farmer said he was about to call the police when their parents showed up later that afternoon.

As the old farmer sat on his back porch swing, he and Red closely watched what was happening by the edge of his cornfield. He, too, was concerned, but not so much for the kids.

Farmer Tucker always had an optimistic outlook; this moment was no exception. Somehow, he knew things would turn out well for the kids. He knew it in his heart.

But what he was more concerned about was all the commotion that was going on right now on his property. It was almost too much for the old farmer. He might even have to sell his farm because of all the trouble this was turning into.

"There has just been too much fuss around here lately—just too many people coming and going," he said to Red.

The old farmer let out a big, long sigh. Then he turned, and the two of them headed into his farmhouse.

It was now time for Tucker to fix something to eat for Red and himself. This would allow them to escape all the commotion on his property.

"Yes, indeed, Red. There's just too much noise and trouble around this place nowadays. Time is almost up anyway. It's almost time for you and me to move on."

Yes, things seemed to get a little busy around his farm now that the kids were lost inside The Woods.

"Things just have to take their course in time, don't you think, Red?"

Red perked his ears toward the old farmer as he heard him say his name. If he could have spoken, he definitely would have agreed with his master.

Even the dog knew that things had to run their course to the end, and this was one of them.

Useful Information

Several hours later, the group arrived at Catton. As expected, Dar was the first to come out and greet them.

Jib walked up to him, and both stood quietly, looking at each other. Neither one of them said a word.

Then suddenly, Dar reached out and put both arms around his brother. Soon, there were tears in both of the brothers' eyes. This seemed to last some time, but finally, they headed toward Dar's hut with the rest following.

They all noticed that Dar was almost half a foot taller than his brother, Jib, who was around five feet eight inches. So, Dar had to bend slightly at the waist when they embraced.

Anyone could see that the two of them were indeed brothers, though. They did look quite similar, but it appeared that Jib was several years older than Dar. Also, Dar seemed in better shape, possibly from being younger.

After the introductions, Jib didn't take long to tell his brother what had transpired and what they needed from him.

"I will help you any way I can. I will go with you on your journey to get them back. I have weapons that might be needed and skilled men to help if a fight is what it comes down to."

When Jib's group heard these words, they felt relief. They

quickly started working on a plan.

"When we get close to Danton, I will send a scout out to check and see if he can tell where the girl and two men are being held. It will be Blane."

Jib shook his head in agreement. Blane was their cousin and the best scout in any situation.

Dar then let the group rest for a while. When they did, Dar had his people gather all the food, weapons, and anything else they might need for the journey. It would take around a day and a half to get there, and then there would be a little more time for Blane to scout it out.

Jib and the rest of his group had gained new hope from this meeting. They were in the dark about how this would all unfold when they left this morning. But now things looked like they might work out. The hard part was coming soon, but at least now, things were moving in the right direction.

Even Hebo smiled a little. He had been so worried about his brother, and he wanted to get him back home and safe with his family.

It seemed that everyone's spirits had been lifted since they arrived here in Catton. There appeared to be a smile on every face as they sat and ate some of the food given to them. Everyone from both villages was getting along, but they knew hard times were ahead.

Jib and Dar went off and talked amongst themselves. It had been such a long time since they had seen each other, so they needed time to catch up on all that had happened since they had been apart.

"This has got to work," Justin thought as he helped some men load a few carts they would take on their journey.

Justin knew that even if the time on the outside were different, his mom would be worried sick by now because they hadn't come home yet. He knew that time was running out, and this journey must be quick and successful.

Weapons were being loaded, and some of Jib's men received training. Hopefully, this would not be needed.

Yes, they were being trained, but mostly, it was just a crash course in self-defense. Jib's group was not ruthless and never would be, so they needed all the training they could get.

Now, the Black Intruders were a different breed altogether. Somehow, the village of Danton had gone from a lovely town to a corrupt one. It hadn't taken that long, either. It seemed that they were a peace-loving village one day, and then the next, they became a place you did not want to visit or trade with.

As Justin watched the men train to fight, he noticed that Dar was the one who did the training. Dar then made it clear to them that this was just precautionary. It may or may not be necessary, but it is better to know how to defend yourself than not.

Hopefully, it would not come down to a large-scale battle, but if it did, they would be better off with some training; even Jib agreed.

With all the carts and supplies gathered, the group decided to bed down for the night. It would be a long journey, so they all needed rest.

Dar had told the remaining people in his village what was about to happen and that they would return as soon as possible.

He then told his villagers that another man would be left in charge while he was away.

"Don't get used to this fellow in charge because I will be back, and you will all have to answer to me."

There were some chuckles throughout the villagers, but mostly, there was a slight nervousness in their glee.

They were all informed about what to expect and how they would do this. They were also told how dangerous it would be but that it was necessary. They would return within a few days if everything went according to their plan.

Then there was something else. Dar gathered many villagers

together, and they all bowed their heads in prayer. It was a touching moment not lost on Jib and the rest of his crew. This seemed to solidify that this quest they were about to embark on would be dangerous and not without the possibility of some fatalities.

***

Cam did not like the way Hess had talked to him earlier. He did not like how Hess ran this village and the clan either. He felt they should attack more towns and more often. But lately, what he saw from Hess was someone who was not as thirsty about pillaging as he should be.

This village and these men needed a more ruthless leader. That way, they could build their town and their supplies up. They would become the envy of the whole valley. Once they got stronger, no other village could stand up against them.

Cam envisioned that someday they would be so big that the surrounding villages would bring workers and supplies in exchange for them not attacking.

"Fear is a powerful tool," Cam said as he looked at the small campfire he had built. He would use fear to his advantage and would do so more often if he were in charge.

As he sat before his campfire, Cam started to think about when and how Hess became their leader.

Reflecting, he remembered that Hess had just shown up one day. The first thing Hess did was to join their clan. When he did, he was immediately at odds with the current leader. What Cam didn't like about this was that the current leader was his close friend. Plus, the leader was very old.

The old leader was going to step down soon, and then Cam would take over, but things changed with Hess coming into the picture.

"They seemed to change rather quickly," he said as he sat there and tried to recall more memories.

It didn't take long for Hess to stir up trouble with the old leader. Everyone could tell that this new man wanted to take over. They could tell this by listening to him talk rudely about the current leader and how he ran things in the village.

The old leader was not a tyrant. He treated his clan and the village of Danton fairly. From what Cam thought, he almost seemed too soft of a leader. That was about the only thing that Hess and Cam agreed on. They thought they should be more complex and meaner to the clan and the villagers. Rule it with fear and strength is what they truly believed.

Then Cam remembered some more things. A short time after Hess joined their clan, he challenged the old leader and made quick and decisive work of him. Their fight lasted around two minutes.

Hess was so much more robust and faster.

Even from the start of the fight, it looked like the clan leader had no chance. At times, it seemed as if Hess was playing with him.

Then, Hess delivered the fatal blow, and no clan member had challenged him since. They were all too scared, for he showed them things that none of them had ever seen. His fighting skills were far superior to anyone in this valley.

But now Cam started thinking about what he could do to take over this clan for himself. That was the one thing he wanted. If Hess had not come along and killed his friend, Cam would have been the leader by now. This is what bothered him the most. He wanted to be the leader and felt he had the right to be.

Another thought came to mind. He started to think back more about Hess and how he had been a great leader initially, but it looked like he had softened as time passed. Cam had noticed this more often, especially with their last attack on the small village.

Something happened when they went there because Cam could see a slight change in Hess when they got back. He couldn't quite figure out what it was, but something did seem different about him.

That was one reason Cam took a couple of his men and attacked the same village later. He wanted to see how Hess would react when he found out what they had done. And, as expected, he got the answer he was looking for.

To Cam, Hess didn't seem as ruthless as one should be when in charge. They could ill afford a clan leader who was soft on anyone. Cam saw these attributes as showing weakness; if valid, it might be the right time for him to take over the clan.

"With me in charge, things will be much different—a lot better. There will be more attacks and more workers and supplies acquired," he said quietly.

Sitting in front of his open campfire, his mind kept coming up with things he would do once he was the leader. But first things first.

Cam quickly called a few of his loyal men over and laid out possible plans to take over the village for themselves and replace Hess.

One thing he was interested in was the weapon that Hess had taken from him earlier.

What did Hess and that Mark guy say it was called? A rifle? Yes. That was it—a rifle.

That weapon looked far superior to their other weapons. The rifle looked as if it could do some real damage.

With it, he might be able to take over this clan and be the

rightful king. His thoughts were now all about himself as the leader. He wanted this so much that he could almost taste it.

As Cam sat by the fire, he was in deep thought. Thinking about his next move, Cam told one of his followers to go and get the new prisoner they had captured.

Shortly, Mark arrived and was told by Cam to sit by the fire with him and his men.

Mark was once again scared because he didn't know what was happening. All he knew was that he needed a strong drink. Many strong drinks. That would help him through whatever was about to happen, good or bad.

Then, the man who had captured him spoke.

"My name is Cam. I am second in command here in this village. I am very interested in one of the things we took from you earlier. It was that weapon that you called a rifle, I believe."

As Cam sat there talking to Mark, he could tell how frightened he was. Cam needed to get information out of Mark and knew that the way Hess did it might not work this time.

Cam decided to try to be nicer to this guy. He felt that if he got on his good side, he might get more information from him.

He then poured some Old Ale for Mark to drink. Cam was sure that with his new approach and the drink, it wouldn't be long until he got what he wanted. He knew this Mark fellow wouldn't want to trust anyone now that Hess had mistreated him.

"I didn't like how Hess treated you or talked to you. He gets that way. Most of the time, he is just plain mean to people. But I'm not like that. I will listen to you if you want to tell me something, like maybe about the rifle that Hess stole from you. How does it work? And what can you do with it?"

Mark took the drink from Cam and guzzled it down. It was the first drink Mark had since he entered the valley. He realized that it was perfect, and it did the trick. It made him loosen up, and he almost forgot where he was and how he got here. It seemed to be a very potent elixir.

The drink numbed his senses, but he didn't care. It was very smooth and relaxing.

A short time later, Mark realized that he didn't know anything about this Cam fellow, nor did he want to. All he wanted was to try and get out of here. He would tell Cam all he knew about the rifle if it helped him achieve that goal. Mark was almost at the point that he would have told him anything so he could leave.

To Mark, this guy seemed more likable than the other one.

"Maybe I can barter with this fellow," he thought.

Once he had thought more about this, Mark felt more at ease.

He then decided to go ahead and explain to this Cam fellow how the rifle worked, but not without a cost.

"I will tell you all I know about the rifle. But I would like a few things in return. If I do this, then is there any way I can go back to where I came from? That Hess guy didn't want to listen to my side or what I wanted. All he cared about was where I got the rifle. There was no room for any bartering."

He thought he saw an opening, so Mark finally sat back and tried to relax. He hoped this guy would let him go once he got some information.

Without hesitation, Cam said aloud, "Granted. Whatever you want, then that is what you will get. I don't believe in capturing and making people work in the fields. That is a cruel and harmful way to treat people."

Mark couldn't see through Cam's lies. He wanted to believe him so much that he started telling him all about the rifle. The Old Ale also helped him give up the information Cam needed.

"A rifle is used for hunting. You can kill anything with it from quite a distance. They shoot things we call bullets. That is what will bring down whatever you are hunting. It kills."

After explaining about the rifle, Mark drank more of the Old Ale. He was sure this guy was on his side and that he was a good man.

The drink was somewhat blurring his vision at this time. It was more potent than almost anything he had ever drunk. Even his thought patterns seemed to be distorted slightly.

With his mind altered, Mark didn't care about the information he had given up so freely. All he cared about was getting out of this place once and for all.

After getting more information, Cam told Mark, "I don't think I can just let you go right now, but when the proper time comes, I will let you know. However, I will make your accommodations here better for you. I must clear your release through Hess; he is still the leader. But something tells me he won't be for much longer. If that happens, you will get to return to where you came from."

Cam looked toward one of his men and then directed him to do whatever preexisting plan he had. The man left, and Mark looked over at Cam.

"Where did that guy go?"

The Old Ale might have hindered Mark's thought pattern a little, but he still knew where he was and mostly what was happening.

Trying to appease Mark's paranoia, Cam said, "He went to clear out another hut for you. This one is better and nicer. You will enjoy it. Plus, you can come and go as you please. Just don't try to leave right now. And stay out of sight of the leader. I will try to make your stay here as pleasant as possible."

Now Mark was lapping it all up. He was so unaware that all Cam wanted him for was more information, not just about the rifle but about how he got into the valley. Also, he wanted to know about things outside of The Woods.

Cam wanted to know all he could so that maybe this information would help him take over this clan. He was now starting to feel like there was a chance for this to happen, which made him a little anxious, but in a good way.

Yes, Cam felt that soon things would come to a head, and he would fight Hess. If this happened, Cam would be the rightful leader; they would never have to worry about Hess again.

But the first thing he had to do was get that rifle. When he did, he knew it would help him take his rightful place as leader of the Black Intruders.

The Plan

They had traveled all day and most of the night to get to Danton. Dawn was breaking as they headed to an area that seemed secluded and off the beaten path.

The group was now only about half an hour away from the village. They had made better time than they thought. They had not encountered a single soul on their quest all this time.

Dar and Jib decided this might be a good time to stop and take cover so that someone passing by didn't find them out. They had to hide over fifty men and several carts in broad daylight. It would be a challenge, but it had to be done. They could ill afford to be caught at this point of their journey.

Since it was daylight, they knew they would have to hide for the rest of the day. Dar wanted Blane to scout the Black Intruders' camp and the village in the dark.

Quickly, they got off the main road and began trying to blend in with the landscape the best they could. This area had many trees and bushes, so it was easier to hide all of them. This took a little bit of time, but less than expected. Most of the villagers knew precisely how and what to do.

Their test on how hidden they were happened just a few minutes after the last cart and Nampo were covered.

Three men came walking down the middle of the dirt road. They were so engrossed in their conversation that they seemed to walk by the trees, hiding most of Jib and Dar's men.

These men were headed toward Danton, so trouble might await them if the group was spotted. Not one word was uttered, nor any animal moved. All that was moving was the wind as it nestled through the trees.

As the men continued down the path, one of the Nampo's did move. When it did, it stepped on a branch that had fallen. The branch then broke in half, which made a slight noise. It wasn't much of a sound, but it sounded like thunder to someone trying their best to hide.

Suddenly, one of the men stopped in his tracks. He was sure that he had heard something that came from the direction of the trees to his left. The other two kept walking ahead, leaving him behind. Standing there, he tried to do his best to listen some more.

Shortly, one of his friends turned and looked back.

"Better hurry up, Jade. We have a lot to do in Danton."

Grudgingly, the man did as he was told, but he gave one last look as he started walking. Convinced that it was nothing, the man caught up with the other two. Thankfully, they only took a minute or two to be out of sight and around a bend in the road.

Then Jade told his two buddies, "I thought I heard something in the trees. It was just a broken branch, I guess."

Thankfully, this was the end of his curiosity.

It was a close call. Hopefully, hiding all of them would be more accessible when night arrived. When it did, it would be like a welcomed friend.

Staying out of sight and hidden was crucial because none knew who they could trust and what might lie ahead.

During the day, most of the men tried to get some sleep, for they all knew that there could be trouble as they prepared to rescue the three captives. They needed all the strength they could muster to have a chance against this ruthless clan.

After discussing their plan some more, Dar and Blane changed it somewhat. They decided it might be better if Blane went and scouted a little during the day and then again later that night.

Dar also wanted Blane to find out information about other possible exit routes. He felt it might be wise to use a different road than the one they arrived on. People might see them on this road, so they needed a less traveled road.

Also, if memory served him well, then there was an old road that they could use to get back home once they got the hostages out. This road was off the beaten path, and no one ever used it anymore.

Over the years, it had been discarded and hopefully forgotten. The main road they came in on was the only one people used now.

A short time later, Blane headed to the village. Being by himself, he felt there would be less chance of someone stopping him and asking questions.

Arriving in the village, he quickly went inside a small store. Here, he saw some trinkets that this place possibly bartered.

Acting like he was interested in some of them, Blane was about to ask the store owner some questions. But before he did, he felt it might be good to change his name and the town he was from. After all, the less this man knew about him, the better.

At this time, Blane walked up to the proprietor and started conversing with him while looking at some of the articles before him.

"Good morning, sir. My name is Cleave. I come from the village of Benton. I heard there was some fine jewelry here in Danton."

Blane felt that this fake name he just used would be okay and that it fit him. He knew he only had to use it here in this village and that he could remember it if need be.

He quickly looked at some of the articles he had seen when he arrived.

The shop owner now thought his little trinkets could pass off as authentic jewelry, so he started conversing with his new customer.

"Good morning to you, sir. My name is Gent. I am the owner of this establishment. I see you are admiring my collection here. Other stores have more jewelry, but mine are the best."

Blane knew just by listening to this fellow that he might not be all that trustworthy and full of hot air. After all, these little trinkets were not jewelry. Most of them were old and used somewhat.

Blane didn't care about these, so it was a moot point.

As Blane gazed more at the trinkets, he saw something appealing. It was sort of a neckless. At first, it was blue, but it quickly changed if you wore it around your neck. It was oval, with a silver chain attached.

"What do you want for this neckless Gent?"

Looking at the article, Gent picked it up and quickly said to Blane, "What do you have that you might want to exchange for?"

Blane had nothing to barter with except one article he always carried. It was a gold knife from his father, which was dear to his heart. His father had given this knife to Blane when he turned fifteen.

With some hesitation, Blane slowly took the knife out of his pocket. He immediately saw that the shop owner was impressed and handed it to him.

Then, acting like he wasn't interested in the knife, Gent said, "Oh, that looks nice. It's probably not worth an even exchange, but I might let the neckless go for your knife and maybe something else you might have."

Blane quickly grabbed the knife and put it back in his pocket for safekeeping.

"No. I'm afraid this is all I have. It would be this knife for your neckless. I came here mostly to look around. I didn't bring much with me, for I travel light."

Feeling that he might lose this customer, Gent interrupted.

"Well, maybe I could trade you for the knife. It would be a slight loss, but I'm in a good mood today."

Now Blane knew beyond a shadow of a doubt that this guy could not be trusted. For all he knew, he might go to the guards that patrolled the village and tell them about this stranger in town.

One thing Blane did not want to do was upset this shop owner. And another thing he did not want to do was trade his knife away. He was now caught between a rock and a hard place.

"Maybe I should never have mentioned the neckless," he

thought regretfully. And maybe I should just leave and not come back."

Blane felt cornered. He wished he had never come into this shop. He could have gone into other shops, but he picked this one for some reason. Impaired judgment, he thought as he moved away from the counter.

As Blane continued looking at the rest of the trinkets, he saw that the shop owner was watching him closely. Even from this distance, Blane could see a slight distrusting look on the shop owner's face.

Blane started to get a little worried but continued to search more of the articles in the shop.

Standing there, he finally realized what he would have to do.

Slowly, Blane took the knife back out of his pocket. He didn't want to lose this, especially to this man, but he felt that this was for a good cause, so he decided to let it go.

Blane had now developed a dislike for the shopkeeper, for he could tell that he was a cheat.

Then, shortly, Blane said words he thought he would never say.

"Then, do we have a deal? My knife for your neckless?"

Once again, Gent tried to act like it wasn't a good trade but slowly took the knife and handed the necklace to Blane.

"Yes. Yes, we have a deal. I think you got the better end, but I'm a fair man."

Gent quickly took his item, put it in a box behind the counter, and moved away to the other side of the store.

It was sad that Blane had lost his cherished knife, but he knew it was the right thing to do now.

Now, Blane had to strike up a conversation to try and get some information from this guy. Hopefully, now that he was apparently on the good side of the shop owner, he might be able to ask a few questions.

"As I said, I am from Benton, south of here. I have never been this far north. I noticed this main road out here. Are there any more roads that someone could use to get here to trade with Danton?"

The shop owner seemed to raise an eyebrow upon hearing this question asked.

At first, Blane thought he might have asked this question too soon.

Gent stood there looking rather suspiciously toward Blane. He then moved from behind the counter and walked over to another table.

"You must have come up this road that leads to our village if you came from the South. Surely, you saw the turn-off on your left."

The shop owner looked at Blane accusingly while displaying a disbelieving expression.

Now, Blane felt a little trapped. He knew he had to come up with something quick. This might alert Gent to get the guards if he said something wrong.

Blane was nervous but quickly responded, "Yes, I did. This main road is a good one to travel. I just saw one that looked abandoned. That must be the one you are talking about."

This answer seemed to appease Gent somewhat. Now, Blane tried to relax a little.

"The one on your left when you entered our village has been abandoned for quite some time. That is the old road connecting the valley's west part to our village. Everyone that comes from the West now uses the new one."

Now Blane knew for sure that there was another road. They would use this one when they headed home tonight after they rescued the captives. If anyone were looking for them, they would never think about searching the old road.

Blane quickly realized that his group would have to go by

the village and head south a bit. Then, they could all take the old road home. It joined the new road after so many miles.

Trying not to appear impatient, Blane slowly continued looking at the rest of the junk in the store.

A short time later, Blane thought about asking more questions when he realized the shop owner was talking.

"Cleave, Cleave. If you are still interested, I have some more stuff in the back of my shop."

But there was no answer from Blane.

A few moments later, Blane realized that Gent was talking to him. He felt that he had to come up with an explanation for not hearing him call out his name.

"Oh, I'm sorry, Gent. I didn't hear you. I have a bad right ear. Now, what were you saying?"

Gents' face looked slightly bewildered, but he cast it off, hoping that this Cleave fellow would barter more trinkets from him.

"I was just letting you know that I have other things in the back of my shop. You may or may not be interested in them, but it's up to you."

Gent quickly showed Blane the articles in the back of his store. There was indeed more stuff in the back, and some looked better than what was on display in the front.

Still, Blane was not interested in any of Gents' jewelry, but he felt he should at least look at some of the articles. That way, it wouldn't seem rude or make the shopkeeper more suspicious of him than he was.

A short time passed, and Blane felt it was time to leave the shop. Some other people had just come into the store, so it kept Gent occupied with them.

Turning to leave, Blane said his goodbye to Gent and thanked him. He poured it on, letting Gent know he was grateful for their deal. He also told him that his wife would love the neckless and that he would be back real soon to do some more bartering with him.

What he just said was the second fib he had told the shop owner. The first was that his name was Cleave. The second one was that he was married, which he was not. So, the neckless was almost entirely useless to him. He had no wife or a loved one to give it to.

Blane then headed away from the shop as far as he could. He wanted to ensure the shop owner couldn't see him and where he was going.

Shortly, he went over to an area that Dar and his group might use once they freed the captives.

As he sat there, he watched the guards closely. He wanted to know how many there were and when, if any, their shift was over. That way, he could tell when the best time to pass this way at night would be.

While he sat in an open area, he ate some fruit he had brought with him, all the while trying to keep a low profile. This might have been hard for most people, but for Blane, it was easy. He was just the kind of fellow that people overlooked.

Slowly leaving this area, Blane wandered around the village a little more. As he searched, he quickly found out where the three prisoner's huts were and how to get to them. The next thing he did was see how many guards there were. Luckily, at least at this time of day, only two guards were on duty.

Now, Blane started to think things out. Since they had to get to the old road, they would have to subdue these guards once they freed the captives.

Knowing he had acquired some valuable information, Blane headed back to their camp. He then told Dar and the rest of the group all that he had found out.

After filling Dar in on the information, he found a quiet resting spot. He knew he would have to be at his best when the time came. Not only to further scout the area but also when they found the captives. His skills would be needed even more.

Besides this morning, Blane had only been to Danton once, but that had been a long time ago and for another matter.

A while back, Blane had come to Danton to check on the new leader of the Black Intruders and find out where he had come from. All he found out was that this man was cruel towards his men and the villagers of Danton. Nobody knew or cared where he had come from. He was here, and no one could do anything about it.

***

Night time fell, and Blane again headed out to scout the area. What he went again for was to make sure nothing had changed, especially with the guards. If there were more guards, then this might pose a bigger problem.

Several hours passed, and Blane was still missing. All of them were getting worried, so Dar put extra guards out just in case Blane had been caught and given away their location. He knew his cousin would never betray them, but it didn't hurt to be cautious.

Then, a short time later, a slight whistle was heard through the trees. Dar knew it was the sound that Blane made when he was approaching and that everything was OK.

Dar then gathered Jib and the boys around a small area they would use to go over their plan of attack.

Jib and Dar then quickly gathered some nearby flowers.

What was so special about these was that they gave off a slight glow when picked, which cast off a type of light. Picking several of them made the glow bigger and lasted for several hours. This was useful when you didn't want to make a campfire or just wanted a soft light at night in a room.

Blane then gave them the layout of the huts that Ronnie, Mark, and Lebo were being held captive in.

"They moved Mark out of one of the huts and put him in another. This one is not guarded. Now Lebo and Ronnie are in huts that have workers inside with them. There is a guard on both of their huts. These huts are away from many other huts, but getting them out of there with the guards watching will still be hard."

Quickly, Dar came up with a plan of attack and informed the others exactly how this would go.

"Blane, you will lead us to the huts. I will take Hebo, Steve, and Justin. Hopefully, the night will keep us from being seen so easily."

Dar then stopped for a few moments, trying to figure out exactly how things would go once they arrived at the huts.

"Jib, you will stay back and let us know if you hear or see someone coming as we go to the huts. The first hut is where Lebo is. Hebo, you will go inside and get him out. If a guard is at the hut, we must take him out. Hebo, you will distract him with a slight noise, and I will come up from behind and get him. Now, Steve, getting your sister out of the other hut will be your job. If there is a guard on that one, we must do the same to him."

All of them shook their heads in total agreement. Then, Dar continued with his plan.

"Justin. Please check out the hut with your stepdad in it. You must convince him to come with you if at all possible. You never know; he might want to stay. There must be some reason he has a better hut and no guard. It sounds like he might be joining them to some degree. So be careful what you say to him. Plus, we need you to wait till we get the first two out and away from the huts before you go and get him."

This plan sounded almost too easy. Of course, they all knew it wouldn't be, but they had to try it, and this plan seemed like it could work. The only problem was that they had to develop it so quickly.

What Dar was relying on was that their enemy had become overconfident, and they would not be prepared for someone to walk right into their camp and take the prisoners. After all, it hadn't been long since the Black Intruders had taken them, so maybe the sooner they acted, the better. If luck was on their side, they might catch them off guard, so to speak, and pull this rescue off.

His last thought sparked a slight smile, but it quickly faded when another idea came to mind.

This thought was something he wasn't ready to tell the others about just yet. He knew that if they did rescue the hostages and got away, the chance of the Black Intruders coming back and attacking their villages would be high.

He also knew the leader would be annoyed at them. Dar was sure that if the plan worked, a few clan members would be demoted. Dar also knew that the Intruders would want their workers back. They would probably do anything to retrieve them. That was the one thing Dar feared the most, but he had not told the others about this possibility yet.

So, once they got home, he would tell the group that they would have to be on the lookout for possible trouble and that things had changed in their villages, especially Jibs.

This was one of the things that had made Jib and his brother come to a parting of the ways so long ago. Hopefully, Jib would understand that defense was needed now more than at any other time.

Nowadays, villages have to be on guard more often and even learn new defenses to combat clans that may attack them occasionally.

It was sad to think that their valley was becoming more dangerous. It all seemed to start when the leader of the Black Intruders took over Danton.

Hate had seemed to infest the valley, at least to a certain degree. If the leader ever left or were removed, maybe their valley would return to how it was before he took over.

Dar had been right about providing better protection for his village. He also knew that if Jib agreed, he would help him with anything he needed to ensure the safety of his villagers.

After telling Dar all he had found out, Blane reminded him about the other road and that there was only one guard at night in the village. This made their rescue mission a little easier. Dar agreed and considered what they would have to do with the guard in that area. The plan had been expanded, but with some luck, this just might still work.

Dar then instructed the rest of their group to get as close as possible to the village. When it was time for them to move out, getting through the town would be easier and quicker, especially at night.

Now, the time to move out was approaching fast. There was no turning back. All these things that they had planned had to work precisely. If they didn't, there was a chance that none of them would make it home.

Standards

As he stood there looking out from the cave, the leader of the Black Intruders had many things on his mind.

Hess could smell trouble in the air and tell that things could change somewhat in his clan. Hopefully, it will be for the better.

"It's all good," he said with a sly smile. He used it when he knew that things would get rough. That is what Hess liked. He liked trouble.

What he liked the most was when his men obeyed him and did as he ordered, but lately, that wasn't happening. Some of his men had now sided with Cam for one reason or another, and Hess did not care for this treasonous behavior.

Cam had been the most rebellious of them all. He had been disobeying his orders lately, almost to the point of no return.

Hess didn't care, though, for he knew that whatever Cam wanted to do was okay with him. He was ready for the fight.

He only needed a few bites of the Silken, and nobody could hurt him. He was invincible when he ate it. He liked it and was probably at the point of being addicted to it. This plant made Hess feel like he could do anything. It made him feel superior to anything and anyone.

"Just bring it on, little Cam," Hess said directly out into the night as he surveyed the village below. "I will be ready for you and whoever you want to bring to the dance."

Laughing out loud, Hess turned and grabbed some more Silken. He could not do without it for very long. Sometimes, he wouldn't even sleep when he ate it. It would keep him awake for two or three days at a time.

When this happened, he got squirrely around his men. The more he ate, the more it consumed him.

Now, sitting alone in his cave, Hess looked up at the full moon, which had crept into full view.

Somehow, he knew trouble was going to happen tonight. He could just feel it. It was like a yearning, a craving that he would sometimes get about certain things.

Hess wanted the fight to happen so badly now that he was more than ready to oblige Cam with this offer.

The Silken herb seemed to give him some insight. Sometimes, he could almost see the future. That was another reason he liked the plant. It helped him in so many ways. He could never see the bad things it did to him—only the good.

Then, his altered thoughts changed to other issues. He began thinking back on some of the attacks recently.

Raiding and pillaging were sometimes fun, but lately, they

lacked something. He couldn't quite understand what it was but felt a piece was missing.

He had felt this way for some time but didn't realize it until he attacked that older man's village. An uneasy feeling came over him when they raided it.

"How could this be?"

The leader was shaking his head as he said this to himself.

"I have got to get my crap together and keep it together. If I don't, then Cam might take me out and become the leader. I feel I am showing weakness, and I'm sure Cam can sense it, too."

Reaching down, he grabbed some more of the herb. He knew this would help, and soon, it did just that.

A few moments later, Hess was back to his old self. Once again, his strength returned, and he could tell the plant was taking over. The euphoria he felt was beyond reproach. Deep down inside, he loved the Silken and knew he would never give it up.

All his senses seemed to return shortly, and hate again filled his heart. He seemed to be back to full strength.

***

The kids had been missing for twenty-four hours. The parents could now file a missing child report, which would help with the search.

Mary was at a complete loss. She and the Williams were reaching exhaustion and needed a break, but they still searched on.

They were so thankful for all their community's support with the food and supplies they received.

Since the missing child report had been filed, more help was brought in. Police dogs and even a helicopter were used to search from the air.

More and more people showed up to help in the search, and by some estimates, there were over a hundred volunteers. It was massive, and with this many, it somewhat renewed the three parents' energy.

Mary had not slept for thirty-two hours straight and was beginning to feel rum-dum. She needed sleep but thought she couldn't leave—not with her boy still out there somewhere. No way.

But shortly, one of the nurses there helping noticed that Mary was sleep-deprived and convinced her to go home and get some rest.

Mary decided the nurse was right, so she told Mrs. Williams that she would go home for a while and see if anyone had called. It was hard for her to leave, but she knew she would be useless to any of them if she were too tired to keep searching.

Mary then left, and Mrs. Williams joined her. She also

needed sleep. Mr. Williams said he would stay longer so the ladies could get some rest, and he would notify them if anything turned up.

Arriving home, Mary broke down in tears. She had a call on her answering machine from the real estate agent. The message he left was that he had sold her house. It was almost too much to bear at this time.

"Wow. Unbelievable," she said to herself. Things had finally changed for the good. Justin and her could leave and never look back. There was nothing to keep them here. She would be free from Mark, and he wouldn't be able to hurt either one of them ever again.

Yes, everything was going great except for one thing. She didn't have her Justin. Without him, life was meaningless. He was all she had left; all she had left of Chris.

Looking back, she remembered that when Chris left, she had promised to take care of Justin and for him not to worry. Mary just wanted Chris to get better so they could be a healthy and happy family again.

A sadness engulfed her now. She felt she had let Chris down somehow. Nothing in her world meant anything to her now. Despair was once again lurking in her corner. How could she keep going if her son didn't come back?

She knew that, somehow, she would have to get some sleep

to continue with the search for the children. She was no good to anyone at this point.

She quietly headed to Justin's bedroom. Looking at everything he had in his room seemed to bring her closer to him.

Mary then laid down on his bed and somehow drifted off to sleep with tears streaming down her cheeks.

***

"The time has come for a new leader of this clan. It is time for me to take my rightful place as the head of The Black Intruders and the village of Danton. I will be so much better than Hess. His time has come to an end. Never again will he be in charge. Never again will he boss us around."

Once the speech was over, Cams' faithful followers shook their heads in total agreement. Even Mark agreed but didn't care either way.

All Mark cared about was getting out of here and back to The Woods. He might feel he could stay longer if things got better here, but they would have to improve.

And one thing had. He had got a bigger and better hut. He only saw it from a distance, but hopefully, the word of this Cam fellow was good.

Deep down inside, Mark knew his last thought was a stretch,

and it almost made him chuckle a bit. He had said this to himself in hopes that somehow Cam would be a man of his word, keep his promise, and eventually let him go home.

Cam had also told him something that seemed interesting. He had said that his new hut would not be guarded.

That was about the only thing Cam said that Mark liked. Without being watched, he might be able to sneak out of this place and return to where he belonged.

When the right time came, Mark hoped he would take the chance and head back to the first village he saw around that mountain. He knew that from there, he could follow the mountain, go to the hill, and climb it to the opening. Then, he could get out of here once and for all.

Mark stopped listening to Cam for a moment because, to him, it was nothing more than a boring speech. Sitting back, Mark started to think of more possibilities.

"What if things changed for the better? What if this Cam fellow put me in charge of some workers? That might make me want to stay longer in this valley. This place might not be too bad after all."

A few moments later, Cam had now sat in front of the campfire and became very quiet. He needed to think about all that would transpire tonight. After a short pause, he filled them all in on his plan.

"This is what is going to happen. I will go to the cave first. Then I will fight Hess. Then you two will come into the cave and jump him. Then I will take the rifle. Once I have it, Mark will show me how to use it on Hess. This will end his reign and begin a new one for me."

Shortly, things seemed to be getting a little serious. Mark perked up his ears so he wouldn't miss anything.

He realized that Cam wanted the rifle badly. He also started shifting his eyes to each man sitting by the campfire, wanting to see how they acted when Cam told them his plans.

Then, another thing came to Mark's twisted mind. What happens to me when Cam gets the rifle and takes over the clan? Sure, he says things will be better, but will they?

This was something Mark kept in the back of his mind. He could not bring himself to trust this man completely. He felt this guy was hiding something from him.

If there was one thing Mark knew about, it was how to lie to someone. From how Cam talked, Mark felt this was what Cam was doing to him. His mistrust and paranoia were eating at him now.

Cam stood up and began to pace around the campfire. It

seemed he was trying to muster up the courage he would undoubtedly need to pull this off tonight. It would come down to Hess against him. But if he got that rifle, there wouldn't be much of a fight, and he would be the new leader before the night vanished. He once again looked over at Mark.

"When I get the rifle, I want you to show me exactly how it works. My two men will keep Hess occupied till I can use it and remove Hess. When this is done, you will be granted even more provisions and a higher status in our clan."

Mark was delighted to hear this news. All he had to do was show him how to use the rifle. That would be easy.

Something in how Cam said these things made Mark uneasy and a little on edge. Never was it mentioned that he could leave and go back home. Mark wanted that because all the other stuff, which might be okay for some people, wasn't for him. Cam said he would let him go, so why not now?

Mark had been a little tipsy from the Ale he had been drinking. He finally realized that his thought patterns kept changing back and forth about what to do.

"I have got to sober up a little bit, or I may never get out of this place."

A short time later, the buzz from the drink finally started to wear off. Mark then began to regain some of his senses.

Now that Mark was sobering up a bit, he once again thought about this Cam fellow. Something about this guy didn't sit right with him, and for someone not meeting Mark's standards, this guy had to be pretty bad.

"I think once this Hess fellow is taken out, I will get the rifle from Cam to get out of this place and back to where I belong. There is nothing that these people have that could make me stay. Nothing."

Mark was now staring into the campfire. His thoughts were finally making sense, even to him. That Old Ale had made his mind wander a bit, and it had made him repeat things over and over.

A moment later, Cam took a deep breath, then gave the order, and the four moved out. If they caught Hess off guard, beating him and taking over the clan would be easier.

Cam and his men also knew that even if some of the men loyal to Hess knew what they were about to do, they would likely not help Hess either. Hess had his faults, and not caring for his men was one of them. He did not treat any of his followers well or with respect.

That was the main reason Cam wanted to take charge. Cam knew that if he treated his men slightly better than Hess, they would follow him anywhere.

The stage was set. Now, all they had to do was act. This was their only chance to take Hess out. There was no turning back and no other way to get to him. It would be challenging, but Cam was pretty sure he could do this, and soon, he would be the ruler of this clan and the village called Danton.

The End is Nigh

Reaching the area to get to the prisoners, the group noticed only one guard at this time of night. Slowly, the six of them passed the guarded area. The guard was on a break, so it was easy to get past. They knew they would likely have to subdue him if he were here when they returned this way. There would be more people with them, so it would be harder to get out of here.

It took them a little while to get to the huts with the three captives. Once they arrived, they formulated a plan.

With Blane leading the way, Dar took Hebo, Justin, and Steve. Jib stayed back so he could keep a lookout and wait for them.

Dar had decided that the best way to deal with getting the three of them out was to go to Lebo's hut first.

Slowly but cautiously, Dar and Hebo crept over to it. Then came their test of distraction.

Dar picked up a nearby branch and threw it away from them and the hut. This made a slight noise, and the guard immediately went to see what it was.

As the guard walked over to the wooded area, Dar snuck up from behind and knocked the guard out without making any noise. It was quick and easy. No one had seen or heard anything.

Dar was almost a foot taller than the guard, which seemed to help him subdue him. He simply overpowered him. Dar hoped this fact would help him each time he needed to do it.

"So far, so good." Dar thought to himself as the group headed to the hut with Lebo in it.

Their group had brought some rope and towels with them, for they knew they would be needed to tie the guards up.

Quickly Dar did this while Hebo went inside the hut to get Lebo.

When Hebo went inside, he noticed that everyone was asleep.

Quickly, Hebo covered his brother's mouth, for he knew that Lebo might yell out if he was disturbed and didn't know who it might be at this time of night.

Gently, his brother woke up and realized who it was. Hebo motioned for him to keep quiet and to follow him.

Once they were out, they went back to where Jib was waiting.

At first, Hebo and the rest of the group wanted to warn the people that shared the hut with Lebo. Upon further thought, they realized they shouldn't do this because they did not know who to trust.

Now for Ronnie. Silently, Dar and Steve went to Ronnie's hut. This hut was not in sight of Lebo's, so the guard could not have heard or seen anything that had happened a few moments earlier.

As they approached, they noticed a small light was on inside the hut.

The man who was guarding the hut was in the front. As they watched, they noticed that he seemed to be falling asleep, for his head kept nodding and falling forward. No matter how hard the guard tried, he could not stay awake.

With this guard seemingly falling asleep, Dar felt this might make him more vulnerable to an attack.

Once again, Dar had Steve make a noise to distract the guard. This trick worked a second time, but not without a fight. This guard was more elusive and almost escaped them, but Dar caught and tied him up like the first guard.

A few good things about these two fights were that neither guard yelled for help or had much time to make noise. It seemed nothing had been disturbed, and no others had been awakened.

Everything was still going as they had planned. Only the second guard was a slight setback. Still, now that he was tied up, they continued.

Steve then crept over to the hut and snuck inside to where

Ronnie was. She was awake then, and the joy on her face was beyond measure.

Before she could say anything, Steve put his fingers to his lips, telling her not to make a sound. She quickly got out of bed and headed outside with Steve.

Once again, they did not make any noise or wake any other occupants in the hut.

Steve took Ronnie and headed back to where the others were waiting. It was time for them to return to the group and head home.

This rescue mission had gone smoothly. Everything went as planned. Now, all that was left was to find Mark.

Blane had said he was in another hut, so he quickly led them to it. When Justin found it, he looked inside, but Mark was not there. This was something they did not expect. They all knew that time was not their ally. The longer they were here, the more chance that they may be found out.

Justin then decided to wait a bit longer. He wanted to give Mark a fair chance to return with them so a few more minutes might not endanger them.

Time passed, and there was still no sign of Mark. Justin then felt that it had been long enough. He turned and started to leave the hut area and go back to his group so they could head home.

Suddenly, he heard an almost cringe-worthy laugh. It was unmistakable. He had listened to this wretched laugh for nearly a year now. It was Mark.

This made Justin stop in his tracks. He then thought about what needed to be done, and it had to be done quickly.

"Dar, you and Blain should leave and lead the group back. I can now find Mark. I will see if he wants to come with me. With everyone heading back, there might be a chance that we can get out of here. I will be alright. Just make sure you get them all home safely."

Dar almost seemed a little choked up when he heard Justin say this. But quickly, he shook his head in agreement.

He was at a loss for words hearing this from Justin. At this moment, he realized this kid was among the bravest young lads he had ever met.

***

Leaving Justin behind, Dar and the rest of the group returned to the others. Only one obstacle was left to get past: the guard they had passed earlier.

As they approached the area they had entered earlier, the guard had returned from his break.

Dar had to come up with something fast. As they all crept

closer to the guarded area, Dar told Blane and the rest of their group to walk on through. This was unexpected; all the guard did was tell them to stop.

That was the last thing he said tonight, though, for Dar had crept up behind him and knocked him unconscious.

What was different with this guard was that they would have to take him with them. There was no place to hide him.

They quickly tied him up. Once they met up with the large group, they put the guard in one of the carts. As silently as possible, they headed down the main road.

The third time was a charm for Dar. He had somehow taken all three guards out without much interference and felt the valley gods were on his side tonight.

Deep down, though, he knew his fighting skills had helped him the most. Someday, he would have to teach Jib and his village more about the art of fighting and defense.

Once again, Dar had to come up with another plan. He was worried about his large group getting past all the shops in town. The only good thing about this was that it was nighttime, so it would at least give them some camouflage.

To get past the shops and this part of the village, Dar divided the large group into three smaller ones.

He then instructed the first group to proceed, and the next would follow in about ten minutes or so. Finally, the third group would head out on the road. Hopefully, passing all the shops would be easy since it was late at night. Plus, smaller groups would be quieter than one large one.

Heading south, the first group reached a bend in the road. This is where they saw another route to their right. This would be the one they would use to go home on. It looked old and discarded, but they knew they must take it.

This road had been abandoned years ago. So much grass and trees overtook the path, but it was barely usable. It would be slow going for a while, but the carts and villagers would be able to make it.

When the first group was at least a mile ahead, they stopped and waited for the other two groups.

Blane was in the third group, and he seemed to be lagging. His group had already left the village, but he had not caught up with them yet. Something significant was on his mind—his knife. He had to get it back.

As he passed the store he was at earlier, he stopped and let the last of his group get out of sight and down the road.

Quickly, he surveyed the shop. What he saw was a rather

large lock on the door. He knew getting it off wouldn't pose much of a problem, for he was bound and determined to get his knife back. But he would not do it if it meant jeopardizing their escape. That was priority one.

It seemed sad that all the shops in Danton had locks. It also seemed strange because, in his village, there were no locks at all. No one here trusted each other. He figured that it was because of the Black Intruders. They seemed to instill not just fear but mistrust.

Blane quickly took a small hammer-type of tool out of his coat. He again looked to ensure his group was out of sight or if anyone was lurking around.

Quickly, he had the door unlocked. He then ran over to the box that had his knife in it. Taking it out, he exchanged the necklace for the blade. That way, maybe the shopkeeper wouldn't be so disappointed. After all, Blane was a scout, not a thief.

Locking the door behind him, Blane slipped quietly into the night. It didn't take him long to catch up to his group. When he did, there was a big smile on his face. He had retrieved the one thing that was special to him.

Now, the whole group was together except for one. Still, they carried on, for they knew they were not out of danger yet. With the young lad on their minds, the group continued toward their home.

***

Once Dar and Blane left, Justin waited five minutes or so. He quietly snuck behind some of the huts and noticed a small campfire with four men sitting around it. Taking a closer look, he saw that one of them was Mark.

While listening to Mark, Justin felt he might not want to leave. He seemed to be enjoying himself as he chatted back and forth with his new friends.

"But I could be wrong," Justin said. "It might be just wishful thinking. I should at least see if he wants to return with us."

Justin waited intently in the shadows of the trees for a chance to see if he could somehow get to talk to his stepdad.

He knew in his heart that he didn't want Mark to return with them, but he also knew that he didn't want him to stay here in this valley either. He was afraid that, somehow, he would ruin this place. There is no telling what he could do with all of his so-called knowledge about things, even limited as it was.

But he also didn't know how to talk to Mark without getting caught, so he waited longer to see if he might return to his hut.

Suddenly, Mark's little group exited the campfire and entered the darkness. They were headed toward a mountain with a cave. This cave was elevated somewhat, but you could see the path leading up to its opening.

Justin could see a small light coming from it and someone peering into the moonlit sky.

Now, he figured Mark had become one of them, so he turned around and headed back to his group.

When Justin was almost back to the shops in the town, he heard a loud noise cut through the air; from this distance, it sounded like a gunshot.

After a short pause, Justin knew it was a gunshot; after all, he had just gone hunting with Mark a few weeks ago, so he knew the sound of a rifle being fired.

As Justin stood there in the dark, he wondered if that shot had come from Mark's weapon. It must have, he convinced himself.

Now, something didn't feel right to Justin. If that was a gunshot, then what could it mean?

The guardian of the Tree had said that Mark had some type of weapon with him, and from his description, Justin knew that it was a rifle.

As he stood in the dark, Justin started thinking about what this gunshot might mean. Maybe Mark was showing some of the clan how to use his rifle. If he was, then that might not be a good thing. From what Justin knew, this valley didn't have any guns.

This gunshot changed his departure. Justin felt in his heart that he had to go back and see if Mark was ok and wanted to return with them. Plus, he needed to get the rifle. There was no need for the gun to be with people who didn't know much about them or needed them.

As he headed back, another noise broke the valley's silence again. He could tell that it was another gunshot. This made Justin pick up his pace somewhat. He left caution behind and started running toward the same area he had just left.

***

The Woods extended outward for thousands of acres; now, those acres had all been checked. Every inch of The Woods had been searched. They had bloodhounds, a helicopter, and over a hundred volunteers, but nothing was found.

There was no sign of the kids and nothing to go on except that Mark's truck and the bikes were in front of the hollow.

Two days had passed, but there was no trace of them and no clue to follow. The search party had even dwindled to about twenty or less.

Mary and the Williams family understood. All these volunteers also had a life and needed to return to theirs. Even the police department couldn't keep men here for much longer. They, too, had families and jobs.

But still, the three of them would not give up. They were prepared to search day and night if necessary.

Then, a strange thing happened. Old farmer Tucker came out of his field with his dog. He quickly surveyed the situation and then walked up to Mary when she was alone.

"You might as well go home, ma'am. The kids are all going to be OK. They will return as soon as they finish whatever they are doing. You can take it from old Tucker here that this will end well."

Mary just stood there in disbelief. Who the heck does this old man think he is? How would he know that everything was going to be alright?

Here she was at her wit's end, and this farmer came out and told her everything would work out just fine.

Since the search began, he had hardly gotten off his porch, but now he was advising her. He almost acted as if he knew more than anyone else about the kids' whereabouts and where they went.

He was a strange old man. Likable but strange, Mary thought as she watched him return to his farmhouse with his dog. Deep down, Mary could tell that Farmer Tucker meant well, though. She was sure of this.

At first, when Tucker said this to her, she wanted to tell him off but held back out of kindness. Plus, she knew there was a good chance she would break down if she did, and this was not the time or place to do that. She needed to be strong and show everyone still here that she had not given up.

She prayed that this old man was right and the kids would all come home safe and sound.

It was a lot to take in, but at this point, Mary and the others didn't have anything else to go on. She prayed every chance she got and would keep praying until they were back home safe and sound.

Mary didn't care how long this took, but she wasn't about to give up. Not this time. She had let her husband go off without a fight, but not with Justin. She was going to keep looking forever if that's what it took.

***

Slowly walking up to the cave, Cam knew there were only two ways to get in: from the front or back.

Quickly, he went around the back and closed off that entrance. This made it impossible for Hess to get out unless it was through Cam, and he was sure that wouldn't happen.

He returned to the front entrance, walked up, and went inside.

Hess had his back to Cam as he entered. The leader didn't

need to turn around, for he knew his enemy had arrived. He also knew this would be the night they would fight for the clan's leadership.

There was nothing to be said, so neither one of them did any talking.

Suddenly, Cam charged and hit Hess in the back, which knocked him down. Quickly, Hess was up and smiling.

"That all you got, little man?"

Hess said this in a deep voice while laughing. His eyes had an evil look as he slowly stalked his prey.

Cam was taken back a bit because he had hit Hess with all his strength, which only knocked Hess off his feet for a few seconds. Now, the leader was up and laughing at him.

This was the first moment Cam realized he might have taken the leader too lightly. He might have underestimated him and his ability to fight and take a punch.

This didn't matter to Cam, for he knew that his men would be here to subdue Hess in a few more seconds, and then he would get the rifle. Then Mark was supposed to show up and show him how to use it on Hess.

Two of Cam's men came running a few seconds later and surrounded the leader. They both attacked and, at first, made no headway with their fighting. But then one of them knocked Hess down to his knees. Immediately, the two started hitting and kicking Hess, and the fight was on.

Cam then headed over to where the rifle was and pointed it at the men fighting. He still didn't know how to shoot it, but he didn't think he had time to wait for Mark to appear.

Suddenly, a shot rang out. Cam had pulled the trigger, and somehow, it hit its intended target. Hess was down but quickly got to his feet.

Strangely enough, Hess was shot, but it didn't seem to slow him down, at least not at first. But a few moments later, Hess lost his balance, yet still fought on. His wicked smile never left his face.

Hess knew the Silken was running through his veins, keeping him from bleeding to death. He also felt that it was allowing him to outsmart these men.

It seemed every time the men tried to throw a punch, Hess would block it and smack them both. His strength was something none of them wanted to go up against.

A short time passed, but the fight continued. Cam was getting a little nervous and wanted this fight to end sooner rather than later. So, instead of trying to help fight Hess, he pulled the trigger. Again, the bullet hit its intended target. This time, Hess went down and wasn't moving.

Suddenly, Mark appeared. He then realized that Cam had shot Hess and that he wouldn't be needed here after all.

"Oh, that's great. You shot him, Cam. You did it. I knew you would. I knew you would figure out how to use the rifle without my help. I guess I'm not needed here after all. I might as well just head on home now."

Mark then took a couple of timid steps back to the cave entrance. He was hoping that since Cam had taken Hess out, he would let him go. Gingerly, he continued with his retreat.

Slowly, Cam turned toward Mark and said, "Not so fast, little man. I need to ask you a few things. Like, where were you? Why did it take you so long to get in here?"

Cam was furious at Mark. If he needed a reason to betray this man, then he had found one.

The new leader of the clan continued questioning his prisoner.

"You could have screwed this all up. Well, no matter. I have done what I needed to do. I have realized that I don't need your help anymore. So, after we leave here, you are to return to the first hut you had, and you will start to work in the fields in the morning. Then next month you will be switched to some harder work. How's that sound, Mark?"

Mark could see all of Cam's pearly white teeth as he watched him laugh. Cam's laughter reminded him of his dad so many years ago.

Hearing this news from Cam didn't faze Mark much. Somehow, he knew this Cam fellow had been lying to him all along.

"I knew you would betray me. I knew you were no one to trust. You are nothing but a liar. I should have just run as soon as you and your men came here."

That was why Mark took so long to get to the cave. He was searching for a path out of this area. He hoped that with all the commotion, he could return to the first village he saw.

Now, there was a smug look on Cam's face as he said, "It takes one to know one. And as far as you running, we would have caught you before you made it past the first shop in my village."

Once again, Cam couldn't stop smiling and laughing at Mark.

"Yes, I guess it does," was Mark's reply. "But why don't you just let me go back? I will be out of here faster than you can spit. Just let me go. You don't need me. You can get others to do the job you want me to do."

As Cam listened to Mark whimper, he had a contemptuous

look. He didn't like it when grown men begged and pleaded. And this Mark guy did both and would not stop. The constant whining was too much. It was almost painful listening to the weak little man.

The clan's new leader then looked at one of the men in the fight.

"Take this coward back with you. I can't stand listening to him cry all the time. Make sure you put him in the first hut."

Rising, the man did as he was told.

The leader then looked at Mark and said, "You may still be useful to me. After all, you have come from beyond The Woods, so there might be more information that you have and that I might need someday."

Roughly, the man grabbed Mark by the arm and led him away. Mark was still begging as he was shoved out of the entrance.

As he was pushed down the path, Mark kept shouting and pleading with his guard to let him go. He even tried to bribe him, but that didn't work either. He was almost at the breaking point, and a few tears seemed to be about to fall. He knew he would be treated poorly once he returned to the hut, just like all the other villagers in the huts.

"How did I get myself into this mess? Why did I have to follow that darn kid into The Woods? I should have just stayed home and drank."

Mark was saying these things out loud now, and the guard was the only one with him. All the guard did was start laughing at his prisoner.

Sulking and whining, Mark was thrown into the first hut. What was terrible was that he could see the lovely hut he would have had. It was only about fifty or so yards away from this one. He then realized he would see it daily as he worked in the fields.

"Oh, the irony," he thought as he lay on his bed and prepared to try and get some rest. He had made such a mess of his life, and there seemed no easy way out.

As Mark sat on the edge of the bed, his head was down, and both hands were over his eyes. A few tears came falling.

Suddenly, a slight noise came from the back of the hut. Mark quickly jumped upon the bed to ensure that whatever made that sound didn't get him. For all he knew, some animal might be ready to attack him.

Standing on the bed, he saw a shadow outside the back of the hut window. Then, looking more closely, he saw a shape peering into the hut. At first, he could not make out who or what it was.

"Go away. Please leave me alone, whoever you are. I have a lot of friends around here, and they will help me. All I have to do is shout out to them."

Mark pleaded to the shadowy figure staring through the window at him. He almost shouted these words, and he was sure the guard out front could hear him, for he could hear the guard again start laughing.

This day had been so traumatic for Mark, and now it seemed to worsen by the minute.

A moment passed, and Mark could hear the person in the window say something. In a quiet voice, it said, "Come over to the window. I need to talk to you."

The voice was shallow—so low that it was almost a whisper. Thankfully, Mark was the only one who could hear it.

Somehow, Mark got the courage to step off of the bed. Slowly, he did what the voice told him to. He walked cautiously to the window but was ready to run if needed. He knew there weren't many areas to run, but he would yell to the guard for help.

"I don't think that guard would help me. No way. He's too busy laughing at me to care whether I need help. Heck, it's probably one of his friends pulling a prank on me or something."

But when he reached the window, all his fears were quenched.

It was Justin, and for the first time in Mark's sick and twisted life, he was glad to see the kid.

Two things went through his mind now. One was that if he yelled and turned Justin in, maybe there would be some reward. Or, by turning him in, he might get safe passage out of this place.

"Kind of like a get-out-of-jail-free card in Monopoly," he said under his breath.

No, no way. He was not going to make that mistake. He knew he could never trust that Cam guy ever again.

He also thought that maybe Justin was here to rescue him, and he started giggling at this last thought.

"The first thing I thought of has a better chance of happening than the second. This kid would not come here to try and get me out. No way. At least I wouldn't do it for him."

But he was wrong. He just never realized that this kid named Justin the Just was such a good person. He would do anything to help anyone, even Mark.

When the guard brought Mark to the hut, Justin could tell things had changed for his stepdad, at least since the campfire chat earlier. It seemed Mark was one of them then, but something had changed in the past forty-five minutes.

"Leave it to Mark to mess things up, even for himself," Justin said, shaking his head in disbelief.

Now, his thoughts went back to the guard. Justin had noticed that he had been rough with Mark and even threw him into the hut. The laughter and the words were all Justin needed to see and hear to know that Mark wasn't a friend of these people. He also could tell that he wanted out of there.

Quickly, Justin had to come up with a way to distract the guard. He would be without any backup, making his chances for success even harder. He could try and do the same thing Dar did earlier with the other guards, but he didn't think he could fight this guy. He knew he would have to come up with some other plan.

"Listen, Mark. I am going to try to distract the guard. When I do, I need you to be ready to run. I will get the guard to leave this hut and break the lock off the door."

Mark nodded in agreement with Justin's plan; even though he didn't think it would work, it was better than no plan at all.

Suddenly, Justin's plan changed in a split second. The entire game plan changed. The kid's luck seemed to be finally turning for the good.

What happened was that there was some noise or commotion that seemed to come from the cave above them.

The guard who had brought Mark back to the hut turned and ran toward the noise. Some people still in the cave were yelling a lot.

This was just the distraction Justin needed.

Without hesitation, Justin went to the front of the hut and saw a large rock on the ground. Picking it up, he used it to break open the lock on the door.

Checking their exit route, Justin and Mark started running through the trees. As they continued running further away from the huts, Justin had a few questions for his stepdad.

"What happened up there in the cave earlier?"

It took Mark a moment or two to answer because they were running, and he wasn't in that great shape. Huffing and puffing, he finally replied.

"Hess, the clan leader, fought with some guy named Cam. This Cam guy wanted to be in charge, and now he is. He took my rifle and shot Hess. The leader must be dead because I didn't see him move after he had been shot the second time. Then that darn Cam guy turned on me. He lied to me. He said that if I taught him how to use the rifle, he would get me out of work and better accommodations."

Shaking his head, Mark looked at Justin with disdain and said, "Can you believe that guy? He lied to me. What kind of person lies to someone about something like that?"

Justin was almost in shock at hearing Mark's accusations.

Listening to him call this Cam fellow a liar was practically comical. Now, that was the pot calling the kettle black. It was an old analogy but fitting and to the point.

Suddenly, they heard some noise coming up the path they were on. Quickly, Justin and Mark took cover.

People from the village came up the path and seemed in a hurry.

As they watched the villagers go by, it seemed they were heading toward the cave, which was in the opposite direction they were going. There was still some commotion from the cave area, and it seemed to be escalating.

Something came to Justin's mind as they waited for the right time to leave their hiding place.

"What if this Hess guy is still alive? He must be, for the fighting seems to have continued. If he is, they better move on and get out of here as fast as possible."

While waiting in the trees for the best time to move out, Justin told Mark that they would be walking down the road and would catch up to the group he came here with. He told him the group was about an hour ahead of them, so the sooner they headed out, the better.

Justin and Mark started jogging down the abandoned road in

darkness shortly after. Even though it was dark, Justin couldn't help but keep looking ahead and behind them as they ran.

Then suddenly, Justin stopped in his tracks.

Somewhere in his mind, he knew he couldn't leave here without finding out if the leader was dead. It seemed strange to him, but still, he needed to make sure once and for all that he was.

"Listen, Mark. Just keep following this road as quickly as you can. You will meet up with the group that I came here with. They will let you join them. Don't worry. They will get you back to where we came in, and then you can go home."

Justin wanted Mark to do precisely what he told him; if he did, there was a good chance he would get out of there and return home.

Turning around, Justin looked behind them to ensure they had not been followed. Then he continued trying to tell Mark what to do and what not to do.

"Don't leave this road until you find the group I came with. Tell them that I will be joining them as soon as I can. I have one last thing I need to do. I am going to go back and make sure that the leader is dead. If he is, that might make our passage home easier. If another leader is in charge, he might not care that the three of you have escaped—hopefully not for a while."

Justin was sure Mark would be alright if he did exactly what he told him, but he never knew with him. You could ask him to do one thing, and he would do the other out of spite.

Shortly, Justin left Mark and headed back toward the cave. It may have been an unnecessary risk he was taking, but something drove him on. For some odd reason, Justin had to find out about the leader of the Black Intruders and who was in charge now.

Justin blended into the night as best he could. He was only a few yards away from the cave's entrance. He could see a few people inside, and it looked like a fight was still happening.

As Justin watched, he saw that the man they called Hess was alive. The fight was still raging, but now they were squaring off for one final time.

While Justin watched, he saw blood coming from two wounds on the leader. Presumably, they were from the bullets that this Cam fellow had shot Hess with. The bullet holes looked awful, with all the blood spewing out of them constantly.

Justin figured that Hess must have regained his strength and started fighting again when Mark returned to the hut.

*****

Cam looked scared now as he and Hess fought on. Cam did not have the rifle now, for it had been thrown out of the cave's opening. It had busted all apart when it hit the rocks below.

Still, Cam and Hess continued their battle. Cam hoped that all he had to do was keep moving, and soon, Hess would get weaker from the loss of blood. Then, he would pounce on him and get his reward.

But two or three jabs came out of nowhere, and then a right hand landed squarely on Cam's temple region. Down he went, rolling over from side to side with pain.

Now it was the leader's turn to think the fight was over, but somehow Cam got up and started charging Hess.

Hess was once again hit by Cam with full force, except this time, it did something awful. It drove Hess back into the side of the cave, smashing his back and head against the wall. This blow almost knocked Hess out for a second or two. Shortly, he was once again on his feet.

"How can this man keep going like this? I've given him all I have, yet he still fights on." Cam said.

Only a few people were watching at this time. Justin had been outside in the dark but now took a chance and walked into the cave. Luckily, for the most part, he was unnoticed. He stood there watching as they continued to trade blow after blow.

Justin would make sure that whatever happened, he would

be ready to leave this cave at a moment's notice.

When he entered, Justin hid behind a large rock inside the cave. Once the outcome was clear, Justin decided to slip out as quickly as possible.

Hess had now stumbled to the front of the cave and was barely standing up. The people still watching knew it wouldn't be much longer now.

Then, finally, Cam made a mistake. He charged Hess one too many times. When he charged, all Hess did was step to the side, and Cam kept going to the cave's opening. He could not stop himself from falling onto the rocks below. It was a fall of about fifty feet or so. What made it lethal was the fact that Cam hit the stones with his head and back.

Hess looked down into the rocks and almost laughed out loud. His enemy had been defeated once and for all. There would be no one to challenge his leadership ever again.

Then suddenly, his elation stopped. He slowly looked to his left and noticed someone by the rock inside his cave.

Hess saw someone he didn't know hiding behind the rock. A stranger was in his cave, and he didn't like this.

As Hess turned toward Justin, things changed. The pain and the loss of blood hit him hard. He was becoming dizzy and cold. His thoughts were confused, and things started to become blurry. He knew he was dying, but he didn't care. He had won his last fight, and that was all that mattered.

Hess fell to the ground. At first, he was on one knee, but a few moments later, he was on his back, gasping for breath.

His eyes were now closed, and his breathing had become a struggle. But there was still a slight smile on his lips.

The few remaining people in the cave began to leave. None of them took notice of Justin.

Why should they? Their village would have no leader in a short time. There would be no one in charge to tell them what to do, no one to make the enslaved people work in the fields or do anything else. Everything was collapsing around them.

Justin thought that might be a good thing as he slowly walked over to the leader.

He could now see that Hess was still alive, barely. For some reason, Justin did his best to move him to a nearby bed.

Cam's men turned and ran off when they saw him fall to the rocks below. They didn't want anything to do with the leader and feared that he would punish them severely if he regained his status.

Justin then turned to the only man who was still inside the cave at this time.

"Please get me a Nampo and a cart if you can. I would appreciate it."

The man did what Justin had asked him to do. He had been one of the few who had stuck beside Hess and was still fearful of him and what he might do if he did regain leadership.

In a short time, the clan member returned and brought the cart to the back entrance that Cam had blocked. Once he cleared the debris, he then entered. The two of them put Hess into the wagon that was to be pulled by the Nampo.

Justin planned to take Hess to Jib's village and get him some help. He hoped the herb or plant that helped the young Nampo might work on Hess. It was a long shot, but it was all Justin could come up with.

Sure, he could ask someone from Danton to get help, but he was convinced no one would. They all hated this man named Hess.

After leaving the cave, Justin reached the village shops. He found the old road again and started heading back.

As Justin headed down the road with Hess in the cart, he wondered why he was trying to help this guy.

This man had been very ruthless in his dealings with the villages. Enslaved people had been numerous, articles had been stolen, and people had been hurt. Not to mention all the families that had been separated when people were kidnapped.

Justin didn't know the answer, but he knew in his heart that it was the right thing to do. This was one of the many things that set him apart from many other kids his age. He was true blue to all his friends and gave everyone he met a fair shake.

Somehow, Justin knew that he had to try to help this man. If it worked, there might be some kind of truce between Jibs village and the Black Intruders clan.

Hopefully, this last thought of his would come to pass. If not, then they all would still be at the mercy of the leader of the Black Intruders.

The Journey Back

The end of the second day had arrived. The children were still missing; no clues were left to check out.

Mary could see that all of the hope that everyone had at the beginning was now turning to despair.

Every inch of The Woods had been checked and double-checked. All the resources from the police and other agencies had turned up nothing.

Mary saw that the search party was dwindling as the day ended. It was only a matter of time before everyone would be gone, including the police.

The police were about to start looking in other areas besides this wooded area. Both of the families' homes were checked.

To the parents, it almost seemed strange that their homes were now being investigated for any clues to the whereabouts of the missing children.

"I guess they have to check everything and every possible motive," Mr. Williams said to his wife and Mary.

"They have to ensure none of us could have done something to the kids. It seems strange, but my friend Dan, who helped us with this search, told me they would eventually do this."

Dan was the officer who had caught the kids out that night and was the one Mr. Williams called when the kids were first missing. He had been a great help, especially with the police department and the volunteers.

It had taken a lot of time and effort to have all these people out here, and now it seemed as if they were at the end of the search itself.

Mary knew she would never give up looking for them and that the Williams family wouldn't either. So even if the searchers went home, Mary would still come out here and keep looking. She just knew that her boy would come back.

Mr. Williams approached Officer Dan and asked if he could borrow a megaphone. He told Dan he needed to say a few things to everyone still here and searching.

Trying to clear his throat, Mr. Williams began his speech.

"I want to thank all of you for the time and effort you have put into finding our children. We are sad to report that there has been no sign or clue of their whereabouts. I know we will keep searching, but you no longer have to. We just wanted to let each of you know how grateful we are for your help."

Everyone still listening to Mr. Williams could tell how sad he was. His voice seemed to quiver a little as he tried to continue his speech.

"And also, a special thank you to the Orchard Park Police

Department for their help and resources. As stated before, we will keep searching, but the rest of you don't have to. And once again, thank you from the bottom of our hearts."

Some of the few that were still here began to head on home. Most of them came by, and hugs and thanks were given.

Mary sat on a tree stump and looked around at The Woods. It seemed like an empty forest, cold and lonely since only a few volunteers were left searching.

Mary decided to go home and get some rest, but the three would again go inside and search first thing in the morning. She couldn't give up on them, and she knew that deep down in her heart, she never would.

***

Once again, now that he was free, Mark started to think about how untrustworthy Justin was. He began to talk out loud, mainly to help calm his deepening fears.

"I can't believe I listened to that stupid kid. I have been walking on this road for hours and still haven't seen anyone. He must have lied to me. He probably wants me to get lost, and then he would never have to put up with me ever again. If I ever see him again, I will make him come home with me and show his mother what a liar and disobedient kid he is."

Daylight was approaching, and Mark was still walking down the road. He was getting discouraged and scared, but at least he was away from Cam and his men. He knew being out here in the open air was better than being locked up in a hut as an enslaved person. At least he had that to be thankful for. Finally, the kid did pull through for him.

"Maybe I won't be so mean towards Justin when we get home. Maybe I'll lighten up on him and not punish him as much."

It almost sounded as if Mark had a change of heart towards Justin.

No, that couldn't happen. He was just having a moment of weakness. Soon, he would return to his old self, and punishing the boy would be at the top of his list.

But first things first. He knew they would have to get home before he let the punishments begin. The good stuff would keep till he was out of this place and back to where he belonged.

The first thing he had to do to achieve his goal was to catch up to the group that had come to get them out of their bondage.

Justin had said they weren't that far ahead, but now Mark was beginning to wonder. It seemed to have been hours, but still, there was no sign of anyone.

As he continued his journey, paranoia started to sink in

again. His mistrust of Justin began to escalate.

Time passed, and Mark had conjured up so much hate that he was oblivious to everything around him. He wasn't paying much attention, just wandering down the road.

But a short time later, something made him come out of his daydream. It was a slight sound and seemed to come from some of the trees to his left.

Stopping in the middle of the road, he tried to listen to see if he could hear more. He then looked in the direction that he thought the sound came from. Once again, he started to think the worst.

"Oh no. That kid set me up. He got me to go down this road, and now those animals will eat me. I knew I wouldn't get out of this place alive."

He started to panic so he started to run. He ran as fast as he could, trying to stay on the road even though it was still dark.

Suddenly, to his left and right, he could see movement in the dark areas of the trees. He even saw something on the road up ahead.

Quickly, he stopped running. Turning around, he started to run in the opposite direction. Shortly, he realized that it was useless to do this. Something or someone was coming from behind him. He was trapped.

"Now I know for a fact that Justin set me up. He lied to me.

He wants me dead. The animals are going to get me or some robbers. I knew I would never get out of here."

He was now almost screaming this to the shadows that had surrounded him. Mark started slowly turning in a circle to keep an eye on whoever this was.

Then, like before, his bladder gave way.

"I got to get that fixed," he half-heartedly joked to himself.

But this time, he was not embarrassed that he wet himself, for he had other pressing issues on his mind, like who or what was ahead and behind him. Plus, whatever was moving in the shadows of the trees also seemed to be getting closer.

Now, a few lights were lit, and Mark could see once again all the shadows were upon him.

"No. Please don't hurt me. I am unarmed. I am just a man who has lost his way in this valley. Please, I beg of you, let me go on my way."

Mark was almost crying now. His voice had risen an octave or two, and the fear in his speech was undeniable.

Suddenly, a man came out of the shadows and said, "This is the Mark fellow I told you about, the man that Justin knows."

"I might have guessed that," Jib said as he walked up to the group that had now encircled Mark.

"Where is Justin? Answer quickly and truthfully if you know what is good for you."

Mark could tell this older man was not messing around with him, even in the dark. He could see and feel two glaring eyes upon him. He was not about to make anything up at this point.

"Justin went back to check on the leader of the clan. The leader had been in a fight with a guy named Cam. The Cam fellow shot the leader. The leader looked dead, but I was taken to my hut at this time. When I told Justin this, he went back to check for himself. He then told me to go ahead and try to catch up with your group. He also said once we get back, you will show me the way out of the valley."

Jib was in no mood for lies and deceit, especially from this man. If truth be told, Jib wanted this Mark fellow out of the valley more than Mark wanted to leave. He knew this guy was wrong for this valley and not fit to be here. How he got in was still a mystery. But hopefully, soon, there would be no chance to get in or out. None whatsoever.

"Come on then. You can join us. We are heading back to Catton. Then we will head to my village. From there, I will show you the way out."

At this moment, Jib felt a slight bit of worry. He hoped that the way out was not completely closed up. If it were, this would not be good for the valley.

"If it is, I will chop the forest down and throw this man out myself." This last thought was said under his breath. It may have been just a quip, but every thought always has a little truth.

Jib was worried about this man having to stay here, but he was more concerned about Justin.

Shortly, all the people behind the trees and bushes came out and continued their journey home. It had been slow, but soon, they would all be safe in their villages.

If Mark's account of the Black Intruders was valid, they could be more ruthless now that they may have a new leader. It all depended on the man named Cam.

From what Jib remembered, this leader named Hess had been quite a tyrant and would not be missed; at least Jib and his village would not miss him. He had attacked them several times in the past. He had taken supplies and workers. Whatever the leader of the Black Intruders wanted, he took. He had no remorse and no regrets.

Several hours passed, and now their group was closing in on Catton. They had all kept their eyes and ears open for the Black Intruders.

Jib knew that getting everyone home was what they needed

to do. Another thing he worried about was that he wanted Justin to catch up with them. The longer he was gone, the more something might have happened to him.

Jib had that worried look again as they all finally reached his brother's village. All in all, it had been a successful journey. Everyone was back except one.

"Give him time. I'm sure he will make it back. If anyone can, it will be Justin the Just," Jib told them. Still, Jib could not stop worrying about the young lad.

***

The road back was taking a bit longer now that he had someone with him who was severely hurt.

Justin knew this man would probably not reach Catton, so he took him to Jib's village instead.

Heading toward Jibs would cut a few hours off their journey. Justin knew that the sooner he got this Hess fellow some help, the better his chance of survival.

Catton was out of the way, so this shortcut might help in the long run. Time was not their ally, and it seemed to be fleeting.

Somehow, the leader of the Black Intruders was still breathing. Justin had now bandaged both wounds, but Hess had still lost a lot of blood. At least now, the bleeding was minimal.

When Justin bandaged the wounds, he could tell that an infection was beginning to appear around the two bullet wound sites. The one good thing, if there is a good thing when one is shot, is that the bullets had gone entirely through. One bullet had entered his right side and out his back without touching any vital organs or arteries. The other bullet hit his other side and came out also.

If Justin could get this man to Jib's village, then maybe Jib could get some of the herbs, which could at least stop the infection from worsening. Justin was told this herb was rare and might help, but it didn't seem to help everyone who used it. Jib had alluded to this when the Nampo was saved.

Whether it worked or not, it was still worth a try. There was no other option. At least there is no option here in the valley.

Then, another thought came to the young boy's mind.

"What if I took him to a hospital outside of the valley? Would that mess things up?" Justin had quietly said these things, hoping he could somehow find the answers.

"It sure would," he heard himself say as he shook his head.

Then Justin started thinking about the journey through The Woods. How could they get him up the hill if they somehow got him to that point? And how could they get him over the big rock?

With this in mind, he answered his questions. They couldn't

do it; it would be next to impossible.

Justin knew that this would be the last resort to try if all else failed.

Also, if he took him outside, many questions and forms would have to be filled out. How could he explain to anyone who and where this man came from?

Then, since it was a gunshot wound, the police would have to be involved. Plus, more questions would be asked, and Justin knew he would not have any answers.

It would be a lot of trouble, but saving a life was worth it. So that is what he was prepared to do if it came down to it.

Justin tried to avoid all the potholes as they continued down the dirt road. Hitting these holes would move the cart up and down, and that action always caused Hess to sigh in pain.

But try as he might, it was unavoidable at times. Also, part of his journey was in the dark, making it even harder to avoid them all.

Thankfully, the sun made the trek a little easier. It was a slow journey, but Justin still would not give up.

As time passed, Justin kept praying that this man would hang on until he got the proper help. As bad luck would have it, he had not seen one person on the road. Even if he did meet someone, the chance they could help was slim.

Also, who could Justin trust at this time? For all he knew, if he did meet someone, they might be a friend of the Black Intruders. Then, if that happened, this journey might be over, for they may not know what had happened at the cave and would still be siding with the Intruders clan. They might even think that Justin had hurt Hess somehow.

So many thoughts ran through the young lad's mind as he kept heading back toward Jibs village. Still, he was bound and determined to see this through.

A short time later, Justin saw someone up ahead coming towards them. He thought about moving out of sight but knew that the person was too close and they must have seen him by now.

As the person got closer, he could finally see who it was. It was Jib.

"You didn't think I would leave you behind, did you?"

Jib had that smile that Justin knew all too well and was glad to see. Some hope had resurfaced now that there was someone else with them.

Things seemed to improve. At least they were not alone on this road; if anyone knew what needed to be done, it would be Jib.

He was the leader of his village and one of the most

knowledgeable people Justin knew here in the valley.

Justin then told Jib all that had happened and their current situation. He told him about Cam dying and that this man was still the leader of the Black Intruders.

Getting off his Nampo, Jib addressed the situation. The wound did indeed look bad, and time was running out.

"I see you are headed to my village. That was a good decision. We can then ask the Nampo if they can get herbs to help this man. It may or may not work. He could be too far gone, but we must try."

Jib's face now looked bewildered. He, too, could not understand why Justin wanted to help this man—the same man who was ruthless toward everyone in the valley.

Yet this fourteen-year-old boy was determined to save someone he didn't know and didn't deserve his help either.

A man who probably, once healed, would not change his ways. More than likely, he was the type of person who would be ungrateful and wouldn't give you any accolades at all. It didn't matter, though, for Jib knew that Justin wouldn't want any. That was the way the boy was. He lived up to his name time and time again.

The Goodbye

The group had now reached Catton. Jib had gone back to search for Justin, and if anyone could find him, they knew he would.

Steve and Ronnie were anxious to go home. Their journey was almost at an end now and would be once they arrived back at Jibs village. The two knew their parents would be worried sick by now, and things would take a long time to return to normal.

How would they explain all of this to their parents? How could they explain any of it to anyone, for that matter?

The kids knew they would have to keep quiet, for the most part. There was no way they could ever tell anyone about this valley.

"Mom and Dad are going to kill us," Steve said to his sister. "They probably have search parties out looking for all of us."

Steve and Ronnie sat there waiting to get more supplies from Catton before heading to Jib's village. Once they did, then Hebo and Lebo were going to lead the way back.

Dar wished them all farewell, and gratitude was given to him and his men, but none were needed. He understood, and he was glad to help.

"We all have to stick together. My village and I were glad to help you all. We are just thankful that everyone is safe. If Jib comes by this way, I will tell him you all went to his village. But if he heads home, tell him I will keep in touch now that we see eye to eye."

There was a slight smile on his face as the group headed home. Dar and his men waved to all of them as they left.

Dar then turned and told his men that they would immediately prepare to defend their village now that they had helped free the captives.

He knew that the Black Intruders would not let this go and would likely come looking for them. So, being prepared and ready to fight would be essential.

More than likely, his brother's village would be attacked. The three captives were from his village, so the Black Intruders would naturally go to that village first. Once they learned that Catton had helped with the rescue, his town would be next.

***

A short time later, as they were headed for Jibs village, Ronnie did something that Steve could hardly believe.

"When we return home, I will tell Mom and Dad that it was all my fault and not yours. Maybe that way, it will work out better. I will tell them we got lost, and you saved us."

Steve was at a loss. He was even getting a little choked up from what his sister said. He always knew she loved him, but this went far beyond anything she had ever said to him.

He put his arm around her and said, "No. You don't need to tell them that. We will just say that we got lost. That should do the trick. But it is a fine gesture even from an ugly little runt like you."

They both laughed as their Nampo headed on down the road. Steve kept looking back in hopes that Justin would appear. It wouldn't be the same if they had to go home without him.

How would they explain it to anyone? But mostly, how could they keep Mark from shooting off his big mouth about this place? He would be the one who could hurt this valley by telling people all about their adventure.

Would people listen? Would they listen to the ranting and ravings coming from a man who was drunk most of the time?

One would hope not. This place needed to be kept secret, preserved for the few who lived there.

Steve knew that Mark, Ronnie, and even he did not belong there. But he knew that Justin did. If Justin didn't make it back, then Steve would understand. He would have to find some answers, especially for Justin's mom. She would be the one hurt the most.

Eventually, he would have to tell Justin's mom the truth. When he did, he hoped she wouldn't tell anyone about this place as long as she knew Justin was safe. She could be trusted. It would be a hard sell, but Steve and Ronnie must try. They would have to do it for Justin and all the people in this valley. He just hoped that it wouldn't come down to that.

Still, Steve wanted Justin to go home with them even though he knew his friend should stay. It was selfish, but he still couldn't help himself. Justin was his friend, and he didn't ever want to say goodbye to him.

As their group left Catton, it seemed to move faster. Mainly, it was because they wanted to see their loved ones. Also, they knew that they all would have to try and devise a plan of protection for their little village. Dar had told them that the Black Intruders would likely attack their village once they found out the captives were missing.

Yes, things seemed to be changing in this beautiful valley, but the one thing they didn't want to change was themselves. So, if changes were happening, then they could all live with that, but if they changed, then that would not be a good thing.

***

"I have got to go back in one more time," Mary told herself as she watched the remaining volunteers leave.

It was a beautiful day, but it still looked gloomy without Justin. She would give it her all this time in The Woods. She would search and search until she dropped if it came down to it.

"I will never give up." She vowed this last thought with conviction. So much that she seemed to shake a little when it was said.

Once again, the three of them went to The Woods. There were no volunteers, officers, or reporters; no one was still there, or so it seemed.

Old farmer Tucker was over by the farmhouse again. This time, he and Red were watching intently. The old man smiled slightly, and even Red seemed happy, if possible.

Even though the area looked gloomy inside The Woods, there was a feeling of hope in the air. It was as if today would be a great day that they all would remember. Even the dog knew something was about to happen because he just barked and barked.

Once they were inside, they began to search the same places repeatedly. They wanted to look at the same bushes and trees everyone had checked hundreds of times.

The parents noticed that they had searched this area so much that it had been beaten down these past few days. But yet again, this did not stop them.

***

Hess was still unconscious. His breathing was shallow and very slow. Jib shook his head when he checked on him, for he knew it would probably do no good to continue home, but they had no other choice.

The young boy's mind kept hoping for the best. He could never give up on anything or anyone. Justin was the type of person who saw goodness in everyone that he met, even Mark.

He felt that if Mark got help with his drinking problem, maybe he would change, and he and his mom could have a chance at a life together. Justin knew it was probably too late for this, but there was always hope.

All Mark had to do was want to get help. There were programs he could attend and doctors he could see. It was all up to him, so maybe he might do some of these things when they returned to the outside.

With all that Mark had been through these last few days, Justin hoped that he may have changed inside. Perhaps he will try and be a better person.

Yes, this Justin kid was always thinking the best about people. Always wanting them to do their best no matter what the circumstance was.

They were now about five minutes out from Jib's village. One or two of the villagers met them on the road.

As they approached the town, more and more people came

out to greet them. Justin could see Steve and Ronnie waiting patiently for their friend. He could see them smiling from quite some distance.

Off the Nampo he went. Hugging Steve and Ronnie was long overdue. Tears came to all of their eyes.

Justin then helped Jib and a few men carry Hess into his hut. Jib quickly sent a Nampo to find their leader and, if possible, bring back some of the herbs.

Justin couldn't tell how Jeb communicated this to the creature, but he knew somehow he had.

There wasn't much time left, for Hess was now in a coma. There was hardly any movement coming from him. They all could tell that he would not last much longer. He would be dead before nightfall.

Jib hoped that this herb would help save this man. Sometimes, it did, and sometimes, it didn't. They believed it was left up to the Gods of this valley to decide.

Ronnie then walked up to Justin. "It's great that you made it back, Justin. We were worried sick. Thank you for saving me and the rest of us."

Quickly, she wrapped her arms around Justin's neck and hugged him. This continued for some time. Anyone could see that she had a crush on him. Both she and Justin were blushing from ear to ear.

And why not? After all, Justin was her prince charming. He had saved her once again and kept her from harm. He never could pass up on saving a damsel in distress.

The three of them then walked outside and decided that it was once and for all time to go back. Steve looked at Justin, knowing that Justin likely wanted to stay. He didn't want to go through a long, sappy goodbye.

Justin could tell what Steve was thinking, quickly saying, "Don't worry, Steve, I'm coming with you guys. I need to get back home and be with my mom. She has no one, just me. Our parents must be worried sick by now. It's been so many days since we saw them last."

This was true, for when Justin thought about how long they had been here, he realized it must be going on a week.

Time was so different here than where they had come from. Justin was hoping that it had only been a few days on the outside, and if it had, then maybe they could come up with something to tell their parents.

Now, once again, Justin could feel that unbearable sadness coming over him. He did not want to leave. He knew once and for all that he belonged here. Justin had fought this notion many times, but now it was more evident than ever.

These people needed his help in so many ways, but above all, he knew that he would never hinder them. He would ensure their little valley stayed the perfect way it was.

Jib had now come out of the hut. He walked over to the three of them and knew what would happen next.

"Is this goodbye?" he said to Justin.

Jib knew it was, but he asked it anyway to be polite.

"Yes. This is goodbye. I have to get back home. I need to be with my mom. She has no one there for her, and she's got to be wondering where we all are."

Justin then turned and looked over in the direction of where Mark was standing.

"Plus, I don't think that guy will be around my mother and me much longer. I will make sure of that."

Justin knew that when he returned, he and his mom could stand up to Mark if necessary.

"Oh, he might be a little upset from the change of plans, but he will soon move on and go his own way. At least if he knows what's good for him?"

Jib then nodded to Justin in agreement.

"Good luck to all of you," Jib said as he walked along with them to the incline.

Mark was now following a few yards behind them. Jib didn't even acknowledge him. He just waved goodbye as he watched the four of them head home.

Jib had told Justin earlier that this would be the last time they could get back inside, and the forest was closing up and would be closed forever.

This was something that Justin already knew. He had seen this each time he had come back. It was getting harder to find the opening coming in or going out.

Jib also told them the guardian in the willow tree would await them. Somehow, this little man could keep the opening from closing, at least for a while.

Quickly, they reached the river and headed around the weeping willow tree. As promised, the little man was there waiting for them. He, too, motioned them to hurry.

Up the stairs they went. The foliage now had covered almost all of the opening.

Mark was the first one in, and he barely made it. Then Ronnie and Steve went in, and Justin was last.

Since Justin was the last one going in, he did something he had wanted to do for so long. He quickly turned around, grabbed the little man, and hugged him before he slipped away. The little man had disappeared every other time, but not this time. Justin was too quick for him.

Justin then looked out upon the valley one last time. It was so beautiful. He would miss this more than anything, but he knew he must return to his world and his mother. It had been quite an adventure that none of them would ever forget.

***

The guardian of the Tree and Steps was happy at this time. He was so pleased that it made him make a mistake. He left the steps unguarded and returned to the village.

Something moved in the shadows. It was now getting dark, and the specter creature was walking about. Quickly, it headed up the steps. The steps had never been here before, so there was no way up to the opening, but now there was. This would give the creature the chance to escape the valley.

There was a smile on the specter's face as he headed into the dark opening. He had been in this valley for such a long time. It had been so long that he couldn't remember when he came here.

But now he was free to go and do whatever he wanted. Never

again would he return to this valley.

***

The evening was approaching way too soon for Mary and the Williams family. They had once again searched the entire area to no avail. And to think this day had started so promising but now had turned to despair. Going home would be hard for all of them, for it seemed like this was the last time they would ever return to The Woods. Mary knew it wasn't true, for she would never stop coming here and looking for the kids. Never.

The Woods lived up to its reputation this time, for sure. It had been a place you didn't want to enter for several reasons, and now it had one more.

Home

It was a slow process getting through the opening. The thorns and limbs were so thick this time. Justin almost felt that he would not be able to make it through.

If that happened, then what would happen to him? Would he be stuck inside this thicket till he died?

It kind of looked that way for a few moments, but still, Justin pushed on. He kept pulling the bushes and limbs out of his way the best he could. The stems and leaves almost seemed to be preventing him from reaching the other side. It was as if they were grabbing him, trying to keep him from leaving.

Then, when he was almost sure he wouldn't make it through, he saw a pair of hands reaching out and grabbing him. It was Steve.

"I just couldn't let you stay behind. I knew you would try, but that won't happen on my watch, mister."

The three of them laughed as they headed toward the big rock. Justin noticed that Mark had not waited for them and was probably already near the opening of The Woods.

***

It was around six p.m. on this side of The Woods, and it would be dark in about an hour or so.

When Mark came out of The Woods, he noticed something immediately.

"Where in the heck is my truck? Somebody must have stolen it. When I catch up to them, they are in for a world of hurt."

Suddenly, someone came out of the cornfield. It was old farmer Tucker and his dog.

"No. I don't think you will, Mark. No one stole your truck. It is down at the police station. It has been impounded. If you walk up the dirt road and off my property, you can turn right when you reach the paved road. From there, you can walk to the police station to get your truck. Now get going before I give you a ride you won't like."

Mark seemed to take this old man seriously, so he quickly stepped up his stride and almost ran up the dirt road.

"That old man doesn't know who he is messing with. I could whoop him if I wanted to. I just don't want to right now," he said but under his breath.

Then Mark heard the old farmer say, "Now go on, GET." It was loud and to the point.

Mark was now running as fast as he could and didn't stop until he had turned right on the paved road. He didn't stop until he was out of sight of the farmhouse and the field.

A slight smile and chuckle came from the old farmer as he turned around and greeted the kids as they appeared.

"Your bikes are at your homes. Your parents will also be waiting for you."

Justin, Steve, and Ronnie didn't speak to farmer Tucker. For some reason, they just believed him. No other words were exchanged, and none were necessary.

As farmer Tucker returned to the farmhouse, he turned and looked at the field and The Woods.

Then, he had a few words for his dog.

"Well, Red, it might be time for you and me to be moving along. We're not needed here any longer."

Quietly, Tucker and Red walked into their farmhouse and prepared dinner. The evening was about to overtake the day, and the old farmer still had so much to do before bedtime.

***

Have you ever seen a track meet? One with professional runners?

Well, more than likely, you have. If you indeed have, then watching the three kids run home would have made you think this was one of those events. These three kids ran so fast that time, and the cars seemed to stand still.

Mary had just returned from searching and was fixing something to eat. Looking up and out the kitchen window, she saw a kid running toward her house. A kid that kind of looked a lot like Justin.

She had such a strange feeling watching the boy running. She could tell by the direction he was running that he was heading toward her house.

So, standing there in the kitchen, she refused to move. Mary ensured she did not get her hopes up, for there was no way she could take it if it weren't Justin after all.

As Justin hit the front door, he noticed the sold sign out front. He then ran around the corner into the kitchen and stopped.

Mary stood there looking at him. The two of them were unable to move for a moment or two.

For her, it was almost too good to be true. She had searched with no results, and now, standing in her kitchen, was a boy who looked much like her son.

Dare she believe this to be true? Could this boy standing before her be her son, the son that had been missing these past few days?

The answer to this question would not take very much longer to find out.

Justin ran to her, and they embraced. This continued for some time, and the tears and the pleading for forgiveness followed.

No forgiveness was needed. It was just understood between the two of them.

Mary could not be any happier. Nothing in the world could top this. Nothing.

Suddenly, the phone rang, cutting short their tears. Mary was sure it would be Mrs. Williams on the other end of the line.

As the two of them tried to talk to each other, there were so many tears and laughter that Mr. Williams had to take the phone. The funny thing was Mary couldn't speak much either, so Justin took the phone from her.

Mr. Williams just wanted to chat with Mary and ensure everything was alright on her end and that Justin had indeed arrived safely back home.

He also needed to inform them that Officer Dan had called and said Mark had come to get his truck out of the impound yard. Then Dan told them he would be right over to talk to all of them. Reporters would also be on the way, and he warned them that it would be quite the fiasco for a while. He also seemed a little choked up when told they were all safe.

Yes, indeed, the lives of these two families would be disrupted for a short time longer, but they didn't care. All they cared about had returned home, safe and sound.

No punishments would ever be given, for it seemed that somehow the kids had learned their lesson. From this day forward, none of them ever told a lie or half-truth.

Well, only about the Woods, that is. The kids told everyone how they had gone inside and somehow got lost. How they were not found would remain a mystery.

But for Mark, then that was another story. He started going around town and telling anyone who would listen to him that he saved the kids and got them out safely. He also said he was a hero and had fought gallantly against all odds to bring them out alive.

The funny thing is that few people believed him, especially when he told them there was a valley inside The Woods.

Mark had always been a talker. He embellished every story he told, which always sounded more incredible to people and made him look more challenging or more of a man, depending on what point he was trying to get across.

The kids were all safe. Everything was back to normal. Things were looking up for them all. This ordeal had strengthened their friendships.

Justin, Steve, and Ronnie knew this encounter in this forest had forever enriched their lives. They also knew they would be forever grateful for experiencing this and that nothing could top this journey.

Back to The Woods

It had been a month since Justin and his friends had returned from The Woods, and it now seemed that everything had changed for the better.

One good thing was that Mark had come around begging to be a part of their family, but neither Mary nor Justin ever wanted anything to do with him again.

He did say that he was trying to make amends for what he had done to them. He even told them he was in AA and trying to dry out.

That would have been good if he had told them the truth. His temper seemed about the same, though.

Once, Mark got mad at them and tried to break down the front door, but Justin stood his ground against him and backed off.

You see, Justin had grown some in the last month. It seemed he had grown a few inches and put on more weight. There was even talk that he might join the high school football team if they stayed in this area.

He had bulked up quite a bit, and this Mark guy could no longer bully and push him around. Also, Mark wouldn't be mistreating his mom anymore, either. She didn't want anything to do with him and had told him so.

Things were finally looking better for Justin and his mom. Their house had sold, and now all they had to do was pack some of their belongings. All of their furniture would stay with the house; if there was anything else, a yard sale was planned to eliminate the rest.

The two of them hadn't decided where to move yet. They did plan on flying to Texas, though. Mary had a brother living there. She and Justin would stay with him until they finally decided where to settle down. Anywhere far away from Mark would be good enough for them. But who knows, they may just choose to come back here and live. They seemed to have all the time to decide now that Mark wouldn't be a part of their world anymore.

It would be good if Mark cleaned up his act and tried to get help. That is what you are supposed to do when you have the dreaded disease of alcoholism.

But if he were lying to them just so he could get back into their good graces, that wouldn't work this time. The two of them were through with him once and for all. Nothing could make his mom change her mind.

Mary had been so happy this past month. Not only did she get her son back, but Mark was out of her life for good.

Thinking of Mark, she knew there was no love loss there. She would never let him control her ever again. Mary would ensure that Mark never had the chance to hurt or even get near Justin. If he did try anything with Justin, she vowed that she would take care of Mark herself and bury him in The Woods if need be.

She knew this last thought was a terrible thing to think of, but that was just how bound and determined she was to set things right with her son. She didn't want Mark messing things up for them ever again.

Sitting in the living room, Justin told his mom about The Woods and what happened inside when they went missing.

Mary sat patiently without interrupting. He told her quite a story. Some of it seemed lovely, and other parts were way past believable. Still, she listened to him.

"So why do you feel this place is somewhere you belong?"

"I don't know, Mom. I just felt at home the very first time I went inside there. It was a great place. If you ask Steve and Ronnie, they will tell you the same thing. However, I will say one thing: not all people seem to belong there. Steve and Ronnie loved being in there but didn't feel the same. At least not like I did. They even told me so."

Mary sat there trying to understand everything that her son was trying to tell her about this valley inside The Woods.

"Now you say that the opening is closed off? That there is

no way to get back inside?"

"That is what the village leader told us. And I could tell for some time that the opening was closing. It was just getting more foliage around it, which would hide the way inside. I barely made it out myself. Steve had to reach in and grab my arms."

Justin went on to tell his mom all about what had happened to them inside the valley. He even told her about the leader of the Black Intruders and how mean and ruthless he was. He also told her how he tried to save him, but he likely died. He didn't know because they left before the Nampo returned with the herbs that might have cured him.

While Mary sat there, she tried to believe her son and his story about this place inside The Woods. It was an unbelievable story, but her son told her this, so she did her best to understand. To call this story far-fetched would be an understatement.

It was almost time now for the two of them to start heading out. This was the last time they would see their house. Neither one of them looked back as they walked away.

Justin and his mom had one more thing to do. Their taxi had arrived, and the driver was told to go to the Williams house so they could say their goodbyes.

Once arriving, the farewells turned into sadness. After all, these two families had known each other for a long time. Now they realized that they might never see each other again. Many tears were shed on this day, but it was expected.

Before he and his mother left, Justin called Steve outside to talk privately.

Steve quickly said, "Don't worry, Justin, I won't tell anyone about what happened inside The Woods."

"No, that's not what I wanted to tell you. I wanted to tell you that I will try to get my mom to go into The Woods. I know the entrance to the valley has been blocked off, but I would like to try one more time, just to make sure. I told her about that place, and she seemed to believe me. Who knows, maybe this is the last time I can return? If I do, I just wanted to let you know so that you wouldn't worry about us if you don't hear from us ever again."

Steve looked at his friend, and a smile appeared on his face. What he saw in Justin was a person who never gave up or surrendered to anyone. When the going was impossible, he kept going anyway. This kid was true blue.

He then answered Justin.

"That sounds crazy, but I wish you two the best. I hope somehow you get back in because you belong there, Justin. You do."

Both boys hugged one last time, and even Ronnie came out

and gave her prince charming a hug and a peck on his cheek.

Now, it was time for Justin and his mom to leave. The next step was to take a taxi to the airport. Mary had sold their car and planned on getting another one when they found a new place to live. She didn't want to take anything with her except a few articles and keepsakes.

As they left the Williams house, they both waved one last time. They had a lot of good memories with them. But who knows, wherever they end up, they may make new memories with other families.

Hopefully, Justin and Mary could start a new life now that Mark wasn't around. It would be fun for both of them, and they couldn't wait to start.

The taxi was heading to the airport, about an hour and a half away. They would have to pass old farmer Tucker's cornfield and The Woods to get there.

Justin knew this and had been thinking about how he could convince his mom to stop at The Woods. This would give him one last chance to see if it was closed forever. If they did stop, then this time, they would do it together. Also, it might give Justin some closure since they would be moving away.

Then, a funny thing happened. Just before Justin was about

to tell his mother what he wanted to do, she said something to the taxi driver.

Mary told the cab driver to pull over when they were close to the cornfield. She told him they would call for another cab when they were ready to leave.

Justin was so surprised by his mom's sudden change of plans that it rendered him speechless.

The driver let them out right at the entrance to Tucker's cornfield. The two of them took the few things they had in a couple of backpacks and headed to the exact spot Justin had used the first time he went inside the hollow.

Mary searched in her backpack and brought out a flashlight. She knew they would stop, and from what Justin told her about these woods, bringing a flashlight would be necessary.

She did not tell Justin that there was no guarantee that the two of them would stay. It would be hard on her because she was used to other things. Still, she was willing to give it a try.

Mary knew in her heart that Justin needed to try one more time. She could almost feel these woods were calling to him. She knew it would be a bad idea to leave and not give him one last chance to see if he could somehow get back into this place he called the valley. The stories he had told were incredible, but she knew he wasn't lying or making them up.

Appeasing him would be the best thing to do. After this, Justin and she could catch a plane and head wherever they wanted.

Slowly but confidently, mother and son walked down the old dirt road by the cornfield.

As they walked, both of them looked over at the farmhouse. But there was no farmer Tucker or his dog.

Word had surfaced that Tucker had moved away to parts unknown and taken his dog with him.

No one knew much about the farmer except that he had lived there for quite some time but now was gone. They could see that the farmhouse seemed to be decaying somewhat, even after such a short time.

It was almost sad to think that farmer Tucker and Red wouldn't be watching him this last time going into The Woods.

Strangely, Tucker seemed connected to these woods. Justin knew that this was a crazy idea and that it was impossible.

Tucker was just the old farmer who owned the cornfield by this wooded area. That's all it was. Still, Justin wished it were true. If it were, that would mean this place was somehow magical.

But no, it couldn't be. Justin quit believing in magic the day his dad passed away. The only reason he ever came to The Woods was to escape people and the pressures of his everyday life.

No, this place was not magical at all. It was just some valley inside here where the people were trying to live away from the outside world. The people in the valley were living off the grid. That's about all it was.

Sure, there were different animals and other things there, but for the most part, it was still just another place to live. A place that only a few knew about. This was the way the valley liked it, and this was the way it would stay.

Animals

Mark had been down on his luck since he returned from The Woods. Justin and his mom didn't want anything to do with him, and he had nowhere to live.

Also, when he went to get his truck out of the impound yard, he had no money, so it stayed there.

He was now on foot and didn't have Mary to fall back on. Things looked pretty bad for him at this moment. Even the shelter where he had been staying kicked him out. They said he was just too hard to get along with. That, combined with his drinking problem, made them concur that it was time for him to move on.

It seemed that he had burned his bridges with just about everyone. Now, there was no place he could go. The only thing he could think of was to go to his sister's house. She lived in another town, and he was sure he could stay there until he could come up with another plan.

Mark had tried to get help with his disease but now had fallen off the wagon again. It was just too hard for him to stop his drinking and stop the hate that had filled his heart over the years.

Things didn't look too good for him. He had no job, no money, and no place to live. One would say he did this to himself, but he wouldn't; he blamed everyone else, especially Justin.

He couldn't stand the kid. Even though Justin had helped him in the valley once, it still didn't change Mark's thoughts toward Justin.

"If I hadn't followed Justin into that valley, then none of this would have happened. I would still have my truck, a place to stay, and the ability to correct Justin when he disobeyed. So, you see, this is all Justin's fault."

He had said these last few remarks while walking down the road leading out of town.

While drinking his last beer, he continued with his fragmented thought process.

"Good times for one and all," he shouted as he continued walking out of town.

He had been talking to himself a lot lately. Most of it was just incoherent babbling coming from a heartless little man who only cared about one person: himself.

A short time later, Mark realized precisely where he was. He was adjacent to the field and The Woods. He had not been back here since leaving that day.

"And I never want to go back in either."

Again, he was talking out loud, glaring at the cornfield and The Woods.

Looking over at the opening where they had entered The Woods, Mark couldn't help but blame Justin again.

"I can't stand this forest. Things have gone wrong ever since I entered it. Maybe I'll burn it down, and then that little runt will have nowhere to play."

Now, his hatred for Justin expanded to The Woods themselves. Lately, he seemed to hate everyone and everything.

Mark seemed tired now, so he stepped off the side of the road and lay down in a tall grassy area. He knew he could rest there for a while.

As he lay there, he started thinking again about going to the next town to stay with his sister. He knew he could mooch off of her and then move on.

While finishing his last beer, something happened that changed his luck—or at least, he thought it would.

He saw a taxi pull over to the side of the road right in the same area of The Woods, by farmer Tucker's cornfield.

"No. It can't be," he said as he watched them leave the taxi and head down the dirt road.

Keeping out of sight the best he could, he quietly said to himself, "Now, where are they going? Has that little punk tricked his mom into going inside? No way! Even I know that the opening to the valley is closed off. We barely made it out."

Still, he watched them as they disappeared into the hollow. Quickly, he got up and started running to the same spot where they had gone inside.

He looked around as he approached the area to see if that old farmer was nearby. If he were, Mark would show him who the boss was once and for all. But he didn't have time for that old man because he was trying to find Mary and her snotty little brat son.

Then, once he was convinced the old man wasn't around, he pulled out a knife he had bought. He had lost his gun and the other knife in the valley when Cam had stolen them from him. This new knife was a lot better and sharper.

Silently, Mark crept into the hollow. He wanted to catch them, but he knew that when he did, he would make them both pay for not letting him back into their lives.

After searching a little, he heard some people talking up ahead. It was Justin and Mary; he was sure of that.

He knew he had them now. Once again, that ugly, worthless smile appeared on his face.

He did his best not to be seen, for he knew when he did come out, he had to make sure he could get to Mary. Once he had her, he could control Justin more easily.

As he watched from about twenty yards behind, he saw them go over the top of the rock. Cautiously, he did the same.

Then, when he was at the top, he knew it was time to appear.

Without waiting another second, he slid down and was on them. This happened so fast that Justin didn't have time to react to Mark's arrival.

"Well, well, well. Look at what we have here," Mark said with a menacing grin.

He then showed them his knife and grabbed Mary before she could run away from him.

"What are you two doing in here? How come you never let me come with you? Come on now, tell me the truth, you little piece of crap?"

Justin had been caught off guard. Now, the very thing he swore would never happen again was happening. His mom was in harm's way from Mark. He had to come up with something and fast.

"We were just going to look inside to see if the opening was completely blocked off. That is all. I told my mom about this place; she wanted to see it herself. Then we were going to come and get you."

Mark then made sort of a growl, which turned into laughter.

"Oh, isn't that sweet? Now you have your son lying so he

can try and protect you. That isn't a nice way to raise a child, is it?"

This rhetorical question was lost in their fear. All Justin wanted to do was get that knife away from his mom's throat.

"Well, I'll tell you what, Justin. Let's all three go over to the area where the opening was. If it is still open, we all can go inside and live happily ever after. Wouldn't that be lovely?"

Mark started to laugh and almost dropped his knife. Justin moved forward, but Mark regained his composure and flicked it at Justin.

Justin then moved back and out of range of the blade.

"Oh. Now, look at little Justin. He's growing up. He's trying to save his mommy. If you try that again, boy, I will cut her good. You understand me now, Justin?"

"Yes. Yes, I understand. I won't try it again."

Justin could not believe that this was happening. When things seemed to be turning for the good, they appeared to be falling apart.

"Now move. Both of you. Let's go see if the opening is still there."

Sadly, finding the exact spot where the entrance used to be was easy. As they searched, Justin kept a close eye on Mark. There was no telling what he might do if the opening was closed.

Then it hit Justin. What would they all do? Justin and his mom had their plans but didn't include Mark.

Mark, on the other hand, had no plans and no future. His only goal was to keep sponging off Mary and never let her go.

The two of them searched for quite a while in earnest. Mark just stood there supervising, all the while making sure neither one of them would run.

After thirty minutes or so, they realized that it was useless. The opening was closed for good.

Shortly, they gave up. As they stopped looking, they suddenly noticed something. There was no sound in this area. No crickets or animals were making any noise at all.

Also, there was a stillness inside these woods. It seemed to cast off an eerie overture, almost as if something terrible was about to happen.

Mark was the first to notice just how motionless things were. After all, this was the place so long ago that he got lost and was scared to his wit's end. This was still The Woods, maybe not the same part, but it was still the place that haunted his memories even today.

It was the place where he and his dad shot that animal. The one that Mark thought would someday pay him back for shooting it.

He was still afraid after all this time. These woods gave him the creeps. And now the silence he remembered from so long ago was back and deafening.

Then it happened. A sound broke the silence. It was a sound Mark had forgotten about because it had been so many years ago— the same sound he had heard when he first shot the animal.

At the time, Mark was so happy that he had shot the animal because he thought it would make his dad proud. But it didn't. Nothing would make his dad proud, and his dad couldn't care less about Mark.

That was one of Mark's biggest problems. It seemed to haunt him even to this day. It shaped him into the man he was. A loathsome, mean and cruel person. One that no one wanted anything to do with.

But it was too late now for Mark. He was who he was. Nothing could change him, and nothing would.

Still, there was that sound. It didn't appear to be going away either. If anything, it seemed to be getting louder and closer.

Mark was aware of this and even tried backing up a bit.

When he did, he inadvertently released Mary, and she went to Justin.

Now, the tables had turned. Mark still had his knife, but he didn't have Mary. When he realized this, he continued to move backward.

As Mark continued to fall back and away from Justin, he started yelling at the top of his lungs.

"See. The opening is closed. There is no way you can ever get back in. They don't want you there anyway, you little punk. We better move on and leave here as quickly as possible."

Now, his long-forgotten fear had returned and was lurking, seemingly blocking any escape, at least in his mind.

He kept yelling obscenities at Justin and his mom while moving further away. Mark wanted them to come with him and escape this forest.

Slowly, Mark inched backward. He kept saying things to both of them, but mostly, it was incoherent ramblings from a scared little man. A man who didn't care for anyone either. He was a miserable person and would never be missed.

It was almost as if the animals inside this area knew this. They knew that this man should never leave The Woods alive.

So, they moved toward him. The gnashing of teeth was heard, making Mark more nervous and scared.

Mark could see eyes peering through the trees and bushes. Things began to move around him, and even a rustling sound was heard. Branches seemed to be breaking and cracking as Mark started to run.

A few moments later, Mark was out of sight, but they could still faintly hear him sobbing as he kept running.

"You think he will make it to the outside, Mom?"

"I don't know. He was such an evil man. It is almost sad that he was so mean and cruel to everyone he met and led such a miserable life."

Justin nodded in total agreement but was glad Mark was away from his mom.

It had been such a close call this time. Things could have turned disastrous, but they had been fortunate.

Justin still had to make sure that Mark wasn't hiding somewhere or following them when they left. He wasn't about to give Mark another chance to hurt his mother.

With Mark gone and wandering through The Woods, they knew it was time to leave and never return. The opening was not there, so the sooner they left, the sooner they could start a new life. It would be a life away from The Woods that Justin hoped would be better now that Mark wasn't in it.

Reunion

As Justin and his mom turned to leave, Justin made sure not to look back to the area that used to have the opening. The kid knew that if he did, sadness would overtake him.

When he thought about the blocked opening, he realized it wasn't just the trees and bushes doing this. It was something else Justin couldn't quite understand at this time. It was almost bewildering.

Well, whatever it was, it would remain a secret forever. It needed to be kept secret to protect the lives in the valley.

In some ways, that was good. The people living in the valley and villages didn't need people like Mark to enter. All he would ever do was harm the valley and the people here.

But in another way, Justin knew he would never see them again. This was almost too much to think about. He had loved the valley and the people inside, and he knew they cared for him, too.

Turning, the two of them headed toward the rock. When they reached it, a most peculiar thing happened. A slight wind began to blow.

The thing that was peculiar about this wind was that the direction it was going was the same direction where the old opening used to be.

Justin then remembered the first time he came to The Woods. There was also a little breeze as he contemplated going inside The Woods that first time.

It was a slight bit of wind, oh so soft, against his skin.

He also remembered what he had thought at that time. Justin felt that even the wind wanted him to go into The Woods. It, too, seemed to know that life would begin if he did. So, he took a chance and went in that day.

But now the wind was back, and Justin felt strange because of its direction. Somehow, he knew it was telling him again, "Go on in. Life awaits you."

It might have been a bit of a stretch, but Justin turned around and headed back to the same spot.

Approaching the area, Justin noticed the wind was going through the bushes and trees where they had just checked.

He then pushed some of them aside, which seemed more manageable this time.

"Too easy," he thought as he continued trying to make a path through the leaves.

Hope had now been rekindled, for he felt that there was a slight chance of an opening still available.

Mary was beside him, and she also started helping him push

the foliage away.

Suddenly, a tiny light appeared that seemed to be coming from the other side of the leaves.

At this moment, Justin knew they had found another opening somehow and that it was daylight again on the other side of The Woods.

The opening was small, but he knew they could make it through. Justin then started pushing and pulling the leaves and branches out of their way so they could get to the other side of the trees. It didn't take long, but when he did, he turned around and helped his mother.

As the two of them stood on the hill overlooking the valley, Justin couldn't help but say, "I told you so," with a slight edge of vindication.

Justin then turned toward his mother and said, "Now, this is the part that may be a little scary to you. You might want to take your time before you attempt this."

But before Justin even finished telling his mom about the slide down the hill, she had already moved past him. And just like he did the first time he slid down, she yelled, "Geronimo."

She was down and looking up at Justin before he realized what she would do.

"And to think I was worried about my mom and the slide." His mom was braver than he gave her credit for, and the kid was amazed at seeing her do this.

As Justin stood looking down at her, he turned around and noticed the opening was entirely closed now. Somehow, he knew it was meant to be like this. He felt he had finally found a home, a place for his mom and him to live the rest of their lives.

Quickly, he slid down the hill and joined her. Then, the two headed off toward the river. As they did, Justin looked over at the weeping willow tree, and sure enough, the little man was there and smiling.

Suddenly, there was a sound that pierced the air. Justin knew it was the alarm that sounded when someone came into the valley. This time, though, it sounded different. It was almost pleasant to his ears.

Walking up to the river, Mary reached down to feel its coolness. It felt great to her touch. She then bent down and grabbed a handful of sand, which felt soft, just like Justin said it would be.

So far, all Justin had told her was true. It wasn't that she hadn't believed her son; it was just that it all sounded unreal. But now she knew why her son wanted to keep this place a secret. It was beautiful, and she, too, felt at home here.

As the two of them walked around the mountain, Justin couldn't wait to reach the top of the little incline and see his mother's look when she first saw the village.

A few short steps more, and the moment arrived. They had reached the top and looked down. Mary looked amazed at the sight of the little village and all the huts. The look was worth the price of admission.

Walking a little further on the path, they both stopped. Jib and someone else were in the middle of the village. Justin couldn't tell who it was from this distance since it was still over a hundred yards away. He could tell that Jib was smiling, though.

Jib was smiling as if he knew something Justin didn't. The more Justin thought about this, the more he realized that Jib always seemed to know more than he let on.

Suddenly, Justin's mom did something he would never forget as long as he lived. She started to stroll toward them.

Then, after a few more steps, she started to run. She ran so fast that she almost fell once or twice.

When she reached Jib and the stranger, she stopped, looked into the stranger's eyes, and started crying.

Then she did another unbelievable thing. She reached up to the stranger and put her arms around his neck, and the two started kissing.

Jib then walked away to give them privacy, but Justin was rooted to the ground.

He could not move, and he dared not move. The only explanation for what was happening was something from a dream, a thought pushed aside long ago.

As Justin walked toward the two of them, he looked closer at the man. Once Justin got a good look at him, he knew who it was.

It was Hess. He had lived, after all. But now he was cleaned up and decent-looking.

That answered one of his questions. The other question was obvious. Why was his mom kissing Hess?

In a way, he knew the answer, but he felt it would be invalid if he said it out loud, and his dreams would be dashed once again.

A few seconds later, Chris and Mary turned and walked toward Justin the Just.

Epilogue

Years had passed since Steve had moved away from Orchard Park in Golden County. He was all grown up now and a very successful businessman. His sister Rhonda also had moved away and had a good life.

All in all, things had turned out well for them. Their parents were still alive and well, so Steve had returned to Orchard Park.

Their dad turned sixty this weekend, so they planned a big get-together. Even Rhonda would be flying in later so she could join the celebration.

This was a rare moment for Steve. The other few times when he returned home, he was always too busy to stop and think about his younger days growing up here.

But now, things seemed to be slowing down a little for him. He had more time to relax and enjoy life a little. Also, he could reflect on his childhood days here in Orchard Park with more time.

The number one thing that Steve had been thinking about recently was his long-lost friend Justin.

What did we use to call him? Oh yeah, Justin the Just. And it fit him, too. That kid was a good kid. He was always doing the right thing, never saying anything wrong or telling any lies.

Wait a minute. That wasn't entirely true. Justin did tell a few fibs. It seems it started when he went into The Woods that first time.

It was understandable, though, Steve said as he sat on his parents' front porch looking at the old neighborhood.

Still reflecting on some of his childhood days, Steve once again thought about Justin. He remembered that his friend was the type of kid who could never give up on anyone or anything. He always had to give it one more try, no matter how hopeless the situation looked.

Sitting there, he wondered if Justin and his mom ever made it back inside the opening and to the valley. Steve and his parents had never heard from them since they moved away. The last thing he remembered Justin saying to him was that he would try and go in again. He wanted to make sure that the opening was indeed closed for good.

Steve hoped he made it because he knew Justin belonged there.

These last few things he had thought of were some things that had been on Steve's mind for quite some time. He missed his friend deeply. But if his friend was happy, then that was all that mattered.

Without realizing it, Steve had left the comfort of his parent's house and started walking down the road. He was again in deep thought, and before he knew it, he was headed toward the area called The Woods.

It had taken Steve about twenty minutes to get here, but as he did, he stopped just outside the premises of old farmer Tucker's cornfield.

Steve then surveyed the farmhouse. It was now all worn down, and he could tell no one had lived here since Tucker moved away when they were kids.

Shortly, Steve looked toward The Woods. He could still see the area in front where they had all gone inside. It looked as if it had not changed a bit all these years. This wooded area still looked dark and mysterious like it did back then.

Being curious, Steve walked down the dirt road to that opening. There was no cornfield, old farmer, or dog watching this time. It seemed strange somehow not having Tucker and Red here. But time moved on, and people did, too.

As Steve walked up to the hollow's opening, he couldn't help but think about the times the three had spent inside this area.

"That has got to be the happiest time in my life, now that I think about it," Steve said aloud. "I will never forget how special it seemed inside the valley. These Woods were fun, and the valley was fantastic.''

Looking inside, he could see how dark and ominous this area was. Even when he was young, the forest looked like this, but his youth hid many pitfalls that could have happened to him.

Oh, how Steve wanted to go back inside and see if he could find the opening to the valley.

"It would be nice to see if Justin made it back inside. But the time moved faster there, so Justin would be somewhat older than I am now. He might not even be alive."

Yes, that was another thing about the valley he couldn't quite understand. When you were inside, time on the outside seemed to slow down. But once you got back outside, time continued as usual.

Maybe that didn't mean it moved faster in the valley after all. Perhaps it just slowed things down on the outside. Or maybe time slowed down inside the valley. Who knows?

Steve just stood there and shrugged his shoulders. He was perplexed about this difference in time. After all, he was a real estate tycoon, not a scientist or Einstein. He didn't know a thing about formulas, equations, or the perplexities of the universe. All he did was buy and sell houses.

Speaking of houses, Steve had just seen a fixer-upper—old farmer Tucker's farmhouse—that he might want to take a closer look at.

"That might be something I would like to check out."

He then pulled his phone out and called his secretary, giving her the details about the location and area where the house was. She said she would get back to him on the price.

"Yes, indeed. I think I will buy this old farmhouse. It might be somewhere I would like to settle down someday. That way, I can watch the next kids who may come this way looking for an adventure. Maybe I will even get an old dog. I can name him Red. Yep. That might be a good thing."

Steve smiled slightly as he turned to leave the area known as The Woods.